Voices

by Josh Langston

Other Books by Josh Langston

Novels
Resurrection Blues
A Little Primitive
A Little More Primitive
A Primitive in Paradise
Treason, Treason!
The 12,000-Year-Old Whisper
Oh, Bits!
Greeley
Zeus's Cookbook
Garden Clubbed!

Non-Fiction
Write Naked!
The Naked Truth!
The Naked Novelist!
Naked Notes!

Short Story Collections
Mysfits
Christmas Beyond the Box
Dancing Among the Starts
Who Put Scoundrels in Charge?

Novels with Barbara Galler-Smith
Druids
Captives
Warriors
Under Saint Owain's Rock

Dedication

At long last I have the opportunity to put my thanks and appreciation—in ink, on paper—where folks can see it. Hopefully, my good friend, Don Wolf, will see it here, too. Without Don's input, and more than a little much-needed nagging, this book likely would never have been completed.

I suspect the adult beverages we both consumed during its incubation added something to the mix, although I hesitate to suggest what that might have been. But the plain truth is, I wouldn't have gotten this one written without him.

So, thank you, my friend. This one's for you.

Chapter One

Sometimes things aren't always as they seem.

Somewhere in Afghanistan – 2010

The taste and texture of dust briefly distracted Andi from the overall ache that plagued her, as if her body had become one gigantic bruise. Concussive sounds grew louder, penetrating her Kevlar helmet–the bark of AK47s from several directions and the consistent short bursts from a Marine M4 somewhere nearby.

She couldn't see who was shooting, but the clang and whiz of flying rounds told her she was a target. Still woozy, Andi managed a belly-down search for her M4 but came up empty. A cloud of oil smoke roiled dark and angry from a burning

Humvee. It took a moment to register it was the vehicle she had been in when the world exploded. "Goddamn hillbilly armor," she muttered. "Useless pile of shit."

She unstrapped her sidearm, a 9-mm Beretta, and clutched it tight, but it wouldn't do her much good against a team of ragheads with RPGs.

Where's Gunny? She crawled toward the flaming wreckage in search of the NCO leading their ridiculously under-sized unit. "Gunny? Gunny!" she shouted. "Tate? Charlie?"

Shut up, girl! What's the matter with you?

Andi froze, not recognizing the voice. "Gunny? That you?"

Hush, damn it. Just listen to me, and I'll get you out of this. Gunny's down.

"Who the hell are you?" she asked, then added, "and *where* the hell are you?"

Shut up and listen, damn it! There's no time to argue. Use a smoke grenade. Lob it at the front of the Hummer. Give yourself some cover.

"But—"

Just do it!

Andi unhooked the cylindrical device from her vest, pulled the pin and tossed it at the wreckage. Dark green smoke immediately billowed up blanketing the vehicle and everything near it. As the cloud spread toward her the voice cut in again. *Your weapon's under the wreck. Done and gone. Gunny dragged you and Tate clear then laid down some covering fire hoping you'd both wake the hell up and join him. Tate's dead, but you can use his gear.*

"You said Gunny's dead, too?"

Yeah. Why are you still sitting here? Move your ass!

Andi moved on her hands and knees, much faster than a belly crawl. She reached Tate's body and quickly checked for a pulse, but his blank-eyed stare told her he was gone. She grabbed his M4 and turned away only to come up short when the annoying and as yet unidentified command voice cut her off.

Grab his frag grenades and extra magazines, too. They'll come in handy. Now hurry!

Though annoyed she couldn't place the voice, Andi followed the directions since they made sense, and she sure as hell wasn't capable of thinking clearly on her own. Not yet, anyway. Besides, following orders was easier.

The voice started in again before she finished raiding Tate's supplies. *There's very little time now.*

Take what you've got and head back the way you came. That smoke cover won't last much longer.

"Where'm I going?"

There's a ditch and some boulders by the side of the road. Hole up there.

Andi didn't question the command and hustled to comply.

Faster! The Hajjis are coming to collect souvenirs.

Andi crawled with dispatch, crabbing hard as if a locomotive were on her tail. She reached the ditch and slithered down into it. Turning, she wiggled back up the short incline for a look at what she'd left behind.

Good girl.

"Who the hell are you?" she asked in an exasperated whisper. "Why can't I see you?"

I'll explain later. For now, just think of me as your overwatch.

"A sniper? Thank God." Snipers were magicians when it came to hiding; that explained why she couldn't see him, but it didn't explain why she could hear him so clearly, as if he were inside her head. In the distance she could see the Ali Babas working their way toward the burning vehicle.

I was a sniper, once. Long time ago. But right now, you're the only one who's going to be doing any shooting, other than those assholes headed our way.

She didn't like the "was" portion of his comment. She needed fire support in a big way. Her sphincter locked itself down, tight.

Stay low. Hold your fire 'til some of that green fog blows away.

Andi stacked the extra mags for her M4 within easy reach. She flipped the safety off and waited. The gunfire had subsided, and she heard nothing but the hiss and crackle of the burning vehicle. She licked her lips to no avail. Death is dry business. She heard voices in the distance, Pashto or Dari. She had no idea which. Could've been Arabic pig Latin for all she knew.

"Am I the only one left?" She feared the answer and fought back tears. If she survived, she could cry later. Tate, a guy she'd known since boot camp, had looked so... dead.

Yep.

"Did you check everyone? There were six of us. 'Easy mission,' they said. 'Low risk.' Goddamn secret squirrels never get it right. They sent us out in a freakin' Humvee for Christ's sake. Might as well have put us on bicycles."

Keep quiet!

Andi clammed up.

There's three of 'em front and center. See the swagger? They wanna be the first to reach the wreckage. You need to let 'em be the first to meet Allah.

Andi squeezed off three rounds, dropping two of the three where they stood. The third ducked behind cover as did those behind him.

Get down!

She inched backwards, out of sight.

Nicely done. Those two are down for good. They're not moving. The rest aren't sure where you are. If you crawl to the far side of the ditch and shoot from there, they'll think they've got more than one little girl to deal with.

Andi wanted to tell him where he could shove the "little girl" reference but prudence dictated she stay quiet and do as told.

Making as little noise as possible she shifted ten feet away and took up a new firing position. She slid the muzzle of her M4 through a clump of heavy weeds and waited for her attackers to show themselves. It wouldn't take long; they weren't about to wait for Yank reinforcements to show up, though that would be delayed since the attack knocked out their communications, and no one back in the camp knew they were in trouble. The ragheads likely didn't know that, however.

One of them shouted and suddenly all of them were on the move. Andi aimed and fired as quickly as she could then dropped back down and crawled to her original position and started firing again. She exhausted two magazines and crammed a third into her weapon.

Get down! Cover up!

Andi did as she was told, curling into a tight ball just as an RPG round cratered the firing position she had just vacated. She waited until the shower of dirt and rocks subsided, then crawled away as quickly as possible.

New problem.

"Swell. What now?" she whispered.

Three of them are trying to get behind you.

~*~

Marietta, Georgia — 2010

Stormy held her coffee cup in one hand and steadied it with the other. Though nearing her 90th birthday, Stormy's shaky hands had nothing to do with her health. What had her nervous and wishing for a quick getaway was the imminent arrival of her youngest child, Margaret or "Mags" as Stormy's late husband nicknamed her. That the girl hated the moniker came as no surprise.

Though nearing retirement age herself, Mags had far more energy than her mother, and every time she came for a visit, she focused that unrelenting, 220-volt current at Stormy. "This place is too big for you! What if you fell down? You don't need to be all alone at your age."

She could go on and on, and usually did, as relentless as a herd of bureaucrats at a taxpayer funded retreat.

After the obligatory two knocks on the front door, Mags let herself in. Stormy put her coffee cup down lest she give in to temptation and accidentally spill it on her visitor. *Oops! Sorry. You'd better go home and change before that stain becomes permanent.* Alas, she was never able to bring herself to act on such impulses, no matter how enjoyable they might be.

"You look tired, Mom."

Stormy resisted the urge to roll her eyes. "Have you gained weight, dear, or are you merely buying tighter clothes?"

"That was just mean," Mags said, sucking her tummy in.

"So was that wisecrack about me looking

tired."

"Can we just put the dueling pistols away and have a pleasant conversation?"

"I'd like nothing more," Stormy said with an almost genuine smile. She knew the possibility of a "pleasant" chat had little chance, but she prided herself on her optimism. Naturally, that's when she started to cough, but at least she was prepared. She grabbed her inhaler from a side table and took two puffs. Relief came quickly.

Mags gave her the condescending look she always used when Stormy had to break out her "puffer." She commented, "I hope you've got more than one of those things lying around."

"I'm good. You don't need to worry."

"Right," Mags said as she settled herself on the sofa and deposited her gigantic handbag on the coffee table in front of it. Hauling that much crap around was likely the only exercise she got, Stormy thought. Lord knew, the girl needed it.

"How long has it been since you last had the house painted?" Mags asked.

Stormy blinked, more out of curiosity than surprise. "I've no idea. Why?"

"Well, I only gave it a quick glance on the way in, but it seems like the spots which aren't faded are peeling. The whole exterior looks awful, probably like it did after the Yankees moved on. I'm surprised the Homes Society hasn't sent someone around to talk to you about it."

Stormy looked forward to a visit from the Marietta Historical Homes Society about as much as she looked forward to a visit from Mags, or a trip to the morgue. "They've been strangely quiet, but if the house looks that bad, I imagine they'll be dropping by soon enough." *Damned busy bodies.*

Mags gestured with both hands in an unspoken, *Well?* "If you moved into a smaller place, it would become someone else's headache."

Stormy nodded agreement. "I'm sure you're right."

"Then, why don't you unload the place and move into something more sensible? There's a wonderful assisted living complex not five minutes from here."

"You say that like it's a good thing."

"It *is* a good thing," Mags said, her face revealing the inner struggle she waged to keep her frustration in check. "I've mentioned it before. I don't know why you won't even give it a look. They have so many activities! Think of the friends you could make."

"I have friends, and I don't need any

assistance, for living or anything else."

"How 'bout the house? Think you're up to painting it?"

"No, but I can still sign a check, and I'll bet I can find a painter who'll take it."

"Aw, Mom...."

"You know I don't want to move," Stormy said. She pitched her voice low in hopes of remaining calm. "Your father and I bought this place shortly after you were born. We rebuilt it from the inside out. I have far too many wonderful memories of living here to ever leave it." *Besides, there are things here which I can't leave behind. Or even tell you about.* "Please, can't we talk about something else?"

"Of course," Mags said as she leaned forward to rummage in her ponderous purse. After a short search, she extracted a folded pamphlet which she held in both hands as if it contained holy writ. "I'm going to leave this with you, Mom. And I want you to promise me you'll look it over."

"Honey, I'm not moving. Ever. If you—"

"Just promise me you'll look at this brochure."

"But—"

"It's not about moving. Jeez, Mom."

"It's not?"

"No. It's about health and safety. Your health and safety. What if your puffer runs out of whatever's inside? Then what? You die, that's what. This outfit provides companions, people who can make sure you're okay. And that's all that matters to me."

"Oh."

"Just knowing you have someone nearby would give me great peace of mind."

Anything to get her off the subject seemed reasonable, so Stormy agreed. "Just leave it on the table, dear. I promise to give it a serious look."

"Today?"

She resisted yet another eye roll. "Yes, dear. Today. I promise."

"And don't forget, you've got a doctor's appointment day after tomorrow. I presume you want me to drive you there."

Stormy wasn't happy about it, but she had to admit her reflexes weren't what they used to be, and she really didn't like dealing with heavy traffic. "I can always call a cab."

"Would you please let me do this much for you, at least?"

She relaxed and gave her daughter a completely genuine smile. "Yes, of course. And thank you. I would appreciate it very much."

~*~

Margaret marched toward her car, scowling and muttering as usual. Conversations with her mother never seemed to end any other way. No matter how carefully Margaret crafted her suggestions about her mother's long-term care, the woman rejected them on the spot. Why was she so damned stubborn? It made no sense for an old woman to live alone in a house she couldn't care for. The place had six bedrooms, for cryin' out loud! How many could she possibly sleep in?

No, Margaret told herself for the millionth time, there was something else at play. She had always pooh-poohed her brother and sister when they talked about their mother's secretive nature. Margaret always assumed they were just making up spooky stuff to frighten their youngest sibling. She never bought into it. At least, not completely. And by the time she went off to college, the skepticism gene she must have inherited from her father kicked in big time. It seemed abundantly clear: Mother had no secrets.

But now that she looked back on her life under Stormy Talmadge's roof, Margaret knew she'd been ignoring something. The difference between

Margaret and her siblings was simple—they didn't completely drop the subject when ordered to. Margaret had been more compliant, and, she admitted to herself, far less curious. When told to drop the subject, she had.

Until now, anyway.

From a very early age, Margaret, her brother, and her sister, all knew about their father's secret room. When the Civil War era house had been renovated, a basement had been dug to take advantage of the slope on which the building stood. The basement provided what their mother called the "terrace" level.

It also housed what became the entire family's secret: the "safe" room. Hidden by a sliding bookcase which acted as the door, the room was undetectable. The children knew how to enter it and lock the door from the inside.

And they might well have had good reasons to hide. Their mother was a journalist and their father was a senior agent in the GBI, the Georgia Bureau of Investigation. His efforts had led to the conviction of a number of high-profile criminals, some of whom had associates well versed in retribution. No one could even mention the safe room to anyone outside the immediate family. Her father had driven the point home on many occasions.

The only thing odd about the hidden room, aside from its very existence, was a large, locked wall cabinet. Odder still, the cabinet was designed to keep even the most determined intruders out, not just curious children with nothing better to do.

Fifty-some years later, Margaret still had no idea what was hidden in that cabinet. She'd asked her mother on several occasions, but her answer had always been the same: "It's nothing illegal; it's just something you don't need to know about."

So much for trust. After all these years, hadn't she earned some? She wasn't being sneaky; she wasn't trying to go behind her mother's back. She was just simply concerned about her. Stormy Talmadge needed someone to look after her. If she fell, God forbid, and broke a hip, it could be days before anyone checked on her. Living alone, at her age, was not only foolish, it was downright dangerous.

The pamphlet Margaret insisted her mother read addressed this problem in very real terms. It spelled out the hazards a senior citizen would likely encounter while living alone. It also offered a plan for in-home companionship, someone who's only job would be to look out for her mother.

It wasn't a question of money. Margaret's dad had left her mother with a substantial stock portfolio. She owned the mansion free and clear; her debts were minimal, and her health, despite Margaret's fears, was excellent for someone going on 90. The woman still rode an exercise bicycle every day.

Margaret's adult life hadn't been as carefree as her mother's. Neither of her marriages lasted much longer than it took to make babies, one per husband. The kids, both boys, didn't like each other, and neither demonstrated any interest in their mother's welfare. That probably fueled Margaret's keen interest in her own parent, and—obviously— for her share of the inheritance when Stormy joined Pete in the Great Beyond.

As all those thoughts percolated in Margaret's brain, one kept surfacing, demanding the lion's share of attention: what, precisely, had her parents hidden in the locked cabinet?

Margaret decided it was high time she found out.

~*~

Stormy sat in the hidden chamber she and Pete had built into their home. The room could only be entered if one knew where to find the access switch. Pete insisted they have the wireless device concealed within the base of a statue of some sort, and Stormy provided one. She selected a small gargoyle modeled after those on the Notre Dame Cathedral. The statue could be moved to any other shelf, and the hidden switch would still work.

Pete hadn't much liked the gargoyle idea, but she persuaded him to go along with it. Stormy's primary means of changing Pete's mind, about anything, relied heavily on alcohol and even more heavily on sex. She suspected he often differed with her solely in anticipation of being swayed. The memories made her smile.

The specially designed room solved more than just Pete's concerns for his family's safety. It also housed Stormy's mirror. As long as the bizarre artifact remained in their home, it had to be stashed where no one would accidentally discover it. Never had the couple been more of one mind than when they designed the hideaway.

As a senior member of the GBI hierarchy, Pete had acquired more than his share of enemies. What would have been a source of pride for most people, his success, was a source of concern for Pete. He had no intention of allowing someone with a grudge against him to take it out on his family. The safe room solved that issue as well.

Though tempted to continue daydreaming about the good old days, when she found it necessary to persuade Pete to her way of thinking, Stormy had a more important concern in mind. Pete's death had not come suddenly, and while she mourned his passing daily, she admitted that having time to settle their affairs had been a blessing. Those affairs involved something even more important than planning for the welfare of Pete's dependents.

As a result of her unique mirror, Stormy had been one of Pete's most important information sources. When it came to the subject of capital crimes, however, she was his Number One informant.

She remained a valuable resource even after Pete's death, providing clues and tidbits that led to convictions for murder and other serious crimes. Stormy knew the people with whom Pete worked most closely, and their relationships remained strong until that cadre of professionals retired.

Sadly, they weren't as particular as Pete had been about finding and training protégés. That left Stormy with only one contact in the GBI, a man one-third her age with one-tenth of Pete's savvy: Donovan O'Keefe, the consummate turd.

Just thinking about O'Keefe made her angry. She'd never trusted him. In return, he'd never treated her with the deference of his predecessors. In short, what Donovan lacked in intellect and ability, he made up for in rude behavior and short sightedness. Pete would likely have fired him, or, if informed about his attitude when talking to Stormy, smacked him. Most likely both.

But, damn it all, Stormy had to contact

someone. The information she'd received the day before demanded it. If Donovan would just respond to her messages, maybe he'd accidentally pass the information to someone who gave a damn.

That's when her phone rang and broke her train of thought. She looked at the caller ID and shook her head. *Mags. The girl never gave up.*

~*~

"Behind me?" Andi whipped around and searched for the new threat. "Where?"

See that little ravine? If you crawl through there, you'll see them before they see you.

"How do you know?"

I just do. Trust me.

"Like I've got a choice," she muttered, then did as instructed. In fairly short order she reached the far end of the shallow ditch. Just as promised, she could make out the bad guys headed her way. All three carried AKs.

As she'd learned to do in previous fire fights, Andi took a breath, let half of it out, and concentrated on the first target. She squeezed the trigger and dropped him. His companions both crouched low, but not completely out of sight. She hit the second bandit square in the turban, ventilating his skull.

The third flanker flattened himself on the ground. Andi couldn't see him at all.

Can you see the last guy you put down?

Andi nodded, worried that she'd soon be caught in a crossfire.

Put a couple rounds about ten feet to the left of him.

Andi squeezed off the rounds and was rewarded by a scream of pain.

Excellent! He's done.

"I doubt that. I can still hear him; I just can't see him."

You got him good. He'll bleed out in no time.

"You can *see that?* How? Where the hell are you? Why can't I see you?"

I told you; I'll explain later. For now, your job is to stay alive. To do that, you'll need to turn around and go back to the main ditch.

"They'll be expecting me."

Probably, but they're waiting for a signal from the three yahoos you just took out. You should be able to get another one or two before they realize their pals are lookin' for virgins in Valhalla. Well, except for that one.

"Huh?"

Geezus, do I hafta spell it out? You put a bullet in his junk. Or near enough.

"Oh. Yeah. Sucks for him." Andi felt the urge to grin but shook it off and eased above the top edge of the low embankment. One of the Jihadis peeked out from behind a boulder, the bulbous upper end of his RPG slanted skyward. Andi aimed for his head and fired.

The round went wide and glanced off the boulder, but the ricochet found the target. The wounded bandit pitched sideways, and his RPG went off with a whoosh. The backblast knocked one of his comrades sideways amid screams and a chorus of "Allah Akbar! Allah Akbar!"

There's two more hiding behind the brush eight or ten meters to the right.

"To the right of what?"

The guy you winged. The one with the RPG.

Andi sent two short bursts into the shrubbery.

You got 'em both, but one's still moving.

"How the hell can you tell? I can barely see either one."

I told ya. I'm acting as overwatch. I can see

stuff you can't without making yourself a target. Not that these assholes have to be very good shots. An RPG makes a big hole.

"Any idea how many of them are left?"

Four. I think they're trying to figure out what to do with the guy who was in the shit zone behind that RPG when it went off. He's a mess.

"Now I can't see any of 'em."

Relax, kid. They're moving out.

Andi heard a scream from one of the wounded terrorists and allowed herself a smile of satisfaction. "That's for Gunny," she said. "And Tate, too. And the new guy, Walker."

And the driver. Don't forget him.

"Right. Jablonski. Nice guy, but a thick accent. You think there's a chance either of them made it?"

Sorry kid, they're gone. All of 'em.

"But how can you know that? Did you check each one of them? I got knocked silly."

You got knocked out, completely.

"Yeah, okay, but how do you know the same thing didn't happen to one of them?"

'Cause if I'd had a chance to attach to a guy, I would've done it. You were the only one left alive.

"*Attach?* What the hell does that mean? And, where are you? I wanna see your face."

That's never gonna happen. Hell, I haven't seen myself in years. Maybe decades.

"What're you talking about? Why can't you see yourself? Why the hell can't *I* see you?"

'Cause I'm a ghost.

Andi's mind and body came to a dead stop. She shivered, unable to respond.

Feel that?

"What?"

The cold. It caused the goosebumps on your arms. It's normal.

There was nothing even remotely normal about any of this. "I— Uh...." She rubbed her arms until her skin smoothed out. Normal, she feared, was no longer part of her world.

Don't sweat it, kid. I'm used to it. I don't like it, but there's not much I can do about it.

"But I— How—"

Get some rest. You need it. I'll explain everything later, when you've had a few drinks and you won't shit yourself over the details.

"Uh, okay, I guess."

Just chill. They'll be sending a rescue unit out here sooner or later. I need you to stay alive at least 'til then.

"And then what? You'll attach yourself to someone else? Someone with the proper plumbing?" She shook her head then added, "Who knew ghosts could be assholes."

I would change hosts if I could, but that would require you being dead. Until that happens, you're stuck with me. And I'm stuck with you.

"Oh, swell."

Yeah, well I kinda feel the same way. It's not like either of us had a choice in the matter.

Andi let their conversation sink in. Weird didn't even begin to describe how she felt. After all, the ghost, or spirit, or whatever the hell he was, had saved her life. Probably several times. She hadn't even thanked him.

"You got a name?"

You can call me Will.

"Nice to uhm... Meet you, I guess. I'm Andi. It's short for Andrea." She felt like she was missing something important, like a handshake or a salute. Maybe a hug.

Get some rest, girl. I'll wake you when the time comes.

Though tempted to ask him if he ever slept, Andi let the question go unasked and snuggled into a hollow in the embankment. It felt good to know someone was keeping an eye on her. Will, she thought. Seems like a nice enough sort.

Chapter Two

"In the main, ghosts are said to be forlorn and generally miserable, if not downright depressed. The jolly ghost is rare." —Dick Cavett

Margaret drifted into the electronics store and pretended to examine the consumer products in the display cases. Clocks, digital recorders, TVs, and an array of computerized toys lined the shelves on both sides of the shop. Toward the rear she could see a seemingly endless supply of electronic components sealed in plastic bags hanging from pegboard racks on the walls. She had no idea what function any of the mysterious gizmos provided and assumed one needed to be a nuclear physicist to make use of them. On second thought, her youngest son would probably know what functions they served, but the smarmy little snot would have to be bribed to share his knowledge.

In any event, she didn't need components. She needed something already built. Something covert, and, if at all possible, cheap.

"Can I help you?" asked a pathetically thin, young salesperson of indeterminate sex. The script style lettering on his name tag read *Chad*. Considering his bizarre hair style and the assortment of rings and metal detritus adorning his ears, she would have guessed he'd sport a "New Age" name. Nothing said goth like dark eyeliner and an abundance of skin piercings. Without the name tag, she mused, she would have guessed he was female.

"Uh, yes," she said. "I need a camera."

"Why not just use a smart phone?"

Margaret had no desire to be rude, but his direct stare was off-putting. "My phone? Oh, no." She forced a chuckle. "I want a camera I can stick on a wall. I need to keep an eye on something from a distance."

"Worried about home invaders?" he asked. A head shake sent quivers through the piercings. "Had one bust into my place not long ago. Stole a laptop and broke the glass on my fish tank. Killed my piranha. I'd love to get my hands on whoever did it. Dead wouldn't be the worst of it."

He slithered out from behind the counter and motioned for Margaret to follow him. "The bad guys are gettin' smarter. They see a camera, they don't run any more. They shoot 'em, or knock 'em down and stomp 'em."

"I'm not too worried about that," Margaret said, trying to picture her 89-year-old mother stomping on anything, "but I need something that isn't intrusive. In fact, I'd rather it not be seen at all."

"Like a spy camera? Something really small you can hide somewhere?"

"Yes," she said. "Exactly."

He deftly sorted through boxes in an under-counter cabinet until he had the one he wanted. "This should do the trick," he said, proffering a compact box in one hand.

"That's it?" She hefted the package, surprised by its light weight. "You sure this isn't empty?"

"Positive," Chad said. "The camera's tiny but works great. I know; I've got one."

"How much is it?"

"Two hundred dollars, but it's worth it. Works with any PC. Won't work with a Mac, though, for some stupid reason."

Chad pushed his long, inky black hair past his temples. Margaret wondered if he ever got his fingers caught in the jewelry hanging from his ears. "Why do I need a PC? I thought I could just watch on TV," she said.

"You can, but that won't do you much good if you aren't at home. A laptop PC would be your best bet."

Margaret exhaled heavily. "So, how much will that cost?" She dreaded the answer. Maybe spying on her mother wasn't such a great idea after all. Maybe she should just confront her and demand to know what she had hidden in the Safe Room. *Yeah, like that'd work.*

"There are some cheap PCs available. If all you want to do is check your email and watch the closed-circuit TV, I can fix you up for a little more than the price of the camera. You know how to use the internet?"

"I— No. I just use my phone."

"Hm." Chad seemed to lose focus, unaware of another customer entering the store. After a few moments of rumination there came a nod and a mumbled, "Hang on a sec."

Margaret made way as the salesclerk trotted toward a door at the back of the store and disappeared. She opened the box he'd handed her and dumped the contents into her palm. The camera was about the size of a lipstick, but flat rather than cylindrical. The lens was equally tiny, and she wondered if it could generate a decent picture.

Chad returned with a big smile and coruscating doodaddery in both ears. "You're gonna love this!"

"I am?"

"I know how to send the video signal straight to your phone."

Margaret grinned back. "No shit? I mean, no kidding?"

Chad saluted her. "No shit is right!"

~*~

"Donovan O'Keefe, please," Stormy said into the telephone. "Tell him it's Mrs. Peter Talmadge."

"I'll ring him for you." The person on the other end of the line didn't react to Pete's name.

How quickly they forget.

Stormy waited. O'Keefe never seemed available. Her calls to him usually went to voicemail, to which he rarely responded.

"This is Director O'Keefe."

Stormy smiled. "Good afternoon, Director. This is—"

"I'm very busy today, Mrs. Talmadge. What's on your mind?"

"I wanted to alert you to an incident—"

"Oh Lord, Mrs. Talmadge, I don't have time—"

"You've no time to investigate and apprehend a murderer?"

Her question floated on dead air for one long moment. O'Keefe broke the silence with a prolonged sigh, as if he were being forced to deal with the lowest of all possible intellects. A thought which, coincidentally, percolated in Stormy's mind, too.

"If you witnessed a murder, Mrs. Talmadge, wouldn't it make more sense to call the police? Why bother me?"

"Who said anything about witnessing a murder? I merely have information about one. I would gladly share it with the local police, but I don't know anyone on the force. My contacts there have all retired." *Or died.* "Besides, this calls for someone with better than average detective skills." She stopped talking before she went too far. With any luck, Director O'Keefe would assign the case to someone who really did have detective skills. His only expertise seemed to be office politics. It was the only explanation for his rise within the organization.

"You wasted enough of my time with your last call."

"The one where you failed to find the victim's body? That one? As I recall, the remains were eventually located by a rookie officer with the Bentonville Police. Nice young man, one of four people who make up the entire force. Have you ever been to Bentonville?"

"I really do have to go back to work now, so if you've got something to tell me, this would be a good time."

Stormy could imagine him shifting from foot to foot, staring at his watch, or lusting after a doughnut. *Such a complete asshole.* "Why don't you just let me speak to someone who'll actually do something with my information?"

"You're trying my patience, Mrs. Talmadge. The only reason I'm talking to you at all is out of respect for your late husband."

"I appreciate that, Mr. O'Keefe." *But believe me, I'd much rather be talking to someone competent.* "How do you want to proceed?"

"Give me the information you have, and tell me how you got it. If I think it's credible, I'll put someone on it."

"You know I can't divulge my sources."

"Then you've tied my hands. There's nothing I can do. Go to the local police or call the State Patrol. We've got enough work to do without having to investigate the fantasies of old ladies who don't know what they're talking about."

Stormy took a deep breath before responding. "I've been a resource for the GBI since before you were born. The crimes solved on the basis of my information were anything but fantasies."

"Mm-hm, sure. But like you said, that was before my time. Way before."

"Well then, I suppose we're done," Stormy said. "I've still got some contacts at the *Atlanta Clarion*. They might be interested in knowing the GBI doesn't have time to investigate murders."

"Is that supposed to be a threat?"

You wouldn't know a threat if it kicked you in the head. "Of course not. But the information is too valuable to waste, and if you're not going to use it, perhaps someone at the *Clarion*, or one of their readers, will."

"But—"

"Good day, Mr. O'Keefe."

~*~

The rescue unit didn't arrive until the following morning, and it wasn't difficult for Andi to identify them as friendlies when they finally showed up. Still, she didn't leave her position until she was absolutely certain they weren't Jihadis disguised as GIs. It had happened before.

As they poked through the wreckage of the hummer and collected remains, Andi slowly made her way out of the ravine in which she'd hidden. "Hey, guys! Over here."

Every head swiveled in her direction, every gun raised.

"C'mon, y'all. Do I look like a raghead?"

A marine corporal tipped his helmet back and smiled at her. "Man, is it good to see you! We thought they'd gotten the whole team."

"Not quite," she said, straightening and moving slightly faster. "You got anything to eat? I'm starved."

"Just bottled water and MREs, but help yourself," the soldier said, pointing to the first of three armored vehicles parked nearby. "You know where to look."

Andi settled herself beside the first vehicle, an M1152, basically a beefed-up hummer with a turret-mounted, M2 .50 caliber machinegun. The weapon, affectionately known as a "Ma Deuce" would have come in handy the day before. But then, so would the heavier armor of the machines parked around her. And all the troops who came with 'em. And maybe some kinda instant transport device which might have beamed them all back to base without anyone getting killed.

While she ate, half of the rescue unit scoured the area while the other half stood watch. The NCOIC made notes. Eventually he sauntered toward her and leaned back against the vehicle. "I gotta say, you look pretty damned good for what you've been through."

Andi shrugged, then looked at the bodies of her slain comrades. They'd been arrayed on stretchers, ready to be loaded into one of the trucks. "Those poor guys never knew what hit 'em," she said. "Fuckin' IEDs. We never had a chance. I'd be dead, too, if my Top hadn't dragged me clear. Now he's gone, too." She teared up and didn't care who saw it.

"We found a bunch of dead Hajjis over there," the sergeant said, pointing with his jaw. "You get all of them by yourself?"

"A couple got away," she said, wiping her nose with her sleeve. "I wasn't really up for chasing 'em."

Gimme a break, girl. You'd be dead if not for

me.

Andi winced, anxious about how the sergeant would react to Will's voice. But he didn't react at all. Instead, he gave her an appreciative smile. "What's your name, Marine?"

Andi brushed away the dirt and sand obscuring the stenciled name on her uniform. "It's Vega, sir. Lance Corporal Andi Vega."

He can't hear me, y'know.

"Thank God for that," she muttered.

"Did you say something Vega?"

"No— I— It's nothing. I'm just tired is all. It was a— a rough night."

"Copy that," the sergeant said. "You did good, kid. I'm sorry about your team, but what happened to them isn't your fault."

The sergeant made a notation on his clipboard and went back to collect data on the dead.

You're smart not to mention me.

Like, who in hell would believe me, Andi thought to herself.

I said, you're smart not to mention me.

"Wait. I can hear you in my head, but you can't read my mind?"

Ten-four. If you don't say it out loud, I can't hear it. Which is just fine with me, 'cause I'd rather not know what's goin' on in yer noggin. So, you can think whatever you like. I couldn't care less.

Andi looked around, hoping for a distraction. She tried to find something that looked normal, something that wasn't either burned, blown up, or bloody. There weren't many options. "This is some crazy weird shit."

Bein' out here?

"Having a goddam voice in my head!"

You'll get used to it.

"You gotta be kiddin' me."

Nope.

Andi palmed her temples. How would she ever get used to something so completely insane? With any luck, she'd wake up soon and be curled up in her rack, most likely nursing the mother of all hangovers.

~*~

Armed with Chad's instructions, Margaret hurried back to her mother's house after dropping the older woman off at the doctor's office. Margaret offered a cover story about needing to zip into town on an errand and promised to return quickly so

Stormy wouldn't have to wait.

Almost surprised her house key still worked, Margaret slipped into the old mansion and made her way to the cellar. She found the bookcase with its gargoyle statue and activated the hidden door. It swung away on silent hinges, as it always had, and Margaret stood looking into the secret safe room.

On a lark, she tested the cabinet door she'd never seen opened. It didn't budge, and her house key clearly wasn't made for the lock on it. She briefly considered rummaging around in search of a key, then gave up on the idea. All her previous efforts had come up empty, so she had no reason to think a new search would result in anything different.

Now, however, she finally had a way to find out what was in the cabinet. All she had to do was set up the tiny, closed circuit camera, then sit back and wait for her mother to reveal everything. Or as much as the little camera could capture.

She dragged a stepstool into the hallway just outside the safe room and climbed to the top step. By stretching, she could just reach the crown moulding and used a bit of two-sided tape to adhere the camera to the wall.

The camera had a wide-angle lens, and she could check the image quality and direction before doing the final attachment. Chad said the tape was industrial grade, and the camera would remain in place through a natural disaster. The only such disaster Margaret could think of was the one which would occur if her mother discovered someone was spying on her. That thought caused her to wipe the tiny camera free of any possible fingerprints. Margaret knew only too well Stormy still had connections in the Georgia Bureau of Investigation.

With the camera installed and the picture faithfully reproduced in high definition black and white, Margaret closed the door to the secret room and tripped the locking mechanism. She paused briefly to admire the device. Unless one knew exactly where to look, the little statue hiding the electronic switch appeared to be just another of the ugly little gargoyles like those lining the shelf in the safe room. Why her parents found the hideous things appealing she never understood, but it seemed like they'd added to the collection every couple of years. She'd be quite happy to dump them all at the nearest second-hand store as a donation.

She whistled to herself all the way back to the doctor's office.

~*~

Thankfully, Mags didn't insist on walking Stormy back into her house after taking her to the doctor. Neither of the women cared to engage in the bickering such visits usually featured. Stormy waited until Mags had backed out of the driveway and crept into the sluggish traffic already stalling in front of the house. Satisfied she would remain unobserved, Stormy took the long, circular ramp into the garden and entered the lower level of the house.

She and Pete had both laughingly referred to the area as the "terrace level" ever since they'd seen something similar advertised in the paper. Pete thought the expression utterly pompous and chuckled whenever either of them used it. Now the term seemed more comfortable even if Pete was no longer there to laugh at it. Pausing outside the bookcase which hid the entrance to the safe room, Stormy opened a small refrigerator set against the wall and extracted a bottle of chilled chardonnay. Pete, of course, would have helped himself to a beer, if not something stronger. Neither of them cared to deal with the portal hidden in the safe room without the advantage of an adult beverage. Even after dealing with the bizarre communication device for most of her life, Stormy still found it unsettling.

After pouring herself a generous helping of white wine, she shelved the bottle and opened the safe room door, watching as it rolled silently to one side. She took a sip, turned on some background music—always something meant to soothe the soul—and then opened the cabinet which housed the ancient mirror.

It had been nearly seventy years since she

took possession of the damned thing, and damned it most certainly was. She'd gotten it from a grave digger back during the war—the Big War—and she'd had it ever since. But it wasn't something one "owned." At least, not in the traditional sense. She was merely its caretaker. She had also become a mouthpiece, a voice for those who could no longer speak to the living.

She kept a photo of the little white dog she and Pete had rescued at about the same time she'd taken custody of the mirror. Looking at the photo, she couldn't help but smile. The rascal had been more meaningful to them than she could have ever imagined. They took him everywhere, and he responded with a measure of love beyond anything they could have asked for. Officially named "Little Bit," they shortened it to an affectionate "Bits," a name to which he readily answered. He lived to be 18 and was a favorite of both her kids. She missed him nearly as much as she missed Pete.

He, unlike Donovan O'Keefe, the GBI's Special Moron in Charge, would have known exactly what to do about the problem she'd been alerted to the day before. Some idiot had murdered his estranged girlfriend and was lying in wait for the deceased's current lover to return to Georgia from out of town. Stormy would have simply called the guy to warn him, but she lacked the contact information. That wasn't a terribly unusual omission for the reigning

Keeper of the Portal. Some were better than others, and this one was worse than usual. Fortunately, he was ill equipped to maintain his hold on the position. She hoped his successor would be better. She prayed that when all was said and done, he would stay on the other side.

She had put in a call to her last remaining contact at the *Atlanta Courier*, her former employer. She'd retired as something of a legend after putting in fifty years as a gossip columnist. "Treat this like an anonymous tip," she'd said. "Our potential victim arrives tonight on a flight from the West Coast. I'd really hate to read about him getting shot at Hartsfield International. They get enough bad press as it is. I gave you the shooter's name, but naturally he's in the wind. I'm sure the cops will want to know what he's got in mind, too. With any luck, they'll get to him first."

Sadly, it didn't always work out that way, but there was only so much an old lady could do. Mostly just alert the authorities and hope for the best. As she had done for the past many decades, she flipped the switch to close the door to the secret room and took another sip of wine as she watched it close. Safely locked in, it was time to go to work.

"Moping around isn't going to get anything done," she announced to the empty room. "Might as well find out who's got the biggest problem today." With that she unlocked the cabinet and opened its doors wide, then lowered herself into an easy chair situated perfectly for the coming ordeal. With a pillow supporting her back and her feet elevated comfortably on a built-in footrest, she waited for the Keeper of the Portal to morph into something recognizable.

With a deep sigh, Stormy uttered a refrain she'd repeated many times. "Oh, how I wish I had turned this over to someone else. I'm too old and tired to deal with it anymore."

Had she been completely honest, she would have admitted that the reason she continued to deal with the dead was because it gave her a reason to go on living.

~*~

Andi returned to base and dragged herself to her quarters, an air-conditioned trailer she shared with three other females. They, too, were marines, but unlike her, they had rear echelon jobs and treated Andi with respect. She was, after all, a grunt, and she wore the title with pride. Grunts had been carrying the load for the country for 200-plus years. Being part of that, she felt, was pretty damned cool.

Aw, hell. I hadn't thought about where you'd be sleeping. You got three female roomies, don'cha?

"Yeah. So what?" Andi was in no mood for chatting. She could barely keep her eyes open. If she could do that long enough to take a shower and crawl into some clean underwear, she planned to spend the next week or three sleeping.

They'll be prancing around, sharing lipstick and shit, and talking about romance magazines and birth control. I just don't want to have to listen to it.

"Then don't." Andi got undressed and was about to drop her fatigues in a pile on the floor when she paused. "You can see me, can't you?"

Yeah.

"Well, how 'bout turning around and looking the other way? Or, better yet, go the hell away."

You wouldn't know the difference.

"So humor me. Pretend I can see your ugly, misogynistic mug."

Whoa. Misogynistic? Where'd that come from?

"I learned it in school from a guy whose nose now runs at a funky angle from his face."

So, now that we're outta the sandbox you're all hard ass?

"Nah. I just don't like it when guys try to lord their usefulness over me. That shit's way overrated."

Will chuckled. *Ya know, we might just get*

along okay, you and me.

Screw modesty. Andi let her clothes fall to the floor. Since there wasn't anything she could do about Will seeing her during what should be private moments, she simply decided it wasn't worth worrying about. She didn't have or do anything he hadn't seen a million times anyway. However, since there were others on base she didn't intend to entertain, she grabbed a towel and wrapped herself in it before heading to the showers. Fortunately, it was a short walk.

Nice birthmark, kid.

"Gee, thanks. Now please leave me alone."

I think I'll go find a poker game somewhere.

"Something tells me they won't let you play." She let the shower door slap shut behind her and draped her towel over it. Anyone over six feet tall could peek inside, but did so at their peril. Most of the guys in her unit were protective of her privacy, an honor she'd won by serving beside them. It did not extend to her three roommates who always stood guard for each other whenever they needed to wash up. Andi thought it was funny.

"You still there?" she said in a low voice.

Will didn't respond.

"Awesome," she said, her voice coming out in

a relaxed whoosh. She doubted she'd ever get all the sand out of her hair and scalp while she remained in country, but the effort felt good. It also felt good to be alone.

Found one.

Shit. Time to rinse.

There's a handful of guys in a tent on the other side of these trailers playin' Texas Holdem.

"Swell."

Ya wanna play?

"No. I wanna sleep. You remember sleep, don't you? It's what live people do. Except when someone's buggin' 'em." She turned off the water, grabbed her towel, and dried off. Wrapped in the damp towel, she gathered her kit and started back toward her trailer.

C'mon. It'll be fun.

"Poker is stupid. It's a waste of time and money."

Doesn't have to be. In fact, I can guarantee it won't be. If you'll let me.

"Is there a way to *stop* you? Can I get a giant spray can of shut-the-fuck-up somewhere? You're really gettin' on my nerves."

He sighed. *Okay. You're right. You need rest. I figured you'd slept out in the desert.*

"The bugs make it hard to get comfy out there, especially when the neighborhood is full of religious nutjobs who'd rather whack infidels than whack off." She slipped into the trailer, dropped her towel, and put on clean underwear. The bed looked more inviting than it ever had. She didn't even care that the sheets hadn't been changed in recent memory. All she had left to do was go back out and hang her towel to dry.

Oh, my! You make GI undies look good. Too bad they cover up that birthmark.

"Seriously? I want to take a nap, and you're trying to chat me up like you want a date or something? Get a life." She stopped and giggled. "Get a life. That's actually pretty funny."

I was only trying to be nice. You really do look good.

"I'm sure it's just the wet hair and the olive drab granny panties. Does it every time." She fell into bed and rolled over on her side. "Do me a favor and wake me up if we're under attack. Otherwise go away and leave me alone."

She fell asleep before he could respond.

Chapter Three

"Last night I stayed up late playing poker with Tarot cards. I got a full house, and four people died."
—*Steven Wright*

Stormy knew she had to be patient with the mirror. The soul acting as its keeper may or may not have been ready to be contacted. Connections were always iffy at best. This time, however, she didn't have to wait long. An eerie faced seemed to form out of nothing and replaced Stormy's reflection.

"I've nothing much to pass along," the Keeper said. "Though many clamor for attention, few are worthy. They all seek to send some message to the living."

Stormy nodded in feigned agreement. If only he were alive, the current Keeper could have filled in admirably for Donovan O'Keefe. Neither of them seemed to have the interests of anyone else in mind.

"There is one woman," the Keeper said, "who has been particularly insistent, but I told you about her problem yesterday. Or was it last week? Time has little meaning here."

"It depends on who you're talking about," Stormy said, trying to mask her impatience. "The last person you told me about was murdered by her ex-boyfriend, and she was worried he would try to kill her current boyfriend."

The wraith nodded. "That's her. That's the one. She pesters me constantly."

"Could be she's worried about her sweetheart."

"Why? It's not like she'll be breathing new life into that affair."

What a jerk. "Have a little heart." *Did I really say that? This idiot has no heart at all.*

"Ah well, other than her, I've nothing important to pass on."

"Good," said Stormy, doubting him, but pleased to be off the hot seat. "I'll talk to you again, soon."

Rather than wait for a response, she got up

and closed the cabinet doors, sealing the specter and the mirror in local darkness.

~*~

Tanner Howell walked through the gates of the Georgia State Prison in Penhurst, fourteen years and ten months older than when he went in. According to the Parole Board, Tanner had been rehabilitated. His previous life of crime and all his felony convictions were behind him. Tanner knew better.

For fourteen years and ten months he'd been thinking about ways to get revenge for his convictions. He knew exactly who to blame. He knew without any doubt who had robbed him of his freedom. He even knew where the bastard lived. Unfortunately, the bastard wasn't living there anymore, or anywhere else for that matter. He was dead. Probably died of old age. Tanner hoped he'd suffered some seriously horrible disease, the kind they didn't bother to treat when one of his fellow inmates had them.

On the contrary, he hoped Pete Talmadge got all the treatments modern medicine had to offer. With any luck they only prolonged his agony. As soon as Tanner got back to Atlanta, he vowed to find the righteous bastard's grave and piss on it. When he was done, he would go after everyone Talmadge left behind.

For the time being, however, the only thing he could do was start the long walk to the bus station. Talmadge's grave could wait. It wasn't going anywhere.

~*~

By late afternoon, Andi's roommates returned and napping was no longer an option. Fortunately, she'd had enough, and the only thing she wanted was food. If she had to look at another MRE, she'd puke.

Forward Operating Base DeJarnette wasn't a huge affair, but it wasn't as puny as others she knew of. They had a modest PX, a decent chow hall, and an operations building that housed a handful of secret squirrels—intelligence officers, supposedly—who had a good bit to say about the missions run from the base. After the latest debacle, Andi had even less respect for them, assuming that was possible. Most of the guys in her unit agreed, those butt wipes never went out on a mission unless they choppered in at night accompanied by a swarm of Spec Ops bad-asses to babysit them.

They never got ambushed. Or killed.

Andi would mourn her lost comrades at some point. They would all be recognized in a hurried ceremony before their remains were shipped back stateside. She still hadn't come to grips with the engagement. It would happen in due time, she knew. Now, however, she needed food. Her next stop was the chow line.

Don't eat the potato salad.

"You've gotta stop sneakin' up on me like this," she muttered, already tired of the conversation.

Who's sneaking? I'm always here.

Lucky me. Andi glanced around to make sure no one was watching her talk to the air. "What's wrong with the potato salad?"

The guy who made it has a cold, and he wasn't too careful where he sneezed.

"Aw geez. You tryin' to make me sick?"

Obviously not. I need you healthy. It's better for me. You won't be as moody.

"I'm not moody!"

You're a woman, aren't you?

"And you're an asshole. A male, chauvinist pig asshole."

Though tempted to try the potato salad as a way to show Will who was boss, she decided against it. If she caught a cold, he'd be all up in her shit with one "I told ya so" after another. She needed that like she needed a third elbow. Besides, the burgers looked good.

Toting the Marine's version of a Quarter Pounder with Cheese, Andi grabbed a soft drink and settled down in a corner of the big tent. She hadn't even tasted the burger when two guys from the Ops Center sauntered into the room. She didn't know who was who, but she'd frequently heard their names. Gunny mentioned them often when briefing his team before a mission. One of them was Derrick Benjamin, the other was Bart Massey. Together, they'd said something to the wrong people and got four marines killed for nothing. Marines she knew, and cared about.

Making no effort to hide her scowl, she watched the pair yuck it up as they went through the chow line. Both took generous servings of the potato salad which made her feel somewhat better.

Y'know they're both poker players.

"Makes 'em even dumber than I thought."

Use yer head, girl. It's a way to get back at them. Maybe the only way.

"What are you talkin' about?"

We can kick their butts in poker. Get a little payback for Gunny.

"Beat them at cards? Oh yeah. That'll

definitely make me feel better."

C'mon. Think about it. How much money do you s'pose they make? Doesn't matter. It's way more than you'll ever see.

"Hey—"

So, how would you like to take every penny they have? Put it in your own pocket. Buy yourself something nice when you get home?

"And how do we do that?"

Oh, that's easy; we cheat. The hard part's gonna be getting them to let you play with 'em.

"Something tells me you've already got that figured out."

It's all about greed, kid. First though, we'll need to build up your image, generate some winnings. If they're impressive enough, the big boys will let you in; they'll want some of your money. We want 'em to think they can get all of it.

"You don't understand. I've never played poker in my life!"

~*~

At first, Margaret figured she'd make a fairly decent spy. Her dad had been pretty slick about gathering information and working clues, but after watching the closed-circuit image on her phone for a couple hours, she knew the truth: she sucked at spy stuff. Patience had never been her strong suit, and that had never been more apparent than now.

What she needed, she finally realized, was a camera that only came on when someone approached the hidden door. It hadn't occurred to her before, but even if she did witness something on the tiny screen of her crummy little flip phone, it couldn't record much of anything. So even if she was watching when her mother entered the safe room, Margaret wouldn't be able to review it later. Much as she hated the idea, another visit to Chad and the electronics store suddenly became a critical need.

She congratulated herself on thinking to call ahead.

"E-Zee-E-Lectronics," intoned the bored voice which answered her ring.

"Is Chad there?"

"Hang on. I'll see."

The phone clattered annoyingly then went nearly silent. Margaret could hear people talking in the background, but she couldn't make out what they were saying. Someone moved the phone, and she heard the sounds of a cash register drawer opening and closing. More talk. More clatter. And then, a familiar voice. "Hello?"

"Chad!"

"Speaking. What can I do for ya?"

Margaret reminded him of her recent purchase and how he'd been so very helpful. "I hate to bother you again, but I've run into a little problem."

"It's your phone, right? You can't record much."

"How'd you know?"

He chuckled, though the pitch seemed higher than she remembered. "I guess I'm psychic. I thought about mentioning the storage issue to you, but you didn't look interested in a phone upgrade. Sorry 'bout that."

"You're exactly right," Margaret said. "I need a better phone. One that will record whatever the closed-circuit camera transmits."

"You don't need to record non-stop. If there's nothing going on, what's the point?"

"Right! Can my camera be set up to do that?"

"I doubt it," he said. "It's pretty basic. We've got some newer CCTVs that're much better. You can get color, and sound, too. Who likes silent movies anymore?"

Margaret could feel her savings drain away

with every new feature. "I don't suppose there's an entry level camera thingy, is there?"

"That's what you have now," he said.

"Any chance I could return it and get an upgrade? I've only had it a couple days."

Chad sounded wistful. "The company's got a really sh— I mean, *crummy* policy when it comes to returns."

"I should've known better. This sort of thing always happens to me."

"And there's more to it. The better gear is a little harder to install. You might need to hire somebody."

Margaret felt the weight of defeat bearing down on her. Her tears hadn't begun to flow, but it wouldn't be long before they did. "Hiring someone sounds expensive."

"Maybe, maybe not. It depends."

"On what?"

"On who does it." Chad cleared his throat. "I've been known to take on a side job now and then. I don't charge nearly as much as some do. It doesn't require a master's degree."

"Well," Margaret said after a deep breath. "You know what I need. Can you work up a package deal for me?"

"Sure," he said. "Lemme see what I can do. Can you give me a few minutes?"

Margaret tried not to look worried while she waited, and was pleasantly surprised when he handed her his quote. The price he intended to charge for his labor appeared to be a mistake. She wouldn't cross the street for a figure that low, but if it wasn't an error, she imagined he was embarrassed by the high price of the new equipment she'd have to buy. Fortunately, he credited her for the return of the first camera. She decided Chad was either a very decent sort or the most devious salesperson she'd ever met.

She might end up broke, but she'd finally learn the big secret about the safe room and the mysterious cabinet within. Now all she had to do was figure out how to lure her mother out of the house long enough to remove the old camera and install the new one. If only she knew someone who'd be willing to—

Suddenly Margaret smiled. She knew just who to call, someone she never thought she'd have to speak to again.

~*~

Will directed Andi to a neighboring tent. The music emanating from within was too loud, but then, it seemed like anything and everything in Afghanistan—"the Stan"—was extreme. She slipped through the opening and cleared her throat to gain the attention of the soldiers inside. They seemed to be evenly divided between napping and card playing.

"Yo, guys! We got company," one of them said as he rolled off his rack to a standing position. He gave her a slight bow and waved his arm as if to usher her into their domain. "Welcome aboard. We don't get many ladies in here," he said.

"That ain't no lady, bro," said another. "That there is a marine."

Andi felt an unfamiliar moment of discomfort, as if she didn't belong.

"C'mon, man. She's too cute to be one of us," said a bare-chested soldier in workout shorts. Andi guessed he was from the East Coast somewhere, but her grasp of linguistic geography was thin at best.

"You wanna git yer ass kicked, son, just try something with her," said one of the card players without even turning around. "And if she don't do it, I will."

Andi believed him fully capable of backing up his words with action. His biceps were bigger than her thighs. "Thanks," she said. "But I can look out for myself."

Ask him if you can join their game.

Andi tried not to react visibly to Will's voice.

They're playin' Texas Holdem. Ask if you can play, too.

"What's yer name, sweetheart?" asked the New Englander.

"It sure as hell ain't 'sweetheart,'" she said. "Guess again."

Several of the guys laughed at her bravado. Those who hadn't been paying attention suddenly became intrigued. "Try Ballbreaker," one of them said.

"Back off," said the heavily muscled card player. "That's Andi Vega. She was in Mandeville's unit."

Chatter in the room came to a halt, and someone turned the music down.

"She's the only one who made it back alive yesterday. And the way I heard it, she took out more than her share of bandits. Shot the nuts off one of 'em."

That broke the ice, and Andi smiled, happy she wouldn't have to play the role of hard ass. She didn't mind doing so when it came to civilians or rear echelon types who pissed her off. But she much preferred to be a warrior among warriors. These were her people. And they would very likely be the unit she was assigned to next.

The card game?

"Geez," she muttered under her breath. "Don't you ever give up?"

"Give up what?" asked the grunt she'd mentally nicknamed "Muscles."

She managed a short laugh. "Oh, nothin'. Just talkin' to myself." Moving closer to the table where the cards lay in a disorderly sprawl, she added, "Texas Holdem?"

"Yeah," he said. "You play?"

"Not very well."

"In that case, feel free to join us." He quickly surveyed the four others crowded around a makeshift table. "Any objections?"

There were none, and the men shuffled a bit to make room for her.

Just relax. I'll tell you what to do.

Anything but relaxed, Andi watched as Muscles and the guy to his right each tossed a coin onto the blanket-covered storage case which served as their table. She reached into her pocket for some change, but Will told her forget it.

Not yet. Watch and learn. You'll get your chance. They're just laying down the blinds.

Muscles then dealt out six hands of two cards each, face down. He gave everyone time to examine theirs, then nodded to the man on his left.

"Call," he said, dropping a quarter on the table.

He's matching the big blind.

The next player muttered, "Fold" and tossed his cards toward the dealer.

What a chicken shit. I'd have paid to see the flop, at least. What's at risk, two-bits?

The flop?

The third player dropped two quarters on the table and grunted something that might have been, "Raise." Andi couldn't tell what he was eating, but it appeared to be a gigantic serving of something inordinately chewy. She hoped he wouldn't choke.

When it's your turn, just fold.

Andi desperately wanted to know why, but remained silent until it was her turn, then gracefully turned in her cards with a polite, "Fold."

When they finished the first round of bets, Muscles placed three cards face up in the middle of the table, the ten of spades, the six of spades, and the jack of hearts.

That's the Flop.

Okay. That makes about as much sense as onions on ice cream.

Another round of betting ensued followed by a fourth card laid face up beside the first three, the queen of diamonds.

That last card dealt? That's called the Turn, and it gives Mush Mouth over there three of a kind. Good thing it's not a big pot.

Three players remained in the betting, and Muscles raised the stakes with a crisp fiver which the other two called, then dealt one last card, face up: the ace of clubs.

That's called the River.

Of course it is, Andi thought. *Who makes this shit up?*

He's betting on a pair of sevens and trying to scare the other two off. Ain't gonna happen. Mush Mouth has three queens. He won't buy it, but the other guy'll fold. He's got nuthin'.

Andi still wasn't sure what she should be looking at, much less betting on. She felt sure she'd never remember all the rules, let alone the stupid names for the cards. Flops and Rivers? Why not animal names or— She couldn't think of anything absurd enough. "Y'know what, guys? I'm still kinda worn-out after yesterday. I'm gonna go take a nap."

What? We just got started. You haven't learned anything yet!

"I've learned enough for one day," she mumbled on her way out of the tent.

~*~

Stormy had just finished reading the *Clarion* when she received a call from Mrs. Olivia Ingram, head of the Marietta Historical Homes Society.

"I'll get right to the point," Ms. Ingram said. Her slightly nasal tone did nothing to disguise her cultivated Southern accent. "I have it on good authority that your house is in decline. We're afraid it will bring down the overall quality of the other homes in our organization. I'm calling to arrange a time when you can go over the findings of our inspection. We'll be happy to help you itemize and address the work which needs to be done."

"That's kind of you," Stormy said, mentally holding her nose as she spoke, "but I really don't need, or want, any help. I'll take care of anything that needs to be done."

"When?"

Stormy let out a tight snort of laughter.

"Whenever I get around to it, I suppose."

"I fear you don't recognize the gravity of the situation."

"Evidently not." Stormy conjured a mental image of the dowdy Ms. Ingram ignoring gravity and floating up into the sky, astride a broom.

"I feel compelled to remind you that many of the homes in the Society are on the National Historic Register. Those of us who have the good fortune to live in them have a civic responsibility to maintain them, wouldn't you agree?"

"I suppose so. Yes."

"Well then, what's the problem?"

"That's funny," Stormy said. "I was about to ask you the same question."

Mrs. Ingram let out a protracted sigh. "There was a reason I dreaded making this call," she said. "I wish you'd take this seriously."

"Believe it or not, I'm trying to do just that."

"You can prove it with a show of good faith. Meet with us so we can go over the report and help you decide the best way to proceed."

"All right," Stormy said, still not fully resigned to her fate. "How about some time next month?"

"How about tomorrow afternoon? We have an opening at two o'clock."

"But, I—"

"Come, come, Mrs. Talmadge. Don't put it off. That'll only make it worse. I presume you know where our offices are?"

"Yes, but—"

"Good, then we'll look for you tomorrow at two. Have a nice day."

~*~

"That went fairly well," Olivia Ingram said as she leaned back in her swivel chair, oblivious to the noises of protest from her vintage perch.

Margaret wondered how many yards of crushed velvet were needed to cover the monstrosity, or if it reached crushed status before or after it was applied. She let the notions slide. "Thank you for making the call. My mother can be a little hard-headed at times."

"Speaking for the Society, we're grateful you brought the issue to our attention. We can't allow all these fine, old homes to fall down through neglect. The owners must take responsibility or this will become just another neighborhood. And I have no intention of ever living in *just another neighborhood*. Or a ghetto for that matter."

The comparison was not lost on Margaret. "I'll call Mother and offer to bring her to the meeting, but I'd appreciate it if you didn't mention I was the one who instigated the review of her home."

Olivia tut-tutted the idea of revealing any confidentialities. "That will remain just between us."

"It's much appreciated," Margaret said already mentally preparing for the call to her mother. With any luck, Chad would still be available to do the camera installation while the house was vacant. She felt a twinge of guilt over revealing the existence of the secret room to an outsider, but told herself it couldn't be helped. Whatever had been going on in that room would soon be revealed. She prayed it was something innocent, but doubted it. The more she dwelled on the possibilities of what Stormy Talmadge did in the privacy of that locked room, the more she feared the worst.

But the worst *what*, exactly?

~*~

Tanner Howell had no intention of ever returning to prison. As his bus slowly worked its way toward his old Atlanta stomping grounds, he thought about the lies he'd told and the commitments he'd made in order to get his release. He'd told them of his conversion to Christianity and his deep and abiding faith in the Lord. He told them how terrible he felt for the horrible crimes he'd committed. He told them anything he thought they might want to hear. He'd even stayed out of trouble for a few years, although bribing a guard or two to keep quiet about a few things had cost him dearly.

But at long last, he was out. Free! Or nearly so. The parole board had given him a handy pamphlet that listed their requirements. He read it again, mostly out of boredom:

> An inmate granted a release by the Board must abide by several conditions. Violation of any condition could result in arrest and parole revocation. Standard conditions which apply to all parolees include following all instructions from their supervision officer, gainfully working, abiding by all laws, remaining in Georgia, receiving permission to change addresses, paying any court-ordered child support, paying a supervision fee or victim compensation fee and, if applicable, paying restitution. Parolees may not possess or own or use a gun or other deadly weapon.

Of course, they'd also told him to lay off alcohol and drugs, stay away from his old pals and anyone else convicted of a crime, yadda, yadda, yadda. So much bullshit. At least they didn't tell him he couldn't have sex, which was the second most important item on his agenda. The first, obviously, was getting revenge.

He'd heard all the crap about how revenge wasn't worth it. How it wouldn't be nearly as sweet as he thought it would be. And truly, since he wouldn't be able to nail the son of a bitch who actually caused him to go to prison, he'd find a way to make the bastard's family pay. And if not them, then the whole damned GBI would take a hit.

Still, the idea of sex—*real* sex, with a *female*—after 14 years and 10 months behind bars, provided a compelling reason to delay his primary impulse. As the bus crawled ever closer to his metropolitan destination, two thoughts fought for primacy: get laid or get a gun.

Decisions, decisions.

Chapter Four

"He who sells what isn't his'n,
must buy it back or go to prison." —Steven Wright

Andi's steps were measured and determined as she made her way back to her quarters. Will's voice rang insistently in her head, and just as insistently, she ignored it.

Except for two syllables and a command: *Aw, shit* and *Get down!*

Andi dropped to the dirt as if she'd been waiting for the order. Seconds later explosions rocked the compound tearing tents and trailers apart and scattering debris in all directions.

"Goddam mortars," Andi growled, scrambling to her feet and racing toward a trio of MRAPs parked near the back of the camp. After a diving roll, she came to a stop beside two other grunts who'd had the same idea.

"Won't last long," said one of them.

He's right. Counter battery's already got 'em ranged. Distant explosions and a sudden quiet footnoted Will's comment.

Andi waited for a full five minutes just to be sure, then rolled out from under the heavily armored truck. Her companions followed suit, and the three of them dusted themselves off as rescue and first aid providers raced through the camp searching for wounded.

"You'd think the bastards would learn," muttered the second marine. "I mean, every time they try this shit they get wiped out."

"But nearly every time they get some of us," Andi said. She would have said more, but the ground nearby suddenly erupted, throwing all three of them hard against the side of the MRAP.

Andi felt herself sliding earthward, but lost consciousness before she got there.

~*~

Edith Parise sniffed the armpits of her E-Z-Electronics uniform shirt and decided she could get another day out of it. Not that she had much choice; it was the only one she had, and there was no time to wash it before she reported to work.

She checked her appearance in the mirror, satisfied with the androgynous look she'd effected. Most of the tacky jewelry she'd had installed in her ears would be gone eventually, thank God. It looked like crap, and she had long since tired of playing the role of a sexually ambivalent store clerk. But it was the price she'd had to pay to get an undercover gig. After five long months posing as Charles "Chad" Pierce, she was eager to shed the disguise and be herself once again. That couldn't happen until she'd worked her way into the confidence of the crew which used the store to cover their real goals: using hidden surveillance on potential targets for robbery or blackmail.

Thus far, the store owners had confined her efforts to legal retail procedures. She'd been shielded from their criminal operations as well as most of the equipment they used to make it happen. Only recently had they suggested there was money to be made as one of their "sideline" installers. Chad had only to prove his technical prowess first.

Playing an undercover role as a male cross-dresser would never have occurred to Edith, but she wasn't given a choice in the matter. The limited information available on the criminal ring they were after suggested it had evolved from an online group called "Meat and Greet" whose membership preferred what the GBI's analyst called "nontraditional" sex practices. Their blackmail targets were yuppies who couldn't afford to have their sexual predilections aired in public.

She was told, "You'll be a lot safer if those assholes think you can't make up your mind about your gender, much less how you like to get off."

Edith had her doubts, but an undercover role seemed to offer the quickest route to senior status, and that was her primary goal. Like many, she thought of the GBI as the FBI's lowly country cousin, but she believed it offered her the best chance for making a move to what she considered the Big Time.

For now, however, she had to deal with Margaret Talmadge. Edith checked the time; she had a half hour before her scheduled arrival in the Atlanta suburb of Marietta, Georgia. She'd already researched the address. The area featured a bounty of Civil War era homes, most of which had housed Union officers during Sherman's occupation near the end of the "great unpleasantness." The territory caused her concern. Edith's electronics background was sketchy to begin with and included only a scant few hours of work in contemporary buildings. She had no idea what to expect in a structure built a 150 years ago.

The only thing she did feel sure about was her customer. Margaret Talmadge seemed like a decent sort, not at all the kind of person who might be the target of a gang, much less a member of it.

~*~

Margaret left Stormy at the offices of the Marietta Historical Homes Society but begged off when invited to come along for the virtual drawing and quartering planned by Olivia Ingram, the head headhunter. For once, Stormy thought, she would have welcomed her daughter's presence. If family loyalty meant anything, Mags might have provided a bit of moral support. *So much for family loyalty.*

"Come in, come in," said the Society's chairwoman. "We're meeting in the boardroom." She bustled from one room to the other, pulling Stormy along as if she were trapped in Olivia's gravitational pull.

Only one other inquisitor occupied the room, but his presence was enough to make the space seem crowded. The massive table with its equally massive chairs all but filled the interior forcing all of them to hunch over it. Stormy wondered how they'd gotten the damn thing through the door.

"Before we get started," Olivia announced, "I'd like to show you a little video I had made to showcase some of the more elegant residences in our organization. The owners have spared no expense to ensure that the historical and esthetic aspects of their homes stand out above the rest." She cleared her throat and looked pointedly at Stormy.

"These are the residences I'd personally like *all* our members to emulate."

Olivia pressed a button on a handheld remote, and a large, wall-mounted, flat-screen TV came to life. Stormy immediately recognized the sound track from "Gone With The Wind." She closed her eyes and prayed for a short production. Instead, it dragged on for thirty tortured minutes.

"Thank you for humoring me," Olivia said. "I just can't get enough of that video."

"How much did you have to pay for the music rights?" Stormy asked.

Rather than answer, Olivia called the meeting to order, and Tom Levin, Olivia's associate troublemaker, quickly produced a list of things they expected Stormy to address. In addition to faded and peeling paint, Levin called her attention to some damaged woodwork, largely decorative, a great deal more in the way of trees and shrubbery than they deemed apropos, and a complete lack of exterior lighting.

"How will visitors ever appreciate your lovely old home if they drive past it at night?" Olivia asked.

"They could start by driving by in the daytime," Stormy said.

Olivia reacted as if she'd been slapped. "You

don't mean it."

"Actually, I do. I don't control who drives by my house, or when. Nor do I care. As for the painting, I'll have to look around and find someone to do it."

"And don't forget the repairs to the woodwork," Levin added. "That's one of the first things we look for in determining a home's true condition."

"Okay then, I'll look into that, too," Stormy said.

Olivia cleared her throat and sat up straight. "I can recommend a landscaper who does beautiful work. You'll have to admit, the structure isn't the only thing that's been neglected."

Stormy took a breath, praying for calm. "My late husband—" She stopped in mid-sentence and began coughing. Mr. Levin looked deeply concerned, and Stormy waved him off before she reached into her purse for her inhaler. She gave it a shake and took two quick hits, then waited to return to normal. It didn't usually take long.

"Are you all right?" Oliva asked.

Stormy nodded, then tried to pick up the conversational thread. "As I was saying, my late husband—"

"Has been gone quite a while," Olivia said. "And you're well past the age when such chores are even possible. Save your energy, dear, especially with that cough of yours. I know just the people who can take care of all those house repair jobs."

Stormy wondered if she could find some people to do a job on Mrs. Ingram.

"Finally," said Mr. Levin, his voice creeping up the scale as he spoke, "there's the whole question of the interior. I'll need access so I can do a thorough inspection there, too."

Stormy stared at him. "What makes you think I'd let you, or anyone else, wander around in my home?"

"Well," began Olivia, "the Society—"

"Can go screw itself," Stormy said, her voice deadly calm. "I'm not letting anyone into my house unless I *want* them there."

An icy silence blanketed the room.

Stormy waited briefly before pushing back from the table and rising in the narrow space available. How Olivia had navigated the passage was a mystery. "I hope that settles things," she said.

"I suppose it does," Olivia said, her back even stiffer than before. "When will you be scheduling the work? Mr. Levin will need to know when to return for a final inspection."

"I'll keep you posted." Stormy nodded to them both and walked out of the room. She waited until she got outside before she retrieved her flip phone to dial Mags.

She let it ring several times, but there was no answer.

~*~

The timing couldn't have been better. Chad, from E-Z-Electronics, was waiting for Margaret when she pulled into her mother's driveway. She signaled for him to follow her and took the exterior walk down to the terrace level entrance.

She felt some remorse over resorting to subterfuge in order to get her mother out of the house, but took comfort from the knowledge that she'd soon learn the truth about the woman's mysterious activity in the safe room. More than likely, Margaret thought, she'd have to do something drastic to put an end to it, whatever it was. At least, she figured, it won't be anything illegal. Her father would never have allowed that.

Chad trailed behind like a faithful hound. Tall and wiry, he had no trouble carrying his tools and the boxes containing the surveillance materials she'd purchased with his assistance.

She fiddled briefly with her keys, then

opened the door for her uniformed accomplice. After locking the door carefully behind them, she headed to a wide hallway in the side of the first room they entered. Chad followed silently.

Margaret flipped on the lights and walked straight to a large, floor-to-ceiling bookcase. She pivoted and pointed to the camera she'd posted across the hall from the book laden shelves. "That'll have to come down."

Chad looked from the bookcase to the camera and back again. "Somebody's been stealing *books*?" He looked closely at the volumes crowding the shelves. "I'm no expert, but they don't look terribly valuable to me. Are they?"

"What? No, not particularly." She reached for the familiar gargoyle statuette her father had used to hide the switch which operated the sliding bookcase/door. A button on the base of the ceramic figure yielded to her touch, and the bookcase slid aside to reveal the safe room.

"Listen," she told him, "I'm counting on you to keep quiet about this. The secret room, I mean. If the wrong people found out... Well, I don't even want to think about that. Just understand, except for my mother, nobody else knows it exists. If something weird happens, I'll know who's responsible." She emphasized her point with a slight jab to his sternum with her index finger.

"No problem," he said as he stepped back and watched the huge bookcase roll to a silent stop. "That's the coolest thing I've ever seen."

Margaret, focused on the task at hand, bustled into the formerly hidden room and pointed to a spot high on the wall across from the locked cabinet doors. "That's where I want the new camera, but you've got to swear to me it won't make a sound."

"It won't," he said. "Unless it falls off the wall or something."

The words triggered a jolt of spinal electricity before she realized he was kidding. "Not funny," she grumbled.

Chad shrugged. "My bad."

"Is there some way to disguise it?"

"Not worth the bother. It's pretty small to begin with. I just don't get what you hope to learn. If you and your Mom are the only ones who can get in here, what is it you wanna record?"

Margaret had anticipated the question, and though her premeditated response was thin, she didn't owe the E-Z-Electronics installer any kind of answer at all. "This is going to sound weird, I suppose, but Mother has the absolute best recipe on Earth for Chicken Kiev."

Chad appraised her as if she'd suddenly birthed an armadillo. With wings.

"The thing is, she won't share it. I've tried for years to figure out how she does it, what secret spices she uses, and how she always gets it to come out perfect."

"Must be some damn fine chicken," he said. "I've never had what you're talking about. At least, not that I recall. Don't suppose you'd be willing to share the recipe once you have it, would you?"

"If this works out as well as I hope, I'll be happy to share any recipes I have." She gave him her warmest smile. "You're going to need a ladder. There's a light-weight one in the storage room; I'll get it and be right back. We've got to hurry. I need this all done before I pick up my mother."

"No problem. I'll get right on it."

Margaret backed out of the room and went in search of the ladder, her mind filled with memories of her mother's countless failed attempts at cooking. She was willing but obviously hadn't been born with a culinary gene. As her late father once observed, Stormy Talmadge was one of the few women in the world who could burn Kool-Aid.

By the time Margaret returned to the safe room, Chad had everything unpacked and ready for installation. "If we don't get the angle right now, you'll have to come in and adjust it later," he said. "It's got pretty good resolution, so you can blow up the image a lot, but I can't guarantee you'll be able to read a recipe."

"We'll see." Margaret kept an eye on her watch as he worked, then put the ladder away while he packed his tools and prepared to leave.

"I couldn't help but notice the little statues you have in here," he said, pointing to a shelf bearing the gargoyle collection. "I saw one in somebody's garden once, but these have so much more detail. They look almost real."

Margaret made no effort to hide her shiver. "They're hideous."

"Well, yeah, sorta. That's what makes 'em cool."

"*Cool?* They're grotesque!"

"I think they're awesome. I'd love to have one. Would you be willing to sell one?"

The very idea took Margaret by surprise. She couldn't imagine anyone wanting one of the dreadful little figures. "I suppose I could run the idea by my mother, but she'd want to know how anyone found out about them. So, on second thought, no; they're not for sale."

"I bet they're valuable, but I can't even

imagine where I'd go to look for one. Online, I suppose. But still, these are fabulous."

"My mother is nearly 90 years old. Come back and see me when she's—"

"How 'bout I trade you the cost of this installation for one?"

"I don't—"

"Come on, there's six of 'em on the shelf, and they haven't been dusted in God only knows how long. I only want one."

"You're serious?"

"Oh, hell yeah. I've never seen anything like 'em. Ever."

Margaret shook her head. How could she ever explain if her mother noticed one of the nasty things went missing? "I'd better not. Y'see—"

"I'll throw in the cost of the camera, too," Chad said, sounding all but desperate. He held a gargoyle in each hand as if comparing their weight. "They're much heavier than they look. Any idea what they're made of?"

Margaret's cell phone rang, and she checked the screen to see who was calling. "I've gotta go. My mother needs me to pick her up. I'll walk you out."

"Hang on a sec. Have we got a deal?"

"You'd trade the cost of the camera gear for one of those vile little figures?"

He nodded.

Margaret shook her head, certain she'd regret what she was about to do, but the money she'd save crushed her resistance. "Okay," she said. "It's a deal. Take your pick."

Chad abruptly put one of the two figures he'd been holding back on the shelf and stared down at the one still in his hands. "This thing looks like it could spread its wings and take off at any moment."

"I'd like a signed invoice showing the balance paid in full," Margaret said as she closed and locked the safe room entrance and restored the hidden switch to its resting spot on the top shelf.

"No problem," Chad said. "That's no problem at all."

The world came into focus slowly which gave Andi a little more time to be alarmed. She lay in a bed in what was clearly a hospital room. Three other beds crowded the room, but only one appeared occupied. She couldn't tell if the other patient was male or female, they weren't moving. That was fine with her, she wasn't in a mood to chat with anyone. Yet.

Well, look who's awake. Again.

"Aw geez," she muttered. "I was hoping you'd gone away."

Sorry kid. It ain't that easy. Like I told ya, we're stuck with each other. For now, anyway.

"Where am I?"

Italy. Ciao bella!

"Any particular place in Italy?"

Does it matter?

"Not really. Just curious. Never been there before."

We're in Naples. Far away from the bastards who hurt you. They're all dead as hammers by the way. Thought you'd want to know. So, you gonna stick around for a while this time?

Andi felt drowsy and made no effort to continue the conversation. Mere moments later, she blinked awake again. The room seemed darker, however. Very little light came in through the windows.

Someone dressed in white was standing over her, talking but not making sense.

"What?" Andi asked. "I—"

The visitor gradually came into focus. He was male and tall and looked about as normal and American as a human could look. "...how you were feeling," he said.

Andi frowned. "About what?" *Such a stupid question.*

He chuckled. "I asked how you were feeling. It's kinda what we do here."

"In Italy, y'mean. Are you speakin' Italian?"

"Nope, English. This is an American hospital, an American Navy hospital to be precise. I'm your nurse."

Andi felt her eyebrows draw down. "But, you're a guy."

"And you're a grunt. Means we're a match made in heaven, 'cept I'm already married. Are you? I didn't see a ring or anything, but then stuff gets lost in transit sometimes."

"Married? No. I'd remember something like that."

You never said anything about it to me.

"Shut up, Will."

"Who's Will?" the nurse asked.

"Nobody."

The nurse held a clipboard in the crook of his arm and scanned through several pages of it. "Says here you've mentioned the name 'Will' several times."

"How? When?"

"Whenever you wake up. You've been drifting in and out of consciousness for several days. You took a massive blow to the head. You're lucky to be alive."

"I— I can't remember—"

"That's normal. Most folks lose a bit of memory after taking a hit like you did. Your memory will come back, sooner or later. Don't worry. You're alive. That's the important thing."

"Yeah, right. I guess."

"Trust me; it is. Now, who's Will? Your boyfriend?"

"What? Good God, no. I don't— Never mind. I don't wanna talk about it."

That's what I get for savin' yer butt? Thanks, kid. Yer all heart.

"Knock it off, Will," she said, trying to make it sound like she'd coughed.

"There you go again," said the nurse. "I suspect the doctor will be asking similar questions.

Try not to blow smoke up her ass, okay? She's pretty sharp. She'll know if you're lying to her."

"I—"

"They'll be around with a light meal pretty soon. I imagine you're starving. A saline drip can only do so much. How 'bout an ice chip?"

"Yeah."

"It's not unusual for patients with head trauma to hallucinate. If Will is part of that, the doctor will understand." He spooned a sliver of ice into her mouth, and she let it dissolve. It barely produced enough liquid to let her swallow. "If Will is a figment of your imagination, that's okay."

"He's—" She forced herself to stop. And think.

I'd shut the hell up if I were you.

"Uh, thanks."

"No problem. Will you need help eating?"

"I don't think so," Andi said, suddenly aware of her empty stomach.

"I'll drop back by anyway. And even though you've been sleeping for a long time, I imagine you're still tired."

"Yeah. How's that possible?"

"Your body's busy healing. That alone is

enough to wear you out. But once the doctor says it's okay, we'll need to get you up on your feet. Got that, Marine? Can't have you goofin' off while the world needs saving."

Andi gave him a smile. "What's your name?"

"Carnahan," he said. "George Carnahan. I'm kind of a big deal around here. You know how it is, saving lives all day and all night. It's tiring, but somebody's gotta do it."

"You're navy, aren't ya?"

"Yep. Semper Fortis."

"Which means?"

Carnahan's laugh sounded more like a bark. "I have no freakin' clue. I empty bedpans and try to help guys who've seen action."

"I've seen my share."

"I thought you got banged up in camp." He consulted the clipboard again. "Says here, Forward Operating Base DeJarnette."

"It was the day after I got back from a mission. Lost some good friends that day."

"Oh geez. I'm sorry," he said. "That was stupid of me. I had no idea. I thought you were—"

"Just a grunt," she said, brandishing a fist.

"Oorah."

Carnahan smiled at her. "Lemme see if I can put a hustle on your chow, such as it is. You look like you can handle it."

~*~

After two weeks in Atlanta, Tanner Howell's limited resources had run out. Though required to check in with his parole officer, he had opted out of the state-run halfway house. Regretting that decision came quickly, but with no resolution. He'd not only run out of money, he'd used up what little good will he had with friends. *Former friends*, he'd discovered.

Prices had exploded since he went to prison. The cost of everything: food, housing, transportation, booze, sex—especially sex—had gone totally mad. He'd been living on the three tasteless meals a day served up with monotonous precision by Georgia's Bureau of Prisons. For the last 14 years and 10 months he hadn't had to think about where his next meal would come from. Overnight, just staying alive went beyond his budget.

He hadn't been living lavishly. His money simply hadn't lasted as long as he thought it would. The job "interviews" the state required him to go on were not only stupid and time-consuming; they were soul-crushing. Dishwasher? Groundskeeper?

Trash collector? That's all he was good for?

Nobody's dumbass, Tanner intended to do well, and cleaning up after someone else had no place in his plans. Furthering those plans required that he stay alive, however, and that required the basics: food and shelter. To secure them he needed money. Therefore, his primary goal became finding both.

Clearly, the neighborhood he once called home offered no opportunities, legitimate or otherwise. He needed to find more lucrative terrain in which to operate. There were plenty of wealthy neighborhoods in Atlanta to choose from, but Buckhead sat at the top of the list. Fat cats occupied every inch from corner bistro to rooftop condo and everything in between.

He had just enough cash to cover the bus fare. What he didn't have was a gun. Fortunately, he knew someone who did.

Chapter Five

"In fact, I have never met anyone who doesn't like gargoyles." —Keith David

Edith Parise removed the tight-fitting band from around her chest and took a deep, unrestrained breath. She never dreamed boob-squishing would be a requirement for detective work, and playing the role of a seemingly male sales clerk took more energy than she'd anticipated. Finding the right balance had been difficult. She wasn't comfortable with male camaraderie, and her disguise seemed to have blunted what little of it existed in the shop. Showing a bit of female sensitivity added to her look, though she often feared she'd overdone it. More than one customer had looked at her with interest when what she'd hoped for was more like disgust. All of which took a toll on her psyche.

Glancing at the gargoyle for which she'd swapped her services, Edith/Chad smiled. She had no idea why the damned thing so fascinated her, but fascinate it did. The exquisite detail on the figure suggested a masterwork rather than some variation of a garden gnome one might find almost anywhere. The object deserved the designation of "art," and had it been rendered in color, it could have easily passed for a living being. Albeit, an ugly one.

She picked it up and hefted it as she'd done many times already, astonished by its weight. "What the hell are you made of?" she asked before inspecting it, once again, for a label, an inscription, or some other clue to its origin. No mold marks, no numbers, not even a copyright or trademark appeared anywhere. *Definitely not Chinese.*

Setting the unsightly *object d'art* on a table, she reached for her phone and dialed Dan Wolfram, her closest friend at the bureau. Dan had been one of the few people at the GBI who took her seriously from the day she arrived, and the two had become good friends. He answered on the second ring.

"GBI Central Lab, Wolfram speaking."

"Dan! It's Edy. I've got a favor to ask."

"Fine, thanks. And how're you?"

She paused at that. "Sorry! Didn't mean to high-step over the greetings. Forgive me?"

"Of course. So, you need a favor? You know it's gonna cost ya."

"So much for the value of friendship. How much will it set me back?"

"Depends on what you want." He cleared his throat. "And whether or not it's legal. Legal's cheaper."

She chuckled. "It's legal. Far as I know, anyway. I've got a little statue thingy I'd like you to examine."

"For trace? Fingerprints?"

"Nothing like that. I want to know what it's made of."

Edy stared at the gargoyle while she waited for his answer. "Dan, you still there?"

"Yeah," he said. "I'm just trying to figure out why you'd care what a statue is made from? Were you thinking of trying to make more just like it? There's probably a copyright issue or—"

"Nope. I'm just curious. What d'ya say?"

He exhaled loudly, but she couldn't tell if it was in relief or resignation. "Thanks, buddy. So, what'll this cost me?"

"A weekend at the beach. I'll get us a place, you bring the food, drinks, and sex toys."

She chuckled. "Will your wife be joining us?"

"Oh, right. Kathy. Darn. Forgot all about her. No, she'll probably stay at home working on some charity thing or teaching folks CPR. You know how she is."

"Indeed. Say 'Hi' to her for me. I'll pass on the beach thing. How 'bout donuts instead. There's a great new place near the Tech campus. I'll grab some on the way over."

~*~

You aren't a very good patient.

Will. Again. Andi suppressed a groan and shut her eyes.

Seriously, you should pay attention to what the doctors tell you. That explosion could've messed you up worse than you know.

"I was kinda hoping it'd knocked you outta my system."

Nah. Doesn't work that way. You've pretty much gotta die to get rid of me.

The good news just never seemed to end. "How 'bout you pretend to get out of my head for a while. Maybe that way I can concentrate on doing just what you're suggesting. I have no interest in staying here any longer than necessary."

So, you wanna go back to the sandbox?

"It's not like I get a choice. They can send me anywhere, but I already know the guys back there." She heard the door open and resolved to ignore him.

"Hey there," said the effervescent nurse Carnahan. "How ya doin'?"

"Great," she said. "But I'm ready to get out of here."

"We all want outta here, honey." He plugged his stethoscope into his ears and pressed the business end toward her chest.

"Honey?" Andi straightened, though the hospital bed didn't make it easy. "Do you address all the grunts that way?"

"Only the cute ones."

I like this guy!

Andi bristled, but in silence.

Carnahan noticed instantly. "Sorry. I didn't mean anything by it. But the fact is, you *are* the prettiest female I've seen in here in ages."

Partially mollified, Andi opted not to lecture him on how hard it was to earn, let alone maintain, the respect of her fellow marines. Looks didn't count for shit in a firefight.

The nurse took her blood pressure, checked her pulse, examined her eyes, and had her follow his finger without moving her head. "Any pains you haven't told me about?" he asked.

"Nope."

"Dizziness?"

"Nada."

"Memory loss?"

How would you even know?

She wanted to scream at Will to shut up, but still, his question made sense. She eyed the nurse. "How would I know?"

"Okay," he said, chuckling. "I should have asked if you have any memory *gaps.* You know, like you can remember getting in a car and going to a party, but you can't remember driving past the Statue of Liberty on the way."

"I've only seen the Statue of Liberty in pictures," she said. "I think I'd remember something like that."

Carnahan just smiled and shook his head. "Still hearing voices?"

"Huh?"

"Voices. Are you still hearing 'em?"

"I never said I was hearing voices."

"So, the conversations I've seen you having were with yourself?"

"You've been *spying* on me?"

Attagirl. Put the pressure on him.

"Hardly. These rooms are designed for observation, not privacy. I glance through the windows from the hall when I walk by if all I need is a quick check on my patients. I look for things like, you know—is she still alive? That sorta thing." He opened his eyes in exaggerated fashion. "This isn't your typical stateside hospital. This is a military facility."

He saw me through the friggin' window? Dear Lord, how many others did, too?

"Hearing weird stuff isn't all that unusual. Especially after being involved in an explosion. What we didn't know until yesterday was that the last one wasn't the first. Your hummer hit an IED a short time earlier."

"Yeah, so?"

He picked up the hospital chart at the foot of her bed and thumbed through it until he found the reference he was looking for. "Uh huh. Thought so."

"What?"

"I'm not supposed to say anything to you about what's in here."

"Give me a break. It's my damn chart, isn't it?"

He sighed in resignation. "Okay, but don't tell the docs you heard any of this from me. All right?"

"Got it."

"Have any of the doctors said anything to you about PTSD?"

Oh, shit. Here it comes.

"Were they supposed to?"

Carnahan shrugged. "Someone will, sooner or later."

"What's that supposed to mean?"

"Post-traumatic stress disorder."

"No. Not that." She resisted the temptation to give him an eye roll; it would have been way too girlie. "What does that mean *for me?* Surely, I won't have to stay here, will I?"

"That's up to the doctors," he said, "but most likely you'll be heading home, especially since you don't have much time left in your enlistment."

Josh Langston

"I'm gonna re-up."

Carnahan briefly chewed his lip. "Well, y'know...."

"What?" She tried to read his expression, but it seemed neutral.

Yeah, what?

"Civilian life isn't all that bad."

"Screw that. I'm a marine. It's where I belong. I'm good at what I do."

Like what? Gettin' blown up?

"I believe you, kid. I really do, but—"

"I'm a grunt, and damned proud of it."

He held up his hands, palms out as if to fend her off. "It ain't up to me. If it were, I'd say fine, go back out and get yourself shot. We've got way too many good-looking marines runnin' around."

"Listen—"

"Fact is, kiddo, it's *entirely* up to the doctors. They know you've been hearing voices. And talking back to 'em, too. I'm sure they'll have a ton of other questions to ask because of that, especially the psych guys."

"But—" She stiffened, and her bruised muscles ached even more.

"It's not all that odd. Explosions can do weird shit to people. No need to be embarrassed."

"I'm not," she said, forcing herself to relax.

"Good. That's great, in fact. Great attitude."

"Will it help me stay in?"

"Probably not," he said, giving her a weak smile. "More than likely you'll get an honorable discharge to go with your Purple Heart and your Silver Star."

"What Silver Star?"

I knew about that but didn't say anything 'cause I kinda felt like I earned the damned thing. Sorry, kid.

"I guess you hadn't heard. I'm told you kicked some serious ass back in Afghanistan. They'll probably wait until they know you're better before they have a ceremony."

"I don't need a damned ceremony! I just want to go back to my unit."

"I know," he said. "I know."

~*~

Though he'd never given much thought to physical fitness, Tanner found that weight-lifting while in prison offered a number of positives. In addition to the company of like-minded cons, his improved strength and stamina meant fewer cons messed with him, and when they did, his survival chances were greatly enhanced. He wouldn't pass for a body-builder like some of the guys, but he was in significantly better shape when he got out than when he went in.

That fact had come as a surprise when he called on an old acquaintance who used to supply his weed. DeAndre' "Little D" Williams had been a small-time dealer when Tanner first met him. In the nearly two decades since then, Little D hadn't improved his lot. He was still small time, and he appeared a great deal older than he had when Tanner last saw him.

Tanner staked out the corner on which he'd formerly done business with Little D, and waited for him to show. It hadn't taken long. The dealer appeared quietly and took up a position from which he could walk to the car window of a passing customer and supply their needs. Fortunately for Tanner, business was slow.

Little D didn't recognize Tanner when he approached. Rat-like in more ways than one, the dealer backed away and began looking for a direction in which to run. Tanner doubted he'd have any trouble catching him if he decided to bolt.

"Lil' D!" he exclaimed. "'Member me? Tanner.

Tanner Howell."

The dealer squinted at him in the fading light. "Thought you was dead, bro."

"Almost. Couple times in fact. Hard to stay alive in the joint."

"How much time you do?"

"Fifteen fuckin' years."

"Sorry, man. I didn't know."

Tanner waved it off. "No problem, my man. I'm out now. That's all that matters."

Little D rushed into a pitch. "Need herb? I kin fix you up, bro, real cheap. It's good shit, too. I should know, I been doing this long enough."

"I know that's right." Tanner laughed to put him at ease, a tactic he'd perfected in prison. "So, yeah. I could seriously use some. How much for a zip?"

"I git twen'y for a whole bag."

"You got it here?" Tanner asked.

Little D motioned with his head toward the back of an abandoned store. "In my office. Wait here. Be right back."

Tanner waited about thirty seconds before following Little D behind the building where he choked him to death. He was surprised by how easy it had been. The rat-faced little shit squirmed a bit, but he didn't have enough strength to offer much resistance. Tanner put him out of his misery quickly, an option he had no intention of offering to his real targets.

A quick search of the dead dealer revealed little in the way of cash or product. Tanner pocketed a few small bills and roughly an ounce of ganja. What made him smile was the .32 caliber Seecamp automatic tucked in the back waistband of Little D's pants. It wasn't a big, scary gun, but it was easy to conceal which made it perfect for what Tanner had in mind, though he'd have preferred a weapon with sights. Using this gun would force him to get close to his target.

Finding car keys in Little D's pocket amounted to a trifecta of good fortune. Who needed a bus when he had a car? Sadly, he wouldn't be able to use it for long; someone would report it stolen. If Little D had any family, they'd be looking for it. That was fine with him. He didn't need to drive any farther than Marietta, and that was way less than an hour away. He already had the address. Now he had a way to get there, assuming he could find Little D's ride.

He clicked the "Unlock" button on the key fob but heard nothing. The rat-like little dealer hadn't parked close. Tanner would have to do some walking before he found it, but he was down with that.

~*~

Margaret held the instruction sheet which came with the miniature camera now mounted inside the secret room in the basement of her mother's house. Though obviously written by someone other than a native English-speaker, the step-by-step procedures weren't too difficult to follow.

She pulled her chair closer to the aging TV set that dominated her living room. Chad had assured her that if she currently subscribed to a cable service, she'd be able to tap into part of the technical mumbo-jumbo/magic that made it work and adapt some of it to her CCTV needs. Between the pigeon-English manual and a phone call to the sales clerk/installer, Margaret finally had access to the answers she had so long desired.

The image on her TV set flickered to life with the opening of Stormy's secret door. It took a moment for Margaret to acclimate herself to the odd camera angle, and she began to sympathize with the view afforded the proverbial fly on the wall now that she'd become one.

Stormy Talmadge set her wine glass on a counter and unlocked the mysterious cabinet.

Margaret discovered she was holding her breath as the doors swung open to reveal a tall, dark mirror surrounded by an incredibly ornate frame. She watched as her mother seated herself in front of the mirror *and began talking to it.*

"Seriously Mother? It's a mirror. You're talking to a goddam mirror!"

Watching as her mother paused to take a sip of her wine, Margaret began to wish she'd thought to bring a drink of her own. When the mirror began to reflect something other than her mother's image, Margaret felt an unwelcome chill and a tightening in her spine. By the time the wavering lines and smoke-like swirls of color coalesced into something that resembled a face, Margaret needed a change of underwear.

Her mother, however, seemed untroubled by the ghastly visage confronting her. Their conversation went on for a good while before Margaret calmed herself and raised the volume.

"...that's all I've got."

"You're sure?" Stormy asked.

"Quite," said the wraith in the mirror.

"Well then, until next time." Stormy nodded and closed the cabinet doors. She then sat back in her chair as if exhausted, and finished her wine.

Margaret remained traumatized, utterly baffled by what she'd just seen and unsure how she would even attempt to address the issue with her mother. No longer worried that Stormy was involved in something nefarious, she began to wonder if the woman wasn't suffering from some sort of dementia, maybe a contagious kind which was at that very moment creeping into Margaret's brain. She shook the thought off as impossible. So, what the hell was up with the mirror?

A talking mirror, for God's sake!

The time had come for more than just a fresh pair of panties; she needed a martini and some aspirin.

~*~

Dan called Edith back the day after she'd dropped off the gargoyle for his inspection. She was enjoying a day off from her undercover role as Chad, quasi-male sales clerk.

"Where the hell did you get this thing?" Dan asked, skipping the opening formalities on which he normally dwelled. It made her smile.

"One of my customers had it. And a few more, too. Why? And what did you find out?"

"This is the strangest damned thing I've ever seen."

She laughed. "I thought so, too. But it's fascinating! The craftsmanship is—"

"Unreal." He paused to cough. "Sorry. It's the smell. I—"

"What smell?"

"Your idol, or figurine, or whatever the hell it is. It stinks."

Huh? That made no sense. "It didn't stink when I had it," Edy said. "What did you do to it?"

"You asked me to tell you what it was made of, didn't you?"

"Yeah."

"Well, I had to take a sample in order to find out. Took me damn near an hour to get one. That's what's so freaky. Hang on while I plug the hole."

"I'm not following you," Edy said.

"Your statue has a coating of some sort that's impervious to most sharp objects. I didn't even realize it was an added layer until I X-rayed it."

"An added layer?"

"Yeah. It's less than a sixteenth of an inch thick, kinda like a layer of skin. I suspect that's why the detail is so— I dunno. Incredible. It might as well be real."

Edith rubbed her eyes. "Skin? Okay. That's a little over the top, don't you think?"

"I guess. Anyway, I have no freakin' idea what the skin is made from."

"But whatever it is, it stinks?"

"No. Sorry. What stinks is the stuff inside. That, as far as I can tell, is pure sulfur. You know, what they used to call 'brimstone' back in the old days."

"I had no idea sulfur was so heavy."

"It's not," Dan said. "And that's what puzzled me. Most of the weight is in that damned coating."

"Could it be lead?"

"Not a chance. It's way too hard. I tried to melt the little sample piece I had, but a gas flame had no effect on it. And it cooled off in nothing flat. Didn't leave a mark."

"Well, if it's not lead, what is it?"

Dan's response was more grunt than laughter. "I have no clue. It's a mystery, a substance I've never seen before. I showed it to a couple other people here in the lab, and they were just as puzzled by it as I am."

Edith remained silent as she tried to think of an explanation. "Is it— Uhm. Radioactive?"

"No, thank God. I thought it might be tungsten, because of its hardness and high melting point. Did you know they make jewelry with that stuff?"

"Stay with me, Dan."

"Right. Sorry. Anyway, it's not tungsten. It's much, much heavier."

"What could it be?"

"I just don't know. I'm stumped."

"So, stumped and stinky. Great combination."

"I plugged the hole I made in the skin with rubber cement. I think it'll hold, and it doesn't smell so bad now."

"Thanks. I think."

"Would you mind if I sent your statue off to another lab? There's a real physics wizard over at Kennesaw State. I'll bet he—"

Edith groaned. "Maybe later. I was just curious. I'll swing by your place after dinner and pick it up. Okay?"

"Sure thing," Dan said, his voice heavy with disappointment. "It's just...."

"What?"

"Nothing. It occurs to me we might get a

better explanation from a priest."

"You've been working too hard, my friend." She made no effort to stifle a laugh. "Thanks for your help."

~*~

Stormy Talmadge eased back in the lounge chair her late husband had loved so much. After many years of constant use, the old chair had grown less and less comfortable. Now Stormy only sat in it as a means to stay awake.

She couldn't help but dwell on her most recent conversation with the Keeper of the Portal. The spirit seemed an unlikely candidate to occupy the post. Most of those with whom she'd worked maintained a keen interest in the world of the living. This one, however, seemed not to care much at all. She doubted he would last long.

Dreams of an earlier Keeper often came to her. She'd never forget Angelica Rohrbach, a woman whose reputation as a syndicated gossip columnist had once impressed Stormy far more than it should have. Angelica had been murdered shortly after Stormy met her, but that didn't end their relationship. Though she never went into detail about how she elevated her position after she landed in purgatory, Angelica hung on to the position for several years, real-world time. Only then did the two women actually click. In fact, they enjoyed the relationship, though it could not have been more bizarre.

Angelica would pass along messages from the recently deceased about a wide range of issues. Stormy had always done her best to deliver such directives and often received a show of gratitude. Sometimes she received information about criminal activities, and it was this data which she passed along to her husband, Pete. He became adept at hiding his beloved source while acting on those tips, and his successes greatly enhanced his career.

Now, of course, her contacts were severely limited, but that fact at least offered her a bit of respite from the guilt she might have felt if the tips she received were of the quality Angelica produced. The current Keeper, she felt sure, must have obtained the position simply by default. Perhaps no other souls were willing to step up. She had no way of knowing. She only wished someone would take the initiative and replace the jerk currently in charge. She often mused about the irony of incompetence at both ends of the spectrum—the Keeper on one hand and the GBI's Donovan O'Keefe on the other, a match most assuredly forged in hell.

How delightful it would be, she reflected, if some aroused spirit were to toss the reigning Keeper back through the portal. Such had been the case numerous times while the curious mirror remained in her possession. When transitions were "gentle," at least in her estimation, no evidence presented itself other than a need for introductions when the new Keeper appeared.

In the cases where Keepers were overthrown—*literally*, as in the case of Angelica's predecessor—the ejected spirit returned to the world of the living in the form of a gargoyle. Stormy had never actually seen one emerge from the uncanny mirror, but over the years she'd found several inside the cabinet where she stored the portal.

It only required one careless incident to teach her to open those cabinet doors carefully. The one time she'd failed to do so, a gargoyle landed on her foot and broke two bones. She hobbled around on a cast for weeks and never did come up with a plausible explanation for how she got hurt.

Just thinking about it now made her wince. It also reminded her that it had been ages since she last dusted the critters, now sitting quietly on a shelf in the hidden room. She made a mental note to deal with them on her next visit.

And with any luck, she might be able to add one to their number.

Chapter Six

"It is forbidden to kill; therefore, all murderers are punished unless they kill in large numbers and to the sound of trumpets." —Voltaire

"Andrea? This is your aunt Margaret."

Andi looked at the phone in her hand as if it were some ancient artifact suddenly come to life. "Aunt Mags? I can't believe it's you." Andi turned her head to track a nurse moving toward a legless grunt in a wheelchair. She hadn't seen him before.

He came in yesterday.

Andi ignored Will and turned her back on the staffers at the nurses' station.

"It's me all right," Margaret said. "How are you? The man I spoke to—"

"How did you know where to reach me?"

"The hospital called. You listed me as your emergency contact. Makes sense. Your grandmother and I are your nearest relatives."

"I'm sorry they bothered you," Andi said. "It's been, I dunno, years. I honestly forgot whose names I listed."

The older woman chuckled. "Bothered? Nonsense. I'm glad they called. We've missed you. How long has it been?"

"Since Dad's memorial service."

"That was what? Two—"

"Three. Three years ago."

"Right."

"I enlisted right after that."

Andi tried to relax her grip on the phone. Eventually, Margaret broke the silence. "I heard you dropped out of school."

"Yeah. I'm not much of a student."

"I heard you had great grades. Your grandmother—"

"What's this about?" Andi asked.

C'mon, kid. Be nice.

"Butt out, Will."

"Pardon me, dear?" Margaret said.

"Sorry. I didn't mean you. There's uh—Someone talking in my ear. Very annoying."

"Is the hospital crowded?"

"It's a rehab center, not a hospital. I won't be here very long."

"That's what I heard. You're coming home!"

She sounds happy, like what a wonderful thing that the Corps dumped me like so much garbage. And their stupid Silver Star is the cherry on top.

"Are you in much pain?" Margaret asked, changing gears.

"Pain? No. Not anymore. Well, maybe. A little. I'm just—" She shrugged in frustration. "Angry, I guess."

You get to go home, dumbass. Not like those poor bastards who got blown up back in the sandbox. Be happy.

Andi clamped her hand over the phone's mouthpiece and whispered, "Sweet Jesus, Will. Cut me some damn slack!"

"I've got a suggestion for you, Andrea," Margaret said.

"It's Andi. With an 'i.' Everybody calls me that."

"Oh. Okay. Andi. It may take me a while to get used to that."

"The suggestion?"

"They said you'd need a place to stay that was close to a VA medical facility. They also said you didn't need to be living alone."

Andi gazed up at the ceiling. She'd heard the same crap earlier in the week and still hadn't gotten used to it. "And?"

"And I'm hoping you'll come back here and move in with your grandmother."

"With *Gran?*"

Oh ho! Lucky you. You get to take care of an old geezer. Sounds perfect.

Andi groaned.

"She needs someone to look after her."

"Since when? She's the most independent woman on Earth."

"She's almost 90. I've tried to talk her into moving into assisted living, but—"

Andi tensed. "Alzheimer's?" She couldn't imagine feisty old Stormy Talmadge with dementia.

The prospect had never occurred to her.

"Her memory's fine. She's just getting old, but she still acts like a teenager from time to time. I worry she's going to hurt herself. If you moved in, you could keep an eye on her, make sure she's eating right. That kinda stuff. You'd be paid, too."

"I'd get paid to take care of my own grandmother?"

"Why not? Pay, plus room and board."

"I'm not a maid. Or a cook. Or a nurse. Or— For cryin' out loud, Aunt Mags, I'm a Marine, not a nanny!"

You tell 'er, kid.

"Damn it, Will," she whispered.

"I know that, but we need you, Andrea. I mean, Andi. Please."

All joking aside, it's not a bad deal. You oughta do it.

"Lemme think about it," Andi said. "How soon do you need to know?"

"As soon as possible."

"Right. Listen, I've gotta go. One last therapy session—to prove I'm still alive, I guess. Give me your number, and I'll call you back." She scribbled her aunt's response on a bit of scratch paper. "Tell Gran I love her."

"I will, dear. Talk to you soon."

Andi hung the phone up without alerting the staffer behind the counter. The sounds of the room came back to her. It seemed as though they'd been blotted out while she was on the line. *Aunt Mags? Gran?* She hadn't thought about them in years.

Easy duty, and you get spending money, plus food and a place to stay. That ain't bad, kid.

"But not exactly what I had in mind."

Yeah, well, join the club.

~*~

Wearily returning to her Chad persona, Edith pulled into the employee lot behind the electronics store and parked her nondescript sedan in the last remaining spot. Though a few minutes late for work, she took a moment to check her reflection in the rearview mirror, loathing the face which looked back at her. Resigned to finishing her assignment, she opened the car door and simultaneously heard and felt an explosion. A blast of heated air slammed the door shut; her ears popped, and she stared in shock as debris hurtled in all directions.

Shaking herself out of a daze, she forced herself to regain focus, starting with the ruined building in front of her.

The rear entry door, a heavy steel affair with a tamper-proof lock, remained attached to the door frame by a single hinge but hung at a bizarre angle. The roof over the store had caved in, and smoke billowed up from inside. Alarms went off in neighboring businesses.

Assuming there had been but one occupant in each of the other cars in the lot, Edith figured everyone else working at the electronics store had been inside when the explosion occurred. She grabbed her phone and speed-dialed her GBI supervisor to report the blast.

"Someone's just destroyed the building," she said when her boss answered. "It's blown all to hell."

"Have you called 911 yet?"

Crap. "No. I—"

"Never mind. I'll take care of it."

Edith waited while he directed someone to make the necessary calls. When he came back on the line he asked, "Could anyone have survived?"

"I doubt it," she said, marveling at the extent of the destruction. "This couldn't have been an accident. Someone deliberately blew the place up. Someone, I suspect, who didn't like being blackmailed."

"Check for survivors," the supervisor said, "but keep an eye out for 'lookie lous.' Our bomber might drop by to check his handywork."

"Yessir."

"And give me an update ASAP." With that, the call ended.

Once again, Edith pushed the car door open and was immediately inundated with a host of odors as the flames roaring through the wreckage burned wood, rubber, plastic, and, she feared, human flesh. She had to shield herself not only from the blaze, but from her own emotions. She harbored no great feelings for the blackmailers, but she worried there may have been innocents hurt in the shops on either side of the electronics store.

She moved as close to the burning building as she could and stared into the inferno, certain that no one could have survived in it. Working her way over and through the debris, she circled the structure and made her way to the front parking lot.

A few cars occupied slots nearest the storefronts and showed signs of damage from material ejected by the blast. Onlookers began to cluster, some taking videos, others chatting and acting as if nothing unusual had occurred. The distant wail of sirens heralded the imminent arrival of police, fire, and ambulances. The crowd continued to grow.

Edith moved closer but hung near the growing mob's fringe where she could look at them and hopefully distinguish the curious from the criminal. Though one's appearance rarely proved enough to warrant an arrest, more than one felon had let his emotions draw the steely glare of an officer.

Most of the gawkers seemed to be of the clueless variety, simply taking advantage of something different in their lives. One or two, however, looked suspicious. Doing her best to avoid being obvious, Edith pulled her cell phone from her back pocket and took pictures of those who had triggered her internal creep detector. One, in particular, radiated smugness and superiority. Wearing a sports coat, sans tie, he could have been a banker or an advertising exec. Though he seemed to be trying, he couldn't keep from smiling at the destruction in front of him.

When emergency vehicles swarmed into the parking lot, Edith moved away. She watched from a distance as uniformed police made sure the public didn't get in the way. With a few quick taps on her phone, she sent the photos she'd taken back to the GBI. They'd know if her suspicions bore fruit.

~*~

Tanner wasted no time stealing a license

plate to replace the one on Lil' D's car. The fool had let it expire, and Tanner had no desire to give the cops a reason to look twice at him. Lil' D's ride was truly a piece of shit, but all things considered, it provided exactly what the ex-con needed: anonymity. Nobody would be giving the dirty, rusted Toyota Corolla a second look.

The inside of the vehicle provided a richer bounty than that carried by its late owner. Tanner found a dozen baggies containing at least an ounce of product each and more than enough cash to tide him over for a month or so, provided he found cheap lodging. Doing that required him to leave the city. Atlanta was for rich folk, and Buckhead housed the wealthiest of the lot. He decided to find a place in the suburbs where he could crash before he looked for a score among the snooty set on Atlanta's north side.

Though her long-distance chat with Andrea had gone much better than she thought it might, Margaret still feared what lay ahead. She had no doubts her mother would react dramatically when she learned Margaret had secured a companion for her. Just thinking about it threatened to give her a migraine. Hopefully, the old woman would be less resentful knowing it was her granddaughter and not a stranger who would be moving in with her.

Logic dictated that things had to change. Just

because Stormy Talmadge didn't like the idea had no bearing on the facts: she was too old to live alone, and she had more house than she could handle. Margaret had somehow managed to shove aside the whole issue of the crazy mirror in the safe room; she had no idea how she'd resolve what that was all about. Ignoring the discovery, at least for the time being, seemed like a wise idea. If need be, she could run it by Andrea—*Andi*, she reminded herself; she'd have to get used to that, too—and maybe the young marine could figure out what to do.

None of that mattered at the moment. Andi would soon be riding the up escalator to the main terminal of Atlanta's Hartsfield-Jackson airport, and Margaret would be waiting for her.

Stormy tried not to stare at her granddaughter's face, but failed. Andrea's time in the marines had transformed her from a child into a strong, mature woman. The resulting changes to her features amplified her resemblance to her grandfather, Peter. Oh, how Stormy longed to have that face back in her life. Pete was the only man she ever loved.

"Gran? Are you sure you're okay with all this?"

"With all what, dear?"

"With me living here. With you. As... I dunno, an employee, I guess."

Stormy couldn't help but smile. "An employee? Never. You're my grandchild. You're family! And I understand why Mags tried to arrange something formal through the agency she's been after me to contact. But we don't need anything like that. You're welcome to stay here as long as you like. And if you're willing to help me out around the house, I'm more than willing to support you with whatever amount the agency would have charged."

Andrea seemed more unsure of the arrangement than Stormy did.

"Why should we give some middleman a slice of your paycheck?" Stormy asked.

"It just doesn't seem right," Andrea said. "That's all. Being paid to care for—"

"Care for?" Stormy sat even straighter. "I'm no invalid. I just need some help around the house. Much as it pains me to admit, your aunt Margaret is right. This is a big house, and it's more than I can handle by myself. But I don't want to leave it. I don't want to live in some miserable, out of the way dumpsite where so many older people end up."

Clearly dismayed, Mags said, "Mom! I never intended anything like that. I couldn't. Ever!"

"Oh, I know, dear. I'm just being dramatic. But even so, I'm serious. As long as I'm still breathing, I'm not leaving this house." She gave long, hard looks to both her daughter and granddaughter. "I mean it."

"Then, I guess it's a deal," Andrea said. She stood and grabbed the heavy canvas handle on her government-issued duffle bag. "Which bedroom would you like me to use?"

"Take your pick," Stormy said. "The one your mother used is in the back, overlooking the garden. Well, what used to be the garden."

Andrea smiled for the first time since the discussion began. "Maybe—together—we can turn it back into a garden again."

Stormy smiled, then looked at Mags who seemed the most relieved of all.

~*~

Derrick Benjamin felt better than he had in days. Stress gave him stomach trouble, and he feared he might be developing an ulcer. But the call he'd just received offered a great deal of relief. The electronics shop that covered for an eavesdropping operation had been taken out, and quite effectively. As far as his contact could tell, not a single one of the bastards who had tried to blackmail him survived.

He'd surveyed the site personally and had no doubts about the survivability of the blast. It was even more secure than the run-ins he had engineered in Afghanistan. He'd felt some guilt over those, at first, but the more of them he managed, the less bothered he felt, even when they went sideways. It was simply business, and besides, he didn't know any of the guys who ended up in body bags. They had, after all, volunteered.

His dismissal from government service ended that phase of his career. And now, only one issue from that part of his life remained, and he intended to deal with it very soon.

~*~

You've really got yourself a sweet deal, kid.

"I dunno. Maybe." Andi heaved her duffle on the double bed and zipped it open. Most of her clothing sported either a camouflage design or some version of olive green and tan. She had a dress uniform once, but she couldn't remember where she'd left it. She'd worn it for a photo she never bothered to pick up. Fatigues served her just fine for the long flight from Milan to Atlanta.

Your wardrobe could use some help.

"So, now you're a fashion guru in addition to being a pain in the ass?"

Just stating the obvious.

"Why bother?"

What's with the attitude? Things are looking up for you.

"Can't you just leave me the hell alone?"

Actually, no. That's not an option since you're the only one I can talk to.

"Lucky me."

Andi separated her things on the bed, then methodically loaded them into the drawers of a dresser, hoping the activity would bore Will into silence. All too soon, she finished, except for a pair of seasonal GI jackets. A light knock on the door provided a distraction.

"It's open," she said.

Her grandmother entered the room and smiled at her. "It's so good to have you here. I can't tell you how much I've missed you."

"It's gonna take me some time to get used to... this. I mean, things are really different where I spent the last couple years."

Stormy's grin grew even wider. "You're unlikely to get shot here."

Or have a mortar round land in yer lap.

Andi shook her head at both notions. "I need some civilian clothes. It's been awhile since I've worn anything but this stuff." She motioned toward

128

her standard barracks attire.

"Would you like me to go shopping with you?"

Do it, kid! You desperately need new threads.

"Maybe later. I'm a little tired."

Bullshit.

Stormy responded by coughing. She held onto the door frame, her face red.

Andi started towards her, but the older woman stopped her with a raised palm. "I'm—" she paused, wheezing. "I'm all right. It's a touch of congestion is all. I've got a puffer." She coughed again. "I probably should use it now."

"Do you need me to do anything? I can go get it for you if you'll tell me—"

"I'll be fine. You stay and finish up in here. Take a nap if you need to. And just—" Once again, she stopped to cough and clear her throat. "Let me know about the shopping. I'd love to poke around a store or two with you. We could do lunch, too."

"Sounds great, Gran. I look forward to it. I hope you feel better."

"I'll be fine." Stormy closed the door behind her when she left.

You definitely need new clothes.

"Geez, Will. What's up with you and my clothes? You see me get undressed every damn day. Why do you care what I put back on?"

I don't, really. Except it'll be easier to scare up a card game if you're not dressed like a drill sergeant.

Andi flopped backwards onto the bed. "Why can't you just leave me alone?"

Because I need you, that's why. That asshole Benjamin's somewhere in the Atlanta area. I guess he got tired of being a secret squirrel.

"So?"

So, a little payback is still in order, don't you think?

"Honestly? I don't give a shit."

You don't care that the guy who got your buddies killed in the Stan is livin' the high life while you don't even have an address of your own? C'mon.

"We don't know he got them killed. I doubt it was deliberate."

I disagree. I know for a fact he had it in for Mandeville.

"Gunny?" She couldn't believe it. The very thought that her unit might have been deliberately set up to fail left her angry and confused. She sat upright on the bed. "How? Why? And how come you never mentioned any of this before?"

I don't know all the particulars, but I know enough. I damned well should; I lived in Mandeville's head before he died. That's when I got shifted into yours. Benjamin had something going on with a local warlord. He even gave the asshole a wedding present. Everybody heard about that and the little girl. Anyway, Mandeville thought Benjamin was involved in some kind of insurance scam, payoffs for troops killed in action. He was trying to find out more so he could blow the whistle on him.

"That's just... I don't believe it. I *can't* believe it. No marine I know would ever get involved in something so shitty."

Don't be naïve. The planet is full of shitty people. And Benjamin wasn't a marine; he was Army Intel.

"So, what're you planning to do? Can you prove he was doing something illegal?"

No. But if he was up to no good in the sandbox, I'd bet anything he's up to no good back here at home.

"And you think you can take him down by beating him at poker? What the hell kind of strategy is that?"

It's just part of a plan. If we can piss him off thoroughly enough, maybe we can force him to take a misstep or two. Then maybe we can take him down.

"You make it sound like we can call in for assistance, air support maybe. But we can't. We're it. Hell, *I'm* it. You're just a voice in my head. A voice that's making me crazy. Maybe the shrinks in Italy were right. Maybe I'm making all this shit up, hallucinating."

You know better than that, kid. At least, you should, by now. You rely on me more than you realize.

"Dear God, I hope not."

Edith Parise concentrated on the email she'd received from her contact within the bureau. Crime scene experts had begun digging through the ashes and what little else remained after the electronics store fire. According to a preliminary report, there wasn't much. They suspected the blaze had been generated using a volatile incendiary substance like jellied gasoline, much like the nasty stuff used in the Vietnam conflict to turn jungles into barren plains.

The man she had photographed at the

shopping mall had been tentatively identified as Gavin Benjamin, formerly an intelligence officer assigned to various marine units operating in Afghanistan. Benjamin had been given an OTH (Other Than Honorable) discharge and returned to civilian life. The email provided no additional details other than a cautionary note stating that facial recognition technology was limited, and any results would need further verification.

In other words, she had pure, unadulterated bupkis to go on.

The weather had turned a bit chilly, and Edith opted to skip her usual daily run. What she needed was some time off to return to a normal lifestyle, one which didn't include hiding her personality or sex. Her supervisor had urged her to take a couple days off to recuperate before digging into whatever might be left of the case they were building against the blackmailers operating out of the electronics store. More than likely, she would be shifting her attention instead to those who had blown that case up, both literally and figuratively.

Her first order of business would be the removal of all the decorative nonsense that adorned her ears for the past several weeks. She couldn't wait for that to be gone, along with the boob-squishing, elastic band which she'd also had to wear. A bra was bad enough; the chest constrictor added insult to injury. They told her Judy Garland had been forced to wear something similar when filming "The Wizard of Oz." At least the actress got to work with some interesting characters.

Edith's list of potentially interesting characters amounted to one, middle-aged woman determined to spy on her aging mother in hopes of learning a secret recipe. That yarn seemed as reasonable as roller skates for snakes. What kept her musing wasn't the recipe story, the woman's desire to spy on her mother, or even the secret room. What got her attention were the mysterious gargoyles. That collection, she felt sure, could provide answers to some questions she hadn't completely formulated.

And then, as she had every time she thought about it, Edith concluded the gargoyles couldn't be that important, or the Talmadge woman wouldn't have been willing to part with one. None of it made sense.

At least, not yet. Perhaps a little peek into the life of Margaret Talmadge would prove interesting. Besides, once she got rid of the atrocious jewelry flapping from her ears, she had little else to do.

~*~

It had been two months since Margaret's mother had been told to use an inhaler whenever she had one of her coughing fits. Stormy had been reluctant to share the directive from her new doctor; she'd outlived the previous two and finally settled for one about a third her age.

The conversation between mother and daughter had been uncharacteristically short but just as contentious as usual. Margaret insisted that her mother agree to let caregivers share her medical history and anything else that might impact her health. Margaret figured she'd won the skirmish by holding off until she knew her mother was too tired to argue. She wished she'd thought of the tactic sooner.

Using the inhaler hadn't been a problem; Stormy welcomed the relief it provided. The issue which proved quarrelsome was when to have her prescription refilled. Margaret argued for having it done automatically. Her mother claimed she was fully capable of requesting a refill when and if she needed one. In the end, they agreed to disagree.

Margaret told herself Stormy would realize she was being foolish the first time she had to go through a cough-filled night with nothing but an empty puffer on her nightstand. With any luck, Andrea—no, she corrected herself, *Andi*—would persuade Stormy to be reasonable. After all, the only thing at stake was the old woman's life.

Chapter Seven

"It does no harm just once in a while to acknowledge that the whole country isn't in flames, that there are people in the country besides politicians, entertainers, and criminals." –Charles Kuralt

Tanner Howell had to satisfy himself with low end accommodations. He thought he'd done well at the first place he stayed. In addition to a fairly decent bed and a dresser he couldn't use, his room in the extended stay motel provided a mini-fridge and a small microwave oven. The latter he intended to use to stretch out his remaining cash. That plan, however, went straight to hell when he tried to microwave popcorn. The bag and its contents caught fire, and the stink in his room was nearly as bad as that from the backed-up toilet in his last prison cell.

For two nights running he'd found hookers willing to come to his room, but neither could stand the aroma. They didn't part ways on the best of terms. One of them even called in her pimp to demand payment, something Tanner found inherently unfair. The pimp's .45 automatic provided the winning argument, however, and Tanner backed down. He didn't even argue when the bastard demanded a tip for his bitch, too.

Tanner took the hint and left the door open all day to air the place out. As a result, he'd gotten the evil eye from the jerk who worked the front desk. Tanner had been smoking a joint just outside his unit, which apparently didn't sit well with management. When confronted, Tanner pleaded stupidity, but when the arrogant little desk clerk tried to intimidate him, Tanner beat him senseless.

That precipitated a change of address. Fortunately, he'd remembered not to leave anything incriminating behind, like his real name or a traceable license tag number.

He did better at the second location, but it was too far removed from the sort of nightlife he preferred. It was cheap, but that alone wasn't enough.

The third place he found was the cheapest by far. In fact, all it cost was the fee to have a trailer hitch mounted on his car. The little travel trailer wouldn't cost him a thing, provided the cops didn't arrest him for stealing it.

Finding a place to park the trailer proved less difficult than he imagined. Once he left Atlanta proper, the suburbs quickly shifted from trendy to functional and then to rural. Unmarked, unpaved, dead-end roads that stopped in the woods proved ideal. He could detach the trailer when he needed to head into town, or he could nestle down in it to eat, sleep, or work out the details of his revenge plans. Such plans weren't limited to the families of former GBI agents. Oh, no, he reminded himself. Not at all.

~*~

Andi lowered the book to her lap, eased her head back on the overstuffed leather sofa, and looked up at the ceiling. The sound of Gran's coughing continued.

The ornate clock on the mantle, always a few minutes behind, would soon strike ten. Gran should have been fast asleep by now. Andi exhaled wearily. She really wanted to finish the book but put it aside instead. She had a job. Stupid and unrewarding as it was, she had agreed to it, and she would do what must be done.

Andi strode toward her grandmother's bedroom, flipping on a hall light as she went. When she reached her goal, she opened the door and let the light from the hall illuminate a sliver of the gloom beyond.

"Gran?"

The old woman responded with a cough, then, "I'm fine. Go back to bed."

Andi smiled. "I'm still up. Where's your inhaler?"

"There," she wheezed, waving a weak hand at her bedside table. "It's empty."

"Do you have a back-up?"

She shook her head. "That *is* the back-up."

"No problem," Andi said. "The pharmacy's open late. I'll get you another."

"It can wait 'til morning," Gran said, but her cough suggested otherwise.

"Hang tight. I'll be back before you know it." Left unspoken was her prayer that Gran would last until she returned.

You'd better haul ass, kid.

"Will the ghost," Andi muttered, "master of the obvious."

Gran's voice barely reached her as Andi went back down the hall. "The car—"

"I know," she called back. Battery's dead. "I'll

jog. I need the exercise."

Don't be foolish. Call a cab.

"Don't try to control me, okay? I'll run. I can make it to the drugstore before a cab could get here anyway."

And back?

"Screw you."

She kept moving, knowing Gran would only stop talking if she thought Andi couldn't hear her. The woman's stubborn streak had served her well all her life, but now it had become a threat. She didn't need to waste breath on communication.

And then there was Will. He was as bad as Gran, if not worse. Just in very different ways.

Andi grabbed her wallet, slid into a jacket, and left the house. The chill night air felt invigorating, though she wished she'd worn something besides tights and a T-shirt. She zipped up the jacket and broke into a distance-gobbling lope. Though not a marathoner, she loved running. The other grunts in her unit always complained when ordered to run. She enjoyed it, and she enjoyed out-running them even more.

The streetlamps cut sharp wedges of light in the general darkness, dramatizing as many shadows as they eliminated. Andi jogged through one such cone of brightness after another, unworried by her surroundings. Her concern for Gran outweighed everything else.

It didn't make her careless, however. She retained the indelible hallmark of her marine training: situational awareness. Though no longer on patrol in Afghanistan, she remained just as vigilant. Traffic was light, both foot and vehicular. Few wished to be out in the unseasonably cold weather which is why the man standing just outside the corner pharmacy seemed out of place.

Andi appraised him as she ran: Tall. Thirties. Rough beard. Most likely fit. Clean, but casual. If he hadn't been staring at her, she might have blown off his presence entirely. She slowed down as she approached her destination.

Watch out for that one.

"I'm not worried."

The man nodded but didn't smile, and as Andi passed him and entered the store, she caught his reflection in the glass door. He appeared deeply focused on her tights.

Cheap thrills, I guess.

The pharmacist recognized her and quickly re-filled her grandmother's prescription. Andi used a credit card to complete the transaction. "Busy night?" she asked.

"Hardly." The elderly druggist yawned. "Might close up early."

Andi smiled as she pocketed her wallet and the inhaler. "Do you know that guy standing outside?"

The pharmacist flipped his glasses down from atop his white-haired head and gazed at the store entryway. "Nope. He came in a while ago and bought some breath mints. Didn't say a word. I think he's waiting for someone."

"Good to know," she said as she turned to begin the trek back to Gran's house.

The druggist called out from behind the counter, "Be safe."

Andi just waved and pushed through the glass entry door. A quick look to either side revealed no one, and she assumed the man's ride must have arrived while she was inside. With a quick breath, she readied herself for the run home.

After a few short steps she broke into a longer stride and passed into a shadow between streetlights. Suddenly she caught her foot on something and pitched forward. Cursing, she caught herself before she landed face first on the sidewalk. Both palms stung from contact with the pavement.

Oh shit. Wake up time, kid. That guy—

"Shut it, Will! Geez."

Suit yerself.

Still muttering about her own clumsiness, Andi gingerly stood and contemplated rubbing her scraped palms on her tights.

"Nice catch," said a male voice from the shadows.

Andi jerked her head toward the sound, but a newer and even more distinct noise caught her attention, the business end of a switchblade clicking into place. As the man from the drugstore stepped closer to the light, she saw the knife in his hand. He carried it lightly, on his fingertips, as if he knew how to use it. He kicked the broomstick he'd used to trip her out of the way.

"You're coming with me," he said waving the blade at her.

"Like hell."

"Shut yer trap, bitch. Say another word or scream, and I'll cut your throat."

Andi curled her hands into fists and assumed a defensive stance. Though shorter and lighter, she figured she had the advantage of training. She'd faced a lot of men, some bent on killing her. This asshole was no different.

Show no fear.

"I've got this," she whispered.

He pointed at a vehicle parked in the shadows of a side street. "We're gonna have a great time in a bit. Just walk yer pretty ass over to my car!" He dangled a zip tie in his free hand.

"Why can't we party right here?"

Careful, kid.

The question took her assailant by surprise. He squinted at her, suspecting he'd missed something.

"C'mon," she said. "Let's see what you've got."

The word "bitch" had barely left his lips as he rushed her. She stepped to one side, pushed his knife hand away, and landed a deft punch to his Adam's apple.

Gasping, he put both hands on his throat as he struggled for air. A hard kick to his groin dropped him to his knees. The knife and zip tie fell from his hands as he curled into a ball on the ground. As she toed the knife beyond his reach and into a storm drain, she contemplated stomping on one or both of his kidneys but figured he'd had enough.

You prob'ly ought not to kill him.

"I won't," she said, staring down at the pathetic, would-be rapist.

"You there!" Another voice cut through the night. "Don't move, or we'll shoot."

Oh, shit.

Andi turned to face the new threat.

Two police officers, guns drawn, made their way toward her. "Hands up!"

She complied instantly. "He tried to grab me! Force me into his car. I was just defending myself."

"Sure you were," said one of the officers as he knelt over the downed man writhing on the ground.

"He had a knife!"

"She attacked me," croaked the cretin on the sidewalk.

The cops kept their eyes on Andi. The one still standing responded, "You say he had a knife? Where is it?"

She looked at the storm drain. "I— It's—"

"You're under arrest lady."

~*~

Edith grew weary of pacing much earlier than she imagined she would. Having to wait for an update on her assignment meant staying ready to respond on short notice. But what would she be responding to, and more importantly, when could she begin?

Her thoughts turned toward what she'd accomplished while working undercover at the electronics store. The list felt less than abbreviated; it felt empty. She knew the other "employees" were engaged in illegal surveillance which morphed into blackmail, but she couldn't prove it. She'd never gained their trust enough to be brought into the scams. The only one she truly had been involved in seemed, by comparison anyway, completely above board.

She wondered if the Talmadge woman ever got her Chicken Kiev recipe, if that was really all she wanted. The more Edith thought about it, the more curious she became.

There's no reason I couldn't take a quick peek at what she found, assuming she stored it on that cheap PC she bought. The machine came with precious little protection from malware, and Edith had instinctively added a program which would allow her to access the machine remotely via the Internet.

Having nothing else to occupy her time, short of watching daytime soap operas, an option that made her shudder, she parked herself in front of her computer and proceeded to invade the PC belonging to Margaret Talmadge, recipe thief, and God only knew what else.

A quick search of the computer's directory revealed that Talmadge had saved only one file with audio/visual content—she had yet to clutter it up with cat videos and other cutesy nonsense. With only modest regrets for violating the woman's privacy, Edith copied the file to her own computer and cut the connection to Talmadge's.

Without taking the time to refresh her coffee, Edith pulled up the video on her viewer and clicked **PLAY**.

Margaret groaned in response to the insistent buzz of her cell phone. *Who the hell calls anyone this late at night?* Her ire dissipated when she realized it might be Andi reporting that something dreadful had happened to her grandmother.

She was only partially right.

"Aunt Mags?"

"Andrea! Is mother all right? Do I need—"

"Please listen, Aunt Mags. I don't know how long they'll let me talk."

"*Let you talk?* Who? What's going on?"

"I'm calling from the police station," Andi said. "I've been arrested."

"What?"

"I went for a short run to the drugstore to get Gran a refill for her puffer. You know the one."

"They arrested you for that? My God! I'll—"

"No, it's even more stupid than that, and I'm so angry I could spit. After I got the new puffer and started back to the house, some asshole with a knife tried to rape me."

"Oh, you poor..." Margaret groaned. She couldn't imagine how distressed her niece was.

"No, no. I'm okay. The little bastard didn't get very far. I put him on the ground pretty quickly and got in a couple good licks, but the cops think *I attacked him!*"

"But you said he had a knife."

"Yeah," said Andi. "He did. A switchblade, I think. But when he dropped it, I kicked it out of the way, and I'm convinced it went into the storm drain. The cops who arrested me didn't think it was worth their time to even look for it."

Margaret had begun to shake, but whether with fear or anger she didn't quite know. As much as she hated to admit it, she needed to get Stormy's input.

"They took the puffer away from me, Aunt Mags. Gran needs it! That's why I'm calling. You've got to get her another one or— Wait. Damn! That won't work. The drugstore's closed by now. The pharmacist said he would leave early anyway, and that was a couple hours ago. Geez. You've got to come to the jail and make them give you the one I bought."

"I'll take care of it," Margaret said. "I know the pharmacist; I'll wake him up if I have to. And I'll get you an attorney. You're going to need one."

"I don't have money for a lawyer. They told me if I couldn't pay for one, they'd get one for me."

"A public defender? No. No way. Forget that! We'll get someone we can actually count on, someone who doesn't have a million other cases to deal with. Just... Sit tight."

"Aunt Mags?" Andrea suddenly sounded very young and not at all like a seasoned marine. "This is all so... weird. I don't know what to do. And I'm... well, scared."

"Don't worry about a thing, you hear me? We'll get this nonsense straightened out in no time. And listen, for now, don't say anything to anyone."

"I already told them it was self-defense."

"Fine. Stick with that, but not another word—

Josh Langston

about anything. Understand?"

"Yes'm."

"Good. Sit tight. Be tough. Reinforcements are on the way. I promise!"

~*~

For once, Stormy was actually relieved to know her daughter had come, even if the woman's arrival through the back door threatened to rattle the whole house. Stormy couldn't have cared less. Her breathing had become an agonizing chore, but one she simply refused to let kill her.

"Mom!" Mags cried as she burst into her mother's bedroom. She clutched an inhaler in one hand and her capacious handbag in the other.

Rather than try to speak, Stormy reached out, trying to cut the distance between herself and the nebulizer. Mags tucked it into her hand and helped her ease back on the bed. Stormy gave the small, plastic, aerosol dispenser a few quick shakes, then put it to her mouth and used it.

Though not instantaneous, relief came fairly soon, and Stormy relaxed for the first time since Andi had left for the drugstore. A quick glance at the clock revealed the girl had been gone over three hours.

"Wh— Where's Andrea?"

"She's okay, Mom. I'll explain in a minute. How are *you?*"

"Fine now, thanks to you." She looked again at the clock and shook her head. "That girl's been gone for hours."

"She's been arrested."

Stormy felt the blood drain from her head, and she feared she might pass out. "I don't... What happened?"

Mags explained as best she could and repeated everything her niece had told her, from buying the puffer to disabling her attacker to getting arrested.

"But it sounds like she was only protecting herself."

Mags nodded. "That's exactly what she was doing."

"Did they arrest the rapist?"

"I don't know. I don't think so. Andrea didn't say."

"Hand me my phone," Stormy said, pointing to the device.

"Who're you going to call at this hour?"

"I'm calling the best damned lawyer in

Georgia." She paused and gave a mirthless laugh. "And just about the only one I know who's still alive."

It had been over a year since Stormy last spoke with Robert Swenson, but she felt confidant the man still had what it would take to get some action, and get it fast. Bobby had been the District Attorney she and Pete relied on for making cases using the leads Stormy provided. Together they had compiled an impressive track record and managed to put quite a few serious felons in prison.

Bobby eventually left his law practice and became a Superior Court Judge, a position he'd held for years and from which he'd recently retired.

"Stormy?" he asked, clearly not awake. "What the hell do you want? It's damned near three—"

"I know it's the middle of the night, Bobby, but I wouldn't have called if it wasn't important."

He sighed heavily into the phone. "This'd better be good."

"It's anything but good. The police arrested my granddaughter for stopping a rape."

"Aw, Christ on a cricket pitch. That can't be right."

"Have I ever lied to you?" Stormy asked.

"Well, there was that time you said the punch

wasn't spiked, and Lynn and I—"

"Aside from that! C'mon. I'm serious. You've got to help us out. My granddaughter is terrified. God only knows who she's locked up with."

She activated the phone's speaker at Margaret's insistence then went on to explain as many of the details as she knew, pausing from time to time for reassurance from her daughter that she'd gotten the story straight.

"I'll go down there first thing in the morning," Bobby said. "That's the best I can do. If I don't get a decent night's sleep, I'm not good for anything."

"And what if it rains?" Stormy asked.

Bobby responded in the voice of a very unhappy magistrate. "What the hell does that have to do with anything?"

"The rapist's knife went down a storm drain. It's likely still there, but it's supposed to rain, and if that happens, it could get washed away."

"And you're sure the police didn't look for it?"

"Positive."

"Well, just shit. They know better than that."

"Apparently not," Stormy said.

"What's this kid's name?" he asked. "I'll make

a couple calls and meet you at the station in an hour."

"Her name's Andrea. Andrea Vega. She's innocent, Bobby; I know she is. She's a decorated war hero for God's sake."

"A war hero?"

"Silver Star, but she doesn't talk about it. And listen, Bobby, I'm really sorry I had to call in the middle of the night. I can't thank you enough for helping us out."

"Thanks, hell. You're gonna buy me the biggest damned breakfast anyone ever ordered."

"Gladly," she said. "See you soon."

~*~

You know it's bullshit. They can't make it stick.

"That's easy for you to say," Andi groused from her seat on a hardwood bench in a jailcell devoid of creature comforts. "It's not your ass in the slammer."

That kinda depends on how you look at it.

"*You're* not locked in here. *You* can wander off, sneak around, go anywhere you want to go."

Within reason.

Andi rolled her eyes. "I have no idea what that means."

It means I can't drift off too far away from you. So, if you're locked up, I'm kinda locked up, too.

"Aw, boo-farkin'-hoo."

A voice erupted from the far side of the cell, "Ah don't know who the hell you talkin' to, but would it kill ya to shut up? Ah'm tryin' to sleep here."

"Yeah, sure," Andi muttered. "Sorry."

Her beefy cellmate, who hadn't shared more than two words with her previously rolled over on her side and faced the wall with her head cradled on her arm. Andi looked away. The lights in the cell had been turned down but not off. Few sounds came from the other cells. Andi concluded It must not have been a very busy night.

Careful with that big momma. She could hurt ya just sitin' on you.

Andi snorted but otherwise didn't respond.

I had an idea.

"Oh, swell. If you're planning a jailbreak, forget it. Aunt Mags said she'd get me a lawyer. I'm sure whoever it is will get me outta here."

Escape? Naw. I wasn't thinkin' about that at

all. You'll be okay once they figure out what really happened. If I could, I'd testify for you. Only— Well....

"Yeah. I know."

But I was thinking. If you got one of those snazzy new phones they have, you know, the kind that fit right on your ear? You could talk to me whenever you liked, and anyone who saw you would just think you're on a call.

Andi considered the idea for a moment. "You may be on to something. That might actually work. Not that I ever really want to talk to you."

It'd save you from having to make up stories to explain that you're not really talking to yourself.

"There's always one other option," she said. "I could just stop answering you altogether."

Good luck with that. I'm too valuable a resource. I know stuff, lots of stuff.

"Oh, you're the bomb when it comes to critical info. Just like you didn't say shit to me about this Benjamin character you think got the guys in my unit killed."

I had my reasons.

"Asshole."

"Will you please just shut the fuck up?" yelled

the cellmate. "If you don't, I swear to God, I'ma pound yo ass inna next week."

You'd better chill. Try to get some sleep yourself. If it looks like she's coming over here to sit on you, I'll wake you up.

"Promise?" she asked in a whisper.

Count on it.

"Right." Andi stretched out on the bench, reminded of nights spent on the ground during missions in Afghanistan. At least back there she had something to sleep on, and if she needed to talk to someone, she could see who they were. All too soon, Will broke the silence.

Don't forget about the phone gizmo.

Andi ignored him.

Okay?

"Yeah. Got it. Now leave me alone."

Chapter Eight

"I'd love to come back as the most annoying ghost ever." –Guillermo Del Toro

Edith watched the video she'd stolen from Margaret Talmadge's computer several times. She'd spent the first viewing open-jawed and stunned by what she saw. The following viewings allowed her to be more dispassionate and gave her the opportunity to try and understand just what in Hell was going on. And she felt certain it actually did involve Hell.

The video was quite clear, nothing obstructed the camera, and its angle took in everything: the cabinet, the mirror, the old woman with her wine glass. It also gave an unrestricted view of the *thing*—the apparition or spirit or whatever it was—that showed up *inside* the mirror.

She thought at first that what looked like a mirror was actually an unusually tall TV screen, but she quickly abandoned the idea. Nobody made TVs that looked like the one she saw. And if it was merely a television, why hide it? Why build a locking cabinet for it inside a room hidden from the world?

It also seemed quite obvious the Talmadge woman didn't know about the mirror or she wouldn't have told Edith, in her Chad persona, anything about the hidden room or her desire to install a secret camera in it. There was a great deal more to this puzzle than she could have ever guessed.

As she looked through the directory on her cell phone for Margaret Talmadge's phone number, Edith's thoughts drifted back to her conversation with Dan in the GBI lab. He'd told her the interior of the gargoyle she'd gotten from Talmadge smelled like biblical hellfire. She couldn't help but wonder about a connection.

She punched the woman's number.

"Hello?"

"Mrs. Talmadge, this is... Uh... Chad. From the electronics store."

She responded instantly. "Thank goodness you're all right! I read about the explosion, and I looked for your name, but I couldn't find it, and I thought—"

"I'm fine. Really. Everything's fine, Mrs. Talmadge—"

"Margaret, please. Mrs. Talmadge is my mother."

"Right. Listen, I— *We*, we need to talk. There are some things I need to explain, and I have some questions I need to ask. Is this a good time?"

"Well, I suppose. I've got a few minutes. What's going on?"

"First off," Edith said, "I need to explain exactly who I am."

Margaret laughed. "You mean the fact that you're not really a male? I figured that out the first couple times I saw you. I figured it was none of my business."

"That's part of it, but only a tiny part." Edith stopped to clear her thoughts before she continued. "My real name is Edith Parise, and I work for the GBI."

Margaret took a sharp breath. "I— What's this about? I haven't done anything illegal. At least, not that I know about. Unless...."

"Please," Edith said. "Allow me to continue. I'll be happy to clear some things up."

"Of course. Thank you."

"I was working undercover at the electronics store, and—"

"Is that something you should be telling me? I mean, undercover. That's... Goodness. What were you investigating?"

"I can't share that," Edith said, "and I probably shouldn't have mentioned anything about my role at the store, so please keep that to yourself."

"I will, certainly. No problem."

"The reason I'm calling is because of the video you took with the camera I sold you."

"What about it?" Margaret's voice echoed her suspicion.

"I watched it."

"You *watched* it? How? It's on my computer. I didn't share—"

"I accessed your PC remotely and made a copy."

After a brief silence, Margaret continued, her voice harsh, "You had no right to do that!"

"I know; I know. You're right. But—"

Margaret's voice rose higher. "You're in *law* enforcement for God's sake. You, of all people, should know better."

"You're absolutely correct. I completely overstepped my bounds, and I apologize. I truly mean that; I wish I hadn't watched it. But that doesn't change the fact that I did, and I saw something so strange, so incredibly weird, I had to talk to you about it." Edith knew she'd have to make this admission, and while she'd dreaded it, she felt better having it out in the open. She thought it best to simply forge ahead. "So, the older woman in the video, that's your mother?"

"Yes," Margaret said.

"And who, or what, exactly, was she talking to?"

"Honestly? I have no idea. I only watched it once; that was enough. I'm not a fan of horror movies. Some fairy tales give me the creeps, and when I saw my mother chatting with whatever was looking at her from inside that mirror, I freaked out."

"My own reaction wasn't much different." Edith paused and took a deep breath. "I think we need to talk to your mother."

"No—we can't! She mustn't know I spied on her. She's kept this secret for as long as I've been alive. I can't just barge in on her and demand to know what she's up to."

Edith shifted tactics. "I get that. But let's stop and think for a moment. How old is your mother?"

"She's almost ninety."

"How's her health?"

Margaret snorted into the phone. "She's almost *ninety*, for cryin' out loud. She's got some health issues. Who doesn't at that age?"

"Exactly. And what happens if she passes away without telling you about the mirror, where it came from, or what it's purpose might be? Will that make you feel better? No. Will it give you any critical information? Definitely not. So, what would you do then?"

"I don't know. I haven't thought about it."

Edith laughed. "You seriously expect me to believe that?"

"No."

"Then let's talk to her, you and I. Give her a chance to explain things. Maybe there's a perfectly good explanation for all of it."

Margaret sounded unsure. "And do you seriously believe *that?*"

"Nope," Edith said. "Not for a second."

"I can't imagine my mother talking about any

of this with me, let alone with someone she doesn't know. But I admit, I've been thinking along the lines you mentioned. At the very least, there's something extremely odd going on, and I'll need to understand it sooner or later."

Edith remained silent.

"So," Margaret said, "I'll try to find a time to talk to her about it."

"Try?"

"No. I will find a time to talk to her about it. And if it's something I think you need to know about, I'll call and tell you."

"That sounds reasonable," Edith said. "But do call me, even if whatever's going on is no big deal. It will set my mind at ease."

"Fair enough," Margaret said. Then she cut the connection.

Edith stared off at nothing, trying to settle herself and become satisfied with Margaret's decision. It wasn't working.

~*~

"Nice work on the electronics shop," said Derrick Benjamin. "I appreciate you keeping me out of it."

"No problem," said the voice on Benjamin's

phone. "You need anything else?"

"Not right now. I've got one nagging little concern, but I'll take care of it."

"Is this something I need to know about?"

"No," Benjamin insisted. "It involves someone from Afghanistan, a marine with an abundance of good luck. There's a slim chance she might cause trouble. It's not a big chance, but I hate leaving loose ends."

"I understand. Just don't do anything stupid. There's a lot of money on the line."

Benjamin chuckled. "You think I don't know that? Relax. I've got it covered."

He clicked off the cellphone connection and slipped the device in his pocket. How convenient that the only surviving member of Mandeville's unit had moved practically into his backyard. He had contacts who had contacts. Finding someone to take care of her wouldn't be difficult.

The lunch crowd swarmed the town square as Stormy accompanied Mags, Andrea, and Judge Bobby to the jail's parking lot. Despite Bobby's best efforts, the police wouldn't release Andrea early. But someone in the department had taken the judge seriously when he threatened dire consequences if they failed to look for the weapon Andrea swore her attacker dropped during their scuffle.

It didn't surprise Stormy at all when they found the knife precisely where Andrea said it would be, and they'd sent it off to check for fingerprints.

"The only thing I'd worry about," Bobby said, looking straight at Stormy, "is if Andrea picked up the knife at some point. If her prints are on it, she'll be in even deeper trouble than before."

Andrea quickly chimed in. "No worries there. I touched it with my foot. With my shoes on. There's no way my prints will be on it."

"I hope you're right, young lady," Bobby said. "Now, see if you can stay out of trouble while the authorities sort through everything." He turned back to Stormy. "Call me if you need me, y'hear?"

"I will," she said, giving him a peck on the cheek. "And what about that big 'thank you' breakfast you mentioned?"

"Later," he said, yawning. "My grandson's coming to pick me up; I'm going straight home to bed."

Just then a car pulled up, and a tall man in his mid-twenties slipped out from behind the wheel. "Hey, Pop! You're right on time."

"Ladies," Bobby said, gesturing toward the new arrival. "This is Erik, my grandson, and heir to..." He paused to chuckle. "...the Swenson fortune."

"That's assuming you don't blow it all in the market," the younger man said.

"Don't be impertinent." Bobby waved to the women, climbed in the front passenger seat, and rolled the window down. "Stand clear. I'm not sure if this child has fully mastered the controls."

Erik got in the driver's seat and appeared to be at a loss for where to insert the car key. He honked the horn and flipped on the wipers instead.

"You see what I have to put up with?" Bobby said, his skull pressed back against the headrest, the back of his hand on his forehead.

Erik smiled and waved, put the car in gear, and pulled smoothly and carefully away.

"He seems like a nice, young man," Mags said as she handed the car keys to Andrea. "Since we didn't think to bring along our own version of Erik, would you be a dear and bring the car around so Mom doesn't have to walk so far."

Stormy stiffened. "I can walk!"

"I know you can," Mags said. "But you don't have to. You've been up most of the night. Save your strength."

"I'm happy to," Andrea said. "It's the least I can do after y'all came to my rescue."

Once the young woman located their car and picked up her passengers—Stormy in the front, Mags in the back—the questions started. Mags went first. "Was it awful in jail? Were there many people in there? Were you able to stay away from them?"

Andrea kept her eyes on the traffic, driving cautiously. "It's not something I'd want to do again. There was only one other woman in the cell, and she was trying to sleep. I tried, too, but I just couldn't. I hope y'all won't mind if I take a nap when we get home. I'm wiped out."

"Don't you think you should take a shower first," Stormy asked. "In case you picked up something while you were locked up?"

Andrea responded with a slight laugh. "They didn't put me in a leper colony, Gran. I'm fine. Really. I'll get cleaned up *after* my nap."

Stormy wasn't convinced, but neither she nor Mags cared to press the point further.

"Do you think you hurt that man badly?" Stormy asked.

"I sure hope so."

"But—"

"When you're fighting for your life, there

aren't any rules. And that's exactly what I was doing. He attacked me. I stopped him. I wouldn't shed any tears if he died."

Mags shook her head. "That's a little harsh, don't you think?"

Andrea shrugged. "Isn't there some proverb about people who live by the sword?"

"Well, yes," Stormy said. "But—"

"Listen, Gran. You, too, Aunt Mags. If someone tried to harm either of you, I'd do whatever I had to do to stop them. If they ended up dead because they picked a fight with the wrong person, that's on them. Do you pity bullies when they get what's coming to them?"

Neither of the older women responded.

"I didn't think so," Andrea said. "I don't either."

~*~

Once her niece had time to settle into bed for her nap, Margaret approached her mother who sat quietly in the living room of the big, antebellum house. "Got a minute?" she asked.

"That depends."

"On?"

"Whether you're still intent on making me leave this house."

"I'm not," Margaret assured her. "But I want to make sure you're up to a discussion. It was an awfully long night for you, too."

"I'll survive," Stormy said. "So, if you're not trying to get me to move to the county farm, what's on your mind?"

"I need to talk to you about the safe room."

Stormy's eyebrows dipped as she looked at her daughter. "Okay."

Margaret settled into a chair. Her knees came close to touching her mother's, and she cast about briefly for a way to start. "For as long as I can remember, you've kept that oddball collection of gargoyles on a shelf down there, hidden from sight."

Stormy nodded.

"And you've got a locked cabinet down there, too. One I've never been able to look inside."

"That's true."

Margaret cleared her throat, then continued. "Don't you think it's about time you told me what that's all about? Are the gargoyle statues so valuable you don't want anyone to know about them? In which case, why keep them at all? What's the point?"

Stormy turned her head and looked out a window, remaining silent.

"Wouldn't you admit that seems a little bit odd, if not downright suspicious?"

"You're beginning to sound like a prosecuting attorney," Stormy said. "Why the sudden interest in something I've shielded you from for your entire life?"

"Because it's time someone understands what you've been hiding all these years. I love you, but you won't live forever. None of us will. It's time you were honest with me."

"I've never lied to you," Stormy said, softly. "Ever."

"You haven't told me the whole truth, either. That's what I can't understand. It's like you can't trust me. If I've done something that caused you to doubt me, you should have said something. You should have told me, given me a chance to make amends."

Stormy sighed and turned back toward Margaret, her face reflecting weariness and defeat. "I didn't want to burden you with it."

"With what? The gargoyle collection? Mom, I can dust them as well as anyone, and as far as I can tell, collecting dust is about all they're good for. Or

Josh Langston

are you talking about what's in the cabinet?"

"Of course I'm talking about the cabinet!" snapped Stormy who quickly settled back down. "The gargoyles are just... artifacts. I've kept them hidden because I'm not really sure what they are, or if they're harmful in some way."

"Harmful?"

Stormy snorted. "Try dropping one on your toes."

"They're heavy; I know. But where do they come from?"

"From inside the cabinet. Or, more specifically, they come from something else inside the cabinet."

"Which is?"

"A mirror," Stormy said. "A very old, very... Uhm... Unusual mirror."

Relief flooded into Margaret's system; she didn't need to admit to spying after all. "Go on," she said.

Stormy did go on. In detail. And when she finished, both women sat back in their chairs as if they'd spent the day at hard labor. The relief that had previously left Margaret feeling so good had long since departed.

"I can't believe you lived with this... this secret, for so long."

"I felt as if I had no choice. And it wasn't as hard when your father was still alive," Stormy said. "We could talk about whatever the Keeper of the Portal told me. Pete knew instinctively whether or not it was something he needed to act on. More often that not, I only needed to deliver a message, and those I could handle on my own."

Stormy's tone shifted as she appraised her daughter. "Is this something you'd be willing to take over for me?"

"Do I have a choice?"

"That depends on your conscience. I didn't think I could walk away and ignore those souls. You may not feel the same way."

Margaret swallowed, hard. "I don't know if I'm up to it. Aren't you frightened talking to the— What did you call it?"

"The Keeper of the Portal. It's not a title or anything; I just didn't know how else to address it, him, them... Whatever."

"Isn't this something that should be turned over to a church?" Margaret asked, hoping for a way out. "Maybe they could form a committee to handle the requests."

"Which church?" Stormy asked. "I'm a Unitarian Universalist. If I took the mirror to my church, they'd likely humor me and then sell it at a yard sale."

"Okay, then how 'bout a Catholic church?"

"They'd probably try to perform an exorcism. These ghosts, or whatever they are, certainly aren't 'holy.' The current Keeper is anything but."

"Wouldn't this be something the government—"

"Don't be silly. The government? They might be interested if they could tax it, or use it to spy on some other government. Besides, I wouldn't trust any bureaucrat on Earth to treat this information the way it needs to be treated. The mirror would end up in a warehouse somewhere, if not a landfill."

While Margaret did not share her mother's deep disregard for politicians and those who flourished around them, she'd seen enough to be wary of them. The government option was out.

"To be completely honest," Stormy said, "I had hoped that this was something Andrea could handle."

Margaret released her breath in a whoosh. "Andrea? You know she's been diagnosed with PTSD."

"Yes, but I haven't seen anything about her behavior that makes me think that diagnosis is accurate."

"I presume you're basing that on your many years as a psychologist," Margaret said, folding her arms across her chest.

"I admit I'm no shrink, and the poor thing hasn't lived here long enough for anyone to make that sort of assessment. But, given what she's gone through lately, and her reaction to it, does she strike you as the sort of person who couldn't handle something like this?"

"Dealing with... I dunno... ghosts?"

"Precisely."

"Maybe," Margaret said, "we just need to ask her."

~*~

Tanner Howell found it amusing that he could look up his next target's name and address in a phone book. Hadn't anyone else ever heard of an unlisted number? Clearly, Robert J. Swenson, esq. was a moron, at least when it came to common sense. His courtroom smarts were a different matter. Swenson had been the one who convinced the sentencing judge to extend his term in prison.

And for that, Swenson would pay. Dearly.

Tanner drove Lil D's car through Swenson's neighborhood several times. Everyone appeared to be staying inside even though the weather hadn't turned that cold. Jeans weather, he thought. Maybe a light jacket. He'd bought one at an Army Surplus store out on Highway 41, the road which used to be the main connection between Marietta and Atlanta, back before the interstate highways were built.

He remembered a time in the past when an old man with a ratty, iron-wheeled, gypsy cart and a big bunch of goats traveled up and down that same stretch. Folks called him the Goat Man. He'd heard somewhere that the old geezer had finally died, and Tanner wondered who got the goats. The thought made him smile. Swenson had sure as hell gotten *his* goat, but there'd be no smiles when Tanner got through with him.

The old attorney's house occupied a big lot in a classy neighborhood, the kind of area where no one did their own yardwork. Tanner parked several streets away from Swenson's house and proceeded on foot.

He hadn't taken the time to formulate much of a plan. The time it took him to walk from his car to Swenson's front door only required a few minutes, but that was enough to decide exactly what he would do—knock on the door, and when someone answered it, he'd start shooting.

With the little automatic hidden behind his back, Tanner reached toward the doorbell and pushed the button.

~*~

Andi managed a few hours' sleep, but it was fitful, mostly because she couldn't darken the room enough. And if that hadn't kept her awake, thinking about the attorney's grandson would have.

The kid's name is Erik. I saw him wink at you.

"Bullshit."

No. I'm serious. He's definitely interested in you.

"Uh huh. Be quiet. I'm tryin' to sleep."

You've been laying there for over an hour, but you haven't been sleeping. You've been fantasizing about him, haven't you?

"What're you now, a mind reader?"

No. I'm just sayin'. The guy likes what he saw; that's the real reason he got outta the car. And it's obvious, to me anyway, that you're interested in him.

Andi rolled over on her side. "I can't wait 'til you start singing the lyrics from 'Fiddler on the

Roof.' How did it go?" She hummed a little then added words, "'Matchmaker, matchmaker, make me a match.'"

Hate to break it to ya, kid, but you're not destined for stardom.

"Go 'way."

If I were you, I'd get my lazy ass outta bed and go find out whatever I could about that guy. See if he's already got somebody in his life. I didn't see a wedding ring on his hand. Did you?

"No."

See! I knew you were checking him out!

"And if I were you, I'd shoot myself."

Fat lot of good that'd do.

"A girl can dream, can't she?"

Yeah, sure. But if you're gonna dream, it might as well be about some young hunk who fancies you as much as you fancy him.

Andi groaned. "Have you any idea how tiresome you are?"

~*~

Edith's superior told her she was no longer assigned to the blackmail case she'd been working on because the whole thing had been escalated to a senior level due to the bombing. When she inquired about the man she'd seen lurking near the blast area, she got a repeat of the first message; she was no longer assigned to that case.

At the behest of someone higher up in the bureau's food chain, a new directive landed in her lap. The client of a former district attorney had apparently been given a raw deal. They wanted Edith to look into it and make sure the case got a proper investigation.

Edith could feel a brush-off as well as anyone, and she had no doubt being reassigned had something to do with office politics. It hadn't been that way when she started working at the GBI, but that had changed dramatically over the past few years. Pushing her distaste aside, she dove into her new project with an open mind.

The facts could not have been clearer: a woman had been arrested and charged with battery; she'd punched the crap out of a man who, she claimed, had tried to rape her. In the scuffle, a knife had been kicked into a storm drain. That weapon had been recovered and the fingerprints on it had been evaluated.

In the interim, no one had been able to contact the alleged victim, and it quickly became clear he had given the booking officer a bogus name, address, and phone number. Oliver Cantrell, the man supposedly attacked by the former marine, was at the very least, a liar. The fingerprints found on the switchblade recovered from the storm drain could only have come from one person, and while those prints weren't in the system, they definitely didn't belong to Andrea Vega.

The DA's office declined to follow the matter further, and Edith assumed she no longer needed to waste her time on it. She didn't change her mind until she found out who had agreed to cover Vega's bail. Margaret Talmadge's name might as well have been written in neon letters.

Chapter Nine

"Most people who went about saying a ghost had poked them with a brolly [umbrella] would be locked up somewhere."
–Pamela Stephensen

Derrick Benjamin rarely summoned his associates to his home; that was sacred turf, and while he might invite someone of stature, he swore he'd never open his private domain to riffraff. On rare occasions, however, it became necessary to ignore his self-imposed dictums. As long as such instances remained rare, he would manage.

The man who called himself Oliver Cantrell embodied the rare exception. He lounged against a wall on the patio of Benjamin's Buckhead estate and, for some reason, appeared quite relaxed.

"You had a job to do, did you not?" Benjamin asked.

"Yeah. Sorry 'bout that. It went sideways."

Benjamin took a seat in a thickly upholstered swivel chair and propped his feet up on a low table. "Tell me what happened."

When his visitor moved to seat himself, Benjamin halted him with an upraised palm. "I'd prefer you remain standing. I like to see if my subordinates can think on their feet."

Cantrell rewarded him with a narrowing of his eyes, but he didn't object. Instead he returned to his spot against the wall.

"Now, go on. Give me the details. How does one manage to screw up a simple thing like an abduction?"

"The bitch knew kung fu, or some other martial arts shit. She's fast, too. And she wasn't scared either. Hell, she *wanted* to fight." He moved his hand absently to his throat. "I didn't think I'd be able to talk again after what she did to me."

"That's it? One punch, and she took you out?" Benjamin snorted and shook his head. "That's pathetic. Actually, no. It's you—*you're* pathetic."

"You weren't there."

"And you were?" His chuckle bore no trace of

humor. "You're at least five or six inches taller and a good forty or fifty pounds heavier. And you had a knife."

"Yeah, well—"

"You're lucky she didn't take that knife and cut your balls off, assuming you have some."

Cantrell pushed off from the wall. "I don't have to listen to this shit."

"I paid you to do a job, and you screwed it up."

"You sayin' you want a goddam refund?"

Benjamin shrugged. "It would've been a nice gesture."

"Screw that. I'll get it done right next time," Cantrell said. "Don't you worry 'bout that."

"I'm not worried in the least. I'll find someone competent enough to actually do what he's paid to do."

"Hey! I—"

Cantrell's voice devolved into a low growl when Benjamin's "valet," a huge, former NFL lineman, got him in a choke hold and lifted him off the ground.

"Down or done?" the giant asked.

"Done. He's of no use to me anymore."

Cantrell's eyes expanded in shock as the big man applied increasing pressure to his throat. The would-be assassin succumbed slowly, his face going purple before his eyes rolled up as if in search of his brain.

"Thank you, Jermontae. Take the usual precautions when disposing of him."

The brute tucked Cantrell under one massive arm and hauled him off the patio. Benjamin sighed as he watched the pair depart. It would have made matters so much easier if Jermontae had two reliable knees. But such was the price of an NFL career. That, and the man's dreadful taste in financial advisors, had brought him into Benjamin's employ.

They even liked each other.

~*~

"Remember," Stormy said, "I'm only doing this because you said you wanted to know about it. I don't pretend to understand how or why it works; it just does."

Mags stayed by her side as the two women made their way down the steps to the terrace level, formerly a cellar, expanded long after the house was built. Pete had also installed a dumb waiter. Large enough for an adult, provided he or she could curl up sufficiently, the device provided access in an emergency. Stormy had never used it and suspected that if she had to now, she'd never be able to contort herself enough to fit inside. And, if she did somehow force herself into such a confined space, she'd likely never get out, much less unfold herself if she did.

When they reached the lower level, they went straight to the safe room. Neither spoke while Stormy pushed the bookcase aside to reveal the hidden space behind it. She then unlocked the cabinet and exposed the mirror.

"Pull up a chair," Stormy said as she lowered herself into the ancient lounger parked directly in front of the dark, flat, enigmatic surface of the mirror. "We may have to wait awhile before the Keeper arrives. If, in fact, he bothers to show up at all."

She looked at Mags. "You nervous?"

"A little." The younger woman squirmed in her chair as she looked from the mirror to the shelves on which sat the collection of gargoyles. "I'm still a little freaked out by what you said about them." She nodded at the squatty, ghoulish figures.

"Don't feel like you're the only one who gets spooked by the damned things."

"Maybe we should toss 'em out."

Stormy glared at her. "If you choose to do that, kindly wait until I've been dead for a few days, at least."

"But—"

"Stand by," Stormy said. "Here he comes."

An image began to coalesce in the mirror. Smoky and indistinct at first, it gradually formed into something vaguely human. The features lacked focus, as if the visage were composed of smoke. The edges wavered even though the room had no moving air currents.

A quick glance at Mags' hands revealed her white-knuckled grip on the arms of the chair.

"Welcome back," said a cultured voice from the apparition. "I've missed our little chats."

I sure as hell haven't. "Same here," Stormy said. "I don't know if you can see past me or not, but—"

"Of course I can. Who is that?"

Was he squinting? She couldn't quite tell. "This is my daughter, Margaret. She's going to be working with us."

"Hmpf."

"Is he always this... Uhm. *Pleasant?*" Mags asked.

"Generally speaking, yes," Stormy said with a trace of an eyeroll before she turned to face the mirror again. "Have you anything new to share?"

"Not much beyond the usual whining and moaning. I shouldn't have to listen to it." His voice rose to a squeaky alto before dropping back to a bass. "I need you to tell my husband I love him; tell my babies I'm sorry; tell my wife that woman meant nothing." He exhaled wearily. "It's all so tiresome."

"How can you not feel sorry for them?" she asked.

"Why should I? Do any of them feel sorry for me?"

They might, if you weren't such a jerk. "So," Stormy concluded, "nothing of interest."

"Well, there is one soul who's been unusually persistent, though I doubt his message involves anything you could act on."

"Let's hear it. If we can do something, we will."

She glanced quickly at Margaret who was leaning forward intently, focused on the hazy face in the mirror.

"He says his name is 'Small D,' or 'Dainty D' or something equally stupid."

Josh Langston

The shadowy face seemed to turn aside briefly, then returned, the voice even more dismissive than before. "It's *'Little D,'* he says, although his diction is dreadful. I can barely understand him. Maybe he meant lower case D. Who knows? Anyway, he claims someone named Tanner killed him and probably stole his gun. The man can't be trusted and will undoubtedly try to kill someone else."

Stormy grimaced. "Did he say who this Tanner person might go after?"

"He doesn't know. He just says the man is crazy."

"That sounds like something we should pass along to the authorities. Did he say where it happened?"

"Somewhere in Atlanta."

"Anywhere in particular?"

"I imagine so. But, then, that's not my problem, is it?"

"Evidently not," Stormy said as she reached out to close the cabinet doors. "Thanks for your help."

The image in the mirror began to fade before the doors closed. Stormy sat back, too tired to even complain about the old chair.

"What a jerk," Mags said.

Stormy nodded. "My thoughts exactly. The problem now, of course, is finding a way to pass this information along to the police. It was no problem when your father was alive, but now..." She exhaled in frustration. "My only contact is the idiot currently running the GBI."

Mags patted her on the shoulder. "Actually, I might be able to help. I just happen to know someone who works there. I could call and tell her."

"Your contact is a *woman?* That's great! It's about time we had more female agents. But how do you propose to share the information without telling her how we learned of it? That's got to remain a secret."

"I think I know a way," Mags said. "And I won't have to say a word about where the information came from. Can you trust me?"

"Of course!" Stormy shifted and pushed herself to a standing position so she could give her daughter a hug. "I can't believe how good it feels to know I don't have to worry about this anymore. Thank you. Thank you so much!"

"It's no problem, Mom," Mags said. "No problem at all."

~*~

Tanner parked his car a block or so from the house Swenson lived in. It wouldn't be difficult to take the old bastard out, even if someone else lived in the house with him. They were all fair game— they earned what they'd get for what Swenson did to him. Payback time had never smelled so good.

Swenson's home sat in the middle of an oversized lot. No doubt the shyster made a fortune in court, conniving with judges and juries to send people to the slammer on the flimsiest of evidence. That Tanner had actually done what he'd been charged with seemed immaterial. Swenson had surely taken decades of freedom from scores of innocent men. Tanner heard their tales repeatedly while in prison. His mission was not just for personal revenge, he'd made the decision to stand up for all those poor slobs who were still locked up. When they discovered that Swenson had gotten his, they'd all salute Tanner for evening the score.

A long drive and a winding walkway led to the front entrance of the huge home. Tanner moved casually. And why not? He had all day. The gun he'd taken from Lil D nestled in his hand which he kept behind his back on the off chance someone might see his approach.

The landing at the top of several broad steps served as a showplace for potted plants of different varieties. Tanner's knowledge of flowers had suffered during his incarceration, but he still knew the difference between a daisy and a dandelion, and none of the pots held either.

With his gun hand still behind his back, he reached for the doorbell, intent on blasting his way through Swenson or anyone else who answered. Instead, someone pushed it open abruptly and with brutal force. The heavy door smashed into Tanner's nose, rammed him backwards, and sent him tumbling down the broad, hard-edged brick steps. Somewhere along the way, he and his stolen .32 automatic parted company.

"What the hell?" Tanner screamed, lying flat on his back. "What're you tryin' to do?"

A lean, young man raced down the steps, grabbed the gun from the lawn, and aimed it at Tanner's forehead. He stood two paces away, and suddenly the bore of the little automatic looked bigger than the opening on a water main. The weapon didn't waver, and the man holding it appeared quite willing to pull the trigger. "Who are you, and what do you want?" he asked.

"I could sue yer ass, ya know that?"

The young man smiled. "And I could shoot yours. Thing is, I get to go first."

"Listen—"

"No, *you* listen, asshole. You think you're the

first idiot to come knocking on my grandad's door with a gun in his hand? I picked you up on video the minute you stepped into the yard. I saw this piece of crap in your hand and was pretty sure you weren't selling shit door-to-door."

"You don't understand! I—"

"Oh, I understand perfectly. And so will the cops when they get here. Shouldn't be more than a couple minutes from now."

"C'mon, kid. You gotta gimme a break. I didn't mean any real harm. I was only gonna try and scare the lawyer that got me put away for fifteen damn years. You understand how long that is? Fifteen years!"

"Chances are, you're lookin' at fifteen more."

"Erik?" The voice of an older man interrupted them. "What's going on?"

"Not much, Pop," the kid yelled back. "Trespasser. I already called 911."

"You gonna let me stand up?" Tanner asked.

The kid inched closer. He held the gun only a few feet from Tanner's head. "Not a chance."

~*~

Margaret went outside to call Edith. She hadn't spoken with her face-to-face since she revealed her true identity. Margaret hoped they would meet in person soon; it would help her replace the image of the sexually vague "Chad" which still occupied her mind.

"It's me, Margaret," she said when Edith answered.

"You okay?"

"Yeah. We're good here. I just wanted to—"

"Is your niece okay, too? I heard she had some trouble with the police."

Edith sounded sincere, something Margaret appreciated. "She's fine, but it was a scary time—for all of us."

"How so? The DA has dropped all charges against your niece. It's Andrea, right?"

"She goes by Andi. But what's troubling me is..." She stopped to exhale. "I talked to my mother about the business in the safe room."

"The crazy mirror stuff?"

"Yeah. And she took me into her confidence. She's been dealing with this insanity for years. It started when she was in her twenties."

"Wait. Your Mom's insanity?"

"No! The mirror. It's— I don't exactly know

how to explain it because it's so bizarre. But trust me when I say that mirror is somehow connected to Purgatory."

Edith didn't respond.

"You still there?" Margaret asked.

"Yes. I'm just... It's kinda hard to wrap my head around. *Purgatory?* You sure?"

"I can promise you one thing," Margaret said. "This is definitely not some elaborate hoax. For one thing, my Mom doesn't have the technical skills. And for another, my Dad wouldn't have allowed it. Say what you will about Peter Talmadge, he was a stickler for the truth."

Edith gave a little gasp. "You're father was Pete Talmadge? Legendary head of the GBI? Holy crap! I had no idea."

"Does that mean you believe me?"

"Well, yes. Of course. Everybody knows about Mr. Talmadge. I never got to meet him in person, but I sure would have liked to."

"He was a good guy," Margaret said. "And a good cop, too. Although I can't help but wonder how many of the tips he acted on came directly from that mirror."

"What d'ya mean?"

Margaret still had vivid memories of her most recent encounter with the mirror. "Do you remember seeing that weird face shape in the mirror from the video? That's the face of the Portal Keeper. That's what my Mom calls him. Or it. Whatever. Anyway, he's a spokesman for the dead, the souls who're hanging around in the nowhere land between our world and the afterworld. It turns out many of them are driven by a need to send a message back to the living. Most of those messages are last words about regret. But some are about crimes that have taken place, or crimes that are about to."

"That's the craziest thing I've ever heard."

"Yeah, well, you oughta try sitting in front of that bizarro Keeper while he rants about having to deal with riffraff."

"What?"

"The Keeper of the Portal is a buffoon. He thinks he's somehow better than all the other souls. He controls the portal, and he acts like a god. Well, he's definitely not a god. He's a butthead."

Edith made a humming sound before she spoke. "Okay then, who put him in charge?"

"Mom thinks any soul can take over the job if they want it badly enough. I don't know exactly how it works, but a Keeper can be overthrown. Literally, kicked out. And that, by the way, is where all those nasty little gargoyles come from."

"They come out of the mirror?"

"According to my Mom, yes. That's exactly where they come from. But she doesn't know what's supposed to come of that. She's never actually seen the mirror spit one out. She's always found them later, after the cabinet's been closed for a while."

"Oh, Lord!"

"What?" Margaret asked, suddenly worried.

"You've got to take that camera down. If I can hack your videos, others can, too. Your mother doesn't know about it, does she?"

"No, but I'm not so sure taking it down is a good idea. I'd rather you just tapped into the video as it's being pumped through the phone lines, or cable lines, or wherever it goes. I won't be needing to save any videos. I'll be seeing that stuff first hand."

"But—"

"But if you're seeing it, too, I won't have to call you every time I hear about something illegal. I don't want to have to make those decisions."

"Well," Edith said, slowly. "I suppose that makes sense."

"It's like this last time. Some guy named Lil D—I presume that's not his real name—claims he was killed by someone named Tanner. I don't know if that's a first name or a last. I told the Keeper I'd pass the information along, and guess what? I just did. The ball's in your court now."

"Gee, thanks."

Edith's sarcasm wasn't lost on Margaret. "You bet," she said. "I gotta go."

~*~

Tanner did his best to tamp down the panic rising in his gut. The guy with the gun had him trapped, but not entirely immobile. He ached in several places from his fall down the front steps, and that served to keep him angry.

"You'll regret this," he growled.

"I doubt it," said the young man as his ambulance-chasing grandfather walked up beside him. "You know this guy?" the younger man asked.

Swenson squinted down at him and shook his head slightly. "I don't know. Maybe. I've prosecuted so many of his kind, their faces tend to run together after a while."

"I sure as hell remember you," Tanner said, grinding his teeth as the words came out.

The sound of an SUV in need of brake pads interrupted their reintroduction as it squealed to a stop in front of Swenson's mansion. Three small children emerged from the vehicle. While two scattered in one direction, the third, a skinny little girl, took notice of Swenson's grandson and ran straight toward him yelling "Daddy! Daddy!" as if she'd spotted Santa Claus or the Easter Bunny.

Tanner got to his knees during the momentary distraction.

"Stay where you are," the kid said in a low voice as he held up his free hand in an effort to keep the child away. "Hold up, Chloe!"

Rather than respond, the little girl slipped out of her pink, cartoon-covered backpack and ran even harder.

"Stay back!" Erik yelled, which caused the youngster to slow down just as she came within Tanner's reach.

He grabbed the child and held her to his chest, facing Erik as he worked his way to a standing position. "You wanna shoot? You go right ahead. Put one through this rug rat and into me why don'cha?"

"Don't you dare move!" Erik said, his voice low and threatening.

"How 'bout this, then," Tanner said wrapping his free arm around the girl's neck. "One little twist and this kiddo's done. I've seen grown men die the same way. It ain't pretty."

"You wouldn't dare," Swenson said, stepping past his grandson who put out an arm to stop him.

"To avoid arrest? To keep from going back to prison? I'd kill a half dozen little brats like this one. She don't mean anything to me."

"Put her down," said Erik.

"Screw that. You put down the gun. Better yet, toss it over here. I'll trade you the girl for it."

"Don't do it," Swenson said. "You can't trust him."

"I *don't* trust him, but what else—"

"Okay, time's up." He could hear the sound of police sirens in the distance. "Have it your way. She's dead."

As he shifted slightly to carry out the threat, Erik yelled at him to stop.

"Then throw me the damn gun!" he yelled back.

Erik complied, and in one motion, Tanner let the girl go as he secured the automatic.

"You'd better get while you still can," Swenson muttered as Erik comforted the child.

"That ain't all, asshole." Tanner raised the gun and fired.

Swenson spun sideways and crumpled to the ground. Erik seemed to be struggling between sheltering the girl, attending to his grandfather, and making a heroic charge. "Bastard!" he screamed.

"Love you, too!" Tanner said, waving the gun as he started running to his car. If he could make it past the house on the corner before the cops arrived, he figured he had a good chance of getting away.

His only regret was that he didn't have time to make sure Swenson was dead.

Chapter Ten

"We don't devote enough scientific research to finding a cure for jerks." –Bill Watterson

Andi hated the fit of the cell phone gizmo mounted on her ear. The absolute latest thing in mobile telecommunications, it felt clunky, and provoked the constant urge to shove a finger through her auditory canal and scratch until her brain bled. Knowing the somewhat impractical nature of that approach, she settled for complaining about the phone to Will. If she had to suffer for his sake, then by God, he needed to feel some pain as well.

"You have no idea how irritating this damned phone thing is. Especially when there's nobody in my life I'd want or need to call."

You don't have to wear the damned thing, y'know. You can just babble on whenever you like

Josh Langston

and ignore the people who think you've lost your mind.

"You're such a comfort. I don't know what I'd do without you," Andi said. "Oh, wait. That's not exactly true. Without you, I'd be the happiest person on Earth."

But you wouldn't be nearly as well-informed.

"Leave me alone," she grumbled.

"Who're you talking to?" her aunt Mags asked as she slipped behind the steering wheel and started the car.

Andi shook her head, only marginally concerned she might dislodge the gadgetry on her ear. "Just some jerk tryin' to sell me something."

The phone makes me a Jerk? Ingrate.

Mags responded with a sympathetic nod. "When I get calls like that, I just hang up on them."

"Me, too, when I can."

Mags kept her eyes on the road during the short drive while she talked. "It's really nice of you to come with me to see Mr. Swenson. I'm not a fan of hospitals and didn't relish the thought of going alone. I know that must sound selfish. Forgive me. I just pray he'll survive."

"No need to apologize. I've seen more than my share of medical facilities," Andi said. "I'm not a fan."

Admit it, kid. You're only going because you

hope to connect with the old man's grandson.

Andi ignored him. "Do you know anything about Mr. Swenson's family?"

"Not much." Mags fell silent as she concentrated on finding an open spot in the hospital's huge parking deck. Once she found one, she continued. "I understand his grandson moved in with him after the young man's wife died. Poor thing. They had one child. A little girl, I think."

"The newspaper article didn't offer too many details."

"They rarely do in cases like this," Mags said. "I asked Mom about it. She said the police often withhold details from reporters. Their favorite phrase is, 'We don't comment on active investigations.'"

"I guess that makes sense." Andi followed her aunt out of the car and through the crowded lot. They enquired about the wounded attorney at a desk in the lobby and were directed to the seventh floor of the North wing. "This could be quite a hike. You up for it?"

Mags groaned. "I'll make it if there's an elevator. I'll be damned if I'm going to *climb* all those dadgum stairs."

"C'mon Aunt Mags. It'd be good for you!"

It'd more likely kill her.

"This way," the older woman said, bustling

into the lift.

When they reached the door to Swenson's room, they were greeted by Erik and a little girl with the skinniest legs and the prettiest face Andi had ever seen. She felt something stir deep inside her heart as the child was introduced as Chloe by her obviously proud father.

"I didn't get to meet you in the parking lot the other day," he said. They exchanged names and pleasantries, but his smile didn't hide the traces of anxiety on his face.

"How's your grandfather doing?" Andi asked.

"He's sleeping," Erik said.

"Grampop's gonna be fine," added the little girl, her tone adamant as she slid in between the two adults. "My Daddy told me so."

Andi knelt down to address her face-to-face. "I'll bet he's right, too. I'm sure your grandfather wants to get well so he can spend more time with you." She smiled and touched the child lightly on her chin with the tip of her index finger.

Chloe looked up at Erik. "I like her, Daddy. You should, too. Maybe she could come with us and help take care of Grampop."

That's an open invitation, kid. Don't blow it!

"I wish I could, sweetheart," Andi said. "But I have my own grandparent to look after. Did you know, she's one of *your* granddaddy's best friends?"

And just like that, another opportunity wasted.

"Did you know that, Daddy?" Chloe asked.

"I do now," he said. "But maybe Miss Andi would like to join us for supper one of these days."

Andi stood and grinned at him. "I'd like that. Very much."

Atta girl!

Mags touched Erik lightly on the shoulder. "Do the police have any leads on the man who... You know...."

"Hurt Pops? Maybe. The guy claimed my Granddad prosecuted him, but Pops said he didn't recognize him."

"This may sound a little crazy," Mags said, "but when he's doing a little better, you might ask him if he recalls anyone by the name of Tanner. It could be either a first name or a last."

"Tanner? Sure. I can mention that name. I just don't know—" He shook his head. "We'll just have to wait until he's better."

Andi leaned closer to Mags and whispered, "*Tanner?* What's that all about?"

"I'll explain later," she said. "In the car."

"Can Miss Andi come to dinner with us tonight, Daddy?" Chloe asked.

"Gee, honey. I don't know. We could be here a

long time, and—"

Andi chimed in quickly. "If you'll give me a call when you're on the way home, I'll rustle something up and bring it over, okay? Leave it to me."

Erik appeared slightly stunned. "You sure?"

"Of course! You both like Italian?"

"Pas'ghetti!" bubbled Chloe. "With balls!"

~*~

Edith reviewed her notes after spending a good bit of time examining trial records, most notably prosecutions by Robert Swenson. There were many more of them than she anticipated, and the task took longer than expected. There was, however, a payoff.

While serving as a district attorney, Swenson prosecuted a man named Tanner Howell for attempted murder. The defendant was found guilty and sentenced to twenty years in prison. After checking a little further, Edith discovered that Howell had been given an early release based on "good behavior."

She wasn't at all sure what constituted "good behavior," but in this man's case, she assumed the worst. If he was the one who shot and wounded Swenson, then whatever he said to sway the parole board in his favor was pure, unadulterated bullshit.

The man had yet to report to his parole officer, and the address recorded for him was as reliable as his "good behavior" story.

Since she'd hit paydirt with the search for "Tanner," she opted to check the records for someone with the nickname of "Lil' D." That search ended quicker than the others. Demetrius "Lil' D" Jackson had been buried in the City of Atlanta's version of a potter's field when no one came forward to claim his remains. According to the autopsy, Lil' D had been strangled to death. There were no leads concerning his killer and no record of Lil' D being a known associate of Tanner Howell.

Edith sat back in her chair, stunned by the revelations. If not for the mysterious mirror in the basement of the Talmadge family home, Tanner Howell would still be free of scrutiny.

She wished she had enough hard evidence to post a BOLO, but that required more than she was willing to reveal. She limited her reported suspicions to Howell. If the GBI wanted someone else to investigate further, they'd let her know. They were pretty good about taking choice cases away from her. She hoped this one would remain under their radar.

Now, if nothing else, she no longer doubted Margaret's profound connection with the afterworld. Still, having grown up a faithful church-goer, Edith couldn't help but wonder what it would cost, in terms of her soul, to use the mirror as a confidential informant. In any case, there was no way in hell she would file any formal paperwork about it.

One other little detail had been made abundantly clear in the trial proceedings for Tanner Howell. The prosecutor had leaned heavily on evidence supplied by none other than Margaret's father, Peter Talmadge.

Suddenly, the presence of the mirror in the Talmadge basement suggested a great deal about what had fueled Pete Talmadge's rocket-like ascension to the top of the GBI.

And now Edith had the exact same thing within her grasp. Or nearly so.

It also suggested that a revenge-minded, psychopathic ex-con might also want to take out his anger on the heirs of the man who investigated him and worked hand in glove with the DA.

Margaret Talmadge and her family were clearly in danger.

~*~

Derrick Benjamin enjoyed the view from his lavish study. He could look out through a massive window wall on the sprawling backyard of his estate. An expansive pool and a waterfall, both artistically done to capture the essence of a natural wonder, sat waiting for him every morning as he read the paper. With the flick of a switch he activated the hidden speakers which brought the sounds of the water feature inside his home without the need to open a window.

Nirvana.

An article in that morning's news caught his eye. A retired judge and former prosecutor had been gunned down in his own front yard. Benjamin smiled, knowing that sort of thing could never in a million years happen to him. His security system would see to that. And if it failed, he had Jermontae as his backup. Anyone foolish enough to face the giant wouldn't last long, armed or not.

Still, the story intrigued him. Evidently, the assailant had been stopped and was awaiting arrest when he managed to break free, disarm the man holding him at bay, and got off a shot at his original target, Swenson, the retired judge. He then managed to elude police and was still at large.

That's just the kind of man I need!

Wasting no time, he called his inside man at the GBI and enquired if they knew the shooter's name.

"Why do you care?" came the reply. "He's got nothing to do with you."

"Nothing *yet*," Benjamin said, quick to make the correction.

There was a long pause on the other end of the line, punctuated by snorts and paper rustling. "This is only a suspicion, mind you. We merely have a name, a person of interest: Tanner Howell. We have no evidence directly linking him to anything except missing an appointment with his parole officer. But, that's enough to put him back behind bars."

"That seems a bit extreme, don't you think?"

"Not at all. Tanner Howell is a bottom feeder, a lowlife. The world's a better place with him locked up."

Benjamin disagreed. "Do me a favor. Don't move too fast on him. Let him be. I'm guessing all the poor slob needs is a good job. And I just happen to have one available."

"A *job?* You're kidding, right? The guy's a total loser, he's—"

"He's in need, that's all. And I can help. Do you have any idea how I might get in touch with him?"

"Don't be ridiculous."

Benjamin cleared his throat. "Let's be very clear about something. You owe me. And I could make your life very difficult. Would you find *that* ridiculous?"

"No," the voice murmured. "Of course not. I was just—"

"*Being* ridiculous?"

"Uh, yeah. I guess so."

"Then don't fuck with me," Benjamin said, his voice low and still threatening. "Or I'll have you dumped with the rest of the trash."

"I get it. Sorry. I—"

"Find out where this Howell character is and let me know. Do not arrest him, understand?"

"Yes."

"Good. Now go do something productive for a change."

~*~

Andi gave Stormy a hug as she headed for the door.

"I think it's sweet what you're doing for Bobby's grandson," her grandmother said.

Ha! She's got no idea what you have in mind, you minx.

As usual, Andi ignored Will. "It's the least I can do. Besides, he's got the cutest little girl in the whole world. I imagine this has been pretty hard on her, too, even though I know she doesn't understand anything that's going on."

She could be smarter than you think.

"Bye, Gran. Bye, Aunt Mags. I won't be out late." Andi made a hurried exit before either of the older women could draw her into speculation about a potential romance with Erik Swenson. That sort of nonsense was way, way, way premature.

So, dinner with the hunky grandson, eh? Nice work!

"Whatever." Silence and civility seemed to be the only thing that actually shut Will up. But maintaining those conditions proved difficult. Will loved to argue. She figured it was a ghost thing.

She made the trip to Constantine's Italian

Bistro in a matter of minutes, blessedly silent ones. After removing the annoying phone contraption from her ear, she cruised into the shop to pick up the family dinner she'd ordered. Erik's timing had been perfect, and she had made sure the dinner included spaghetti—*with* meatballs. The package felt as if it contained food for a dozen hungry Italians. The leftovers would likely come in handy, especially if the elder Swenson's condition didn't improve.

Erik and Chloe met her car as she drove up the long drive to the house. Chloe seemed overly excited and possibly ready to explode. Andi had never had that effect on anyone that she recalled, except for a miniature dachshund which escaped from a neighbor's house when Andi was a child. Though assured later that the little monster tried to bite everyone except its owner, she had her doubts.

"She's here, she's here!" Chloe cried, as if it were an unimaginably fabulous surprise.

"I am, I am!" Andi responded, only a bit less enthusiastically. "Will you help me carry this stuff inside?"

Erik sidled closer and smiled. "I really do appreciate this. And Chloe does, too."

"It's not just the pas'ghetti?"

He chuckled. "Nah. She really likes you."

Andi smiled and shook her head. "I can't imagine why."

"Well I can," he said.

I wish you could see yourself. You're blushing!

Momentarily flustered, Andi turned and followed Chloe up the front steps.

"This way," the little girl shouted. "Hurry, hurry, before everything gets cold."

"Spoken like a little marine," Andi said as the trio entered the kitchen.

She watched as Erik and his daughter unpacked the meal and set it up on a kitchen table.

"I hope you won't mind if we eat in here," Erik said. "The dining room is way too formal for Chloe and me. Fact is, even when Pop's home, we usually eat right here."

"This is fine," Andi said. "I wouldn't know what to do in a formal setting."

"Balls!" Chloe yelled as she dumped out the container containing the sausage lump-laden sauce. "My favorite!"

You have no idea how I miss eating.

An eyeroll was all Andi could spare for Will.

Chloe eventually finished eating, though much of what she'd piled on her plate remained. Erik kissed the top of her head and suggested she go watch cartoons while he and Andi cleaned up.

The little girl gave Andi a hug before leaving the room.

"You are so lucky to have such a sweet child. I was sorry to hear about her mom," Andi said. "It's gotta be hard on her."

"It is, but she's pretty resilient, one might even say tough. Way tougher than I thought she might be. When that asshole grabbed her the other day—"

"*What?* Who grabbed her?"

"The guy who shot Pops did it while we were waiting for the police to arrive. He threatened to kill her if I didn't drop the gun I was holding on him, his gun actually. That's how he got it back and... Well, you know. Anyway, Chloe didn't make a sound the whole time he had her. She just looked at me. She seemed both angry and scared, but mostly angry. She tried to kick him."

Whoa. That's my kinda little girl.

"I had no idea," Andi said, wishing she could get Will out of her head. "The paper didn't mention anything about that." She remembered the little girl piling one meatball atop another on her plate, helping herself to more food than the average grunt could handle at one sitting.

"Think maybe she was a marine in a former life?" Andi asked.

Erik grinned. "Maybe so. I heard you were, too. Right? I guess you're retired now."

"Do I *look* like I'm ready for retirement?" Andi feigned indignation.

"No! No, of course not. I just—"

She laughed. "I'm kidding. I served. Now I'm out. But they say there's no such thing as an ex-marine."

"Are y'all coming, or not? I don't wanna watch all these cartoons by myself!" Chloe announced. "And what're we havin' for bizzert?"

~*~

Tanner Howell finished the last of his Tennessee whiskey while sitting on the ratty little bed in the ratty little trailer he'd stolen from some ratty little asshole he hadn't even met. The darkness of his mood approached a level he hadn't experienced since his early days in the can. This time, however, he aimed his anger directly at himself. He simply couldn't believe he'd let Swenson's kid, or grandkid—whatever the hell he was—knock him flat on his ass. With a fucking door, no less.

How could I have been so stupid? I should've known Swenson, the slimy bastard, would've installed some kind of security system. If that damned kid hadn't seen me coming....

Such thoughts, swallowed with liberal helpings of Tennessee's finest, according to the label, only provoked more anger. When he realized the bottle was empty, he sent it on a short, flat trajectory flight ending on an inside wall. It bounced, unharmed. He needed another.

And he needed to get back in the saddle, something a former cellmate said once too often. Someone needed to pay.

He checked the magazine in the little .32 automatic before slipping it into his pocket for the trip to Marietta and a visit to the former home of Pete Talmadge. If he couldn't get Swenson, he'd have to satisfy himself taking out Talmadge's widow. This time, however, he'd be more careful.

~*~

Margaret got a call from Edith while watching television with Stormy. As soon as she saw the caller's name she stood up and announced, "I'll take this in the other room."

Safely out of earshot in the kitchen, Margaret asked, "What's up?"

"Those two names you gave me, Tanner and Little D? It turns out your source was correct. A guy named Demetrius Jackson, aka Lil' D, turned up on a slab in the Fulton County morgue. He'd been strangled. A quick check of the name Tanner produced a paroled convict whose full name is Tanner Howell."

"That's good, right?"

"Depends on how you look at it," Edith said. "I checked court records to see if Tanner Howell ever had a run-in with Judge Swenson. He did. When Swenson was the District Attorney, he prosecuted Howell who got a twenty-year sentence. The Parole Board let him out after he served about two-thirds of his time. My guess is he's carrying one helluva grudge."

Margaret let out a sigh. "I don't know what to say."

"The thing is, your father is the one who did the detective work. He built the case for Swenson, and there's no question that Tanner Howell knows that. My fear is that he might come after you or your mother. Maybe both of you."

"Oh, hell," whispered Margaret. "You don't really believe that, do you? I mean, Mom and I had nothing to do with it."

"Really? You don't think your mother got some sort of message from that spook inside her crazy mirror?"

"Well, sure, she probably did, but this Tanner character couldn't know that, could he?"

"No," Edith assured her. "But that doesn't matter. If he was the one who shot the judge, then he's definitely out for revenge."

"I can't imagine anyone being so angry they'd try to hurt us. That's just... I don't know. So extreme."

"Here's what I think," Edith said, "You need to have a chat with your mother and bring her up to date. If you've got somewhere else you can go, someplace Tanner Howell wouldn't know about, then I suggest you go there. Right away. Have you got a cabin in the mountains, maybe? A condo somewhere?"

"We don't have anything like that," Margaret said. "But I'm sure we could find a place to stay for a while. Until things cool down or the police catch the jerk."

"Well, do something! You've got to look after yourself. There's no way I could get the bureau to pay for someone to sit outside your house and guard it. If you think about it, a vacation could be cheaper, and safer, than hiring private security. More fun, too."

"Thanks for the warning," Margaret said. "I'll talk to Mom. I sure wouldn't mind a little vacation time."

"Don't forget your niece. She's at risk, too."

~*~

The whiskey seemed to have more impact once Tanner got up and started moving. When he had nothing to do but sit and drink on the trailer's stupid excuse for a bed, the space remained stable, and the only sounds came from frogs, birds, and insects outside.

Little shits should be busy eating each other instead of making all that racket.

Such thoughts vanished when he stood up and discovered the trailer wasn't level. He had to hold his arms out on either side to ensure he remained upright. A few deep breaths seemed to help. Concentrating on each step, he navigated his way out of the trailer and into the darkness beyond.

He reached the car without incident, got in, and drove down the dirt track which led toward civilization. But even with the high beams on, he seemed to hit far more ruts than usual, all of which added to his foul mood.

If I'm going to do this right, I need to get my head clear. He considered going somewhere for coffee but decided against it. As late as it was, the only places open out in the boondocks were the same kinds of places the cops liked to visit for their nightly ration of doughnuts. Instead, he stopped the car and rolled down all the windows, then drove on.

He had driven by the Talmadge home a number of times, just as he had Swenson's. Getting there was no problem, and rather than worry about concealing his car, he just pulled right into the driveway.

Still unsteady as he exited the car, he made his way toward the front of the house where he had seen lights on inside. When he got close enough, he discovered the window sills were above his head. He could see the high ceiling inside the old-time building, but he couldn't see anyone inside. Stepping back to improve his line of sight didn't help and he stumbled backwards when he connected with some shrubbery and landed on his tail.

Muttering obscenities, Tanner got to his feet, pointed his gun at the windows and fired four rounds in quick succession before exhausting his ammunition. He heard screams from inside which brought a smile to his face. He probably hadn't hit anyone, but he'd doubtless scared them shitless.

That thought comforted him as he made his way back to his car and took off. He forced himself to maintain an even speed and not weave. If he encountered cops, he didn't want to appear suspicious, and there was no doubt in his mind that Talmadge's family would call them.

He made it all the way out of Cobb County and into the relative wilds of neighboring Bartow County before he was pulled over.

Chapter Eleven

"I drink too much. The last time I gave a urine sample, it had an olive in it." –Rodney Dangerfield

The drive from Erik's house to her grandmother's felt surreal, and would have even without Will's annoying commentary. Andi turned up the radio though she knew it would never drown out his voice.

You should've spent the night with him.

"Are you nuts? I just met the guy."

So? It's obvious you two click.

"I'm supposed to jump in bed with the first guy I'm interested in? On the first date? Which it wasn't, by the way. It wasn't even close to being a date. It was— I was doing the Good Samaritan thing."

You don't think the Good Samaritan ever got laid?

"Actually, no. I don't recall ever seeing that in the Bible."

You've read the Bible?

"Parts of it."

And that makes you an expert.

"Leave me alone."

Nonsense. I feel it's my duty to guide you, keep you safe. At least until I find a better host. Besides, I've grown fond of you. Sort of.

"That's interesting, 'cause I still think you're an enormous pain in the ass. I'd give anything to have a ghost-ectomy."

That's not a thing.

"It damned well should be! And while we're on the subject of guidance, how would you have proposed that I send little Chloe to bed so I could jump her daddy's bones?"

That would have required some finesse, I admit. But if—

"What the hell?" Andi's hands locked on the steering wheel when she saw police cars all but surrounding her grandmother's house. Uniformed officers stood on the lawn, in the driveway, and on the front steps.

Andi parked at the curb and raced toward the cluster of people standing just outside the front door. Mags and her grandmother were wedged between two officers, one of whom was taking notes while the other questioned the women.

"What's going on?" Andi demanded as she vaulted up the steps. "Are y'all okay? What's—"

"Thank goodness you're here," Mags said. "Someone was shooting at us! We were inside watching TV when bullets smashed through the window."

"Who did it? Have they been caught? You don't think it was—"

"Miss," said the police officer who had been asking questions of his own, "we're almost done here. If you'll let us finish, I'm sure these folks will be happy to answer *your* questions."

"Yes sir," Andi said, automatically. Being a civilian didn't give her the right to be... What? Insubordinate? Disrespectful?

Being quiet is almost always the right move.

Andi backed down the steps and whispered. "Why can't you practice what you preach?"

"Who're you talking to?" Stormy asked when the police turned to leave.

"Nobody, honest."

You're such a snot.

Andi lifted her shoulders in a quick shrug. "Well, nobody important anyway."

Geez.

"We've got some decisions to make," Mags said waving them toward the house. "I know it's late, but we don't have any choice."

"Here we go," Stormy said. She nudged Andi's arm and made a face. "She'll have me in a nursing home before breakfast."

"Don't tempt me," Mags said. "What I'd really like to do is find a nice motel room somewhere. Maybe near a beach."

The three walked back into the house and paused to look at the glass littering the living room floor. "Let's do this in the kitchen," Stormy said. "I could use a cup of coffee. And my inhaler if one of y'all can track the damned thing down. I had it when we were watching TV."

Andi sprinted back into the other room and quickly gathered it up.

I'm sorry I didn't see this coming, kid.

"You mean you could have warned me?"

To be honest, probably not. I'm sure they were outta my range when the shooting occurred. And I couldn't have warned them in any event.

"So, what is your range, anyway?"

I dunno. Fifty, seventy-five meters, give or take.

"Good to know. But listen, give me a break and don't bug me while I'm talking to my Aunt Mags and Gran, okay?"

I'll try.

"Thanks."

Andi hurried into the kitchen and handed the inhaler to Stormy just as she appeared ready to start coughing.

Mags made coffee, and they gathered around the kitchen table. Once Stormy had her breathing under control, they discussed possible options for getting away.

"The beach would be nice," Stormy said, obviously trying to lighten the mood. "But I'll need a new swimsuit. I doubt I still fit in the little two-piece Pete liked so much."

Mags responded with an eyeroll and changed the subject. "Y'know, Mom, this might be the perfect opportunity to let those people from the historical society into the house. Maybe let them coordinate repairs, too."

"I'm pretty sure it's the *Hysterical* Society." Stormy pressed her lips together in a tight line.

"I know it's not my place to say anything," Andi interjected. "But there's a lot of peeling paint on the outside of the house. This place used to be so beautiful. I loved coming here to visit 'cause it reminded me of that big house in 'Gone With the Wind.'"

Tara!

"Tara, I think. But to be perfectly honest, now it looks kinda sad, neglected."

Stormy looked wounded, so Andi rushed on. "I'm not trying to hurt your feelings! It's just... It's more than just the bullet holes in the ceiling that need patching. The whole house could use a tune-up."

"She's right, Mom. And this might be a golden opportunity. It's not like you can't afford it."

"All right. I give in," Stormy said. "But I intend to continue living right here when the work is all done."

Mags smiled for the first time since Andi had returned with the inhaler. "Do you want me to call

Ms. Ingram and make the arrangements?"

Stormy shuddered. "Yes. Please. I don't want to have anything to do with that woman. And don't you dare let her paint over the haint blue ceiling on the porch. That's... historical. Cultural, too, by God." She shook her head, then looked at Andi and shifted gears again as if nothing had happened. "So, how was your dinner date with that dashing young Swenson boy?"

~*~

Derrick Benjamin relaxed in his hot tub as the water bubbled and swirled all around him. It had been a long day, fraught with calls from his agents around the country. Combat deaths of U.S. service members had fallen off sharply, and that meant less insurance money coming in, though his expenses remained the same. What he needed was for the country to get involved in another hot spot. The war in Afghanistan had been a gold mine, but now it appeared to be playing out.

He pushed that from his mind. He had earned the peace and solitude the hot tub afforded so late at night. Finally, he could relax. When his cell phone rang, he scowled but answered it despite the intrusion. He didn't bother to mask his annoyance and barked, "What?"

The caller didn't identify himself, nor did

Benjamin need him to. "I just got word the guy you're looking for got picked up for drunk driving. They're holding him overnight in Euharlee, but because we labeled him a person of interest, they notified us in case we wanted to talk to him."

"*You-Har-Lee?* Where the hell is that?

"It's in Bartow county, north of Atlanta. Small, rural town."

"No shit. Well, tell them you're sending someone to pick him up."

"I don't have anyone I can—"

"No, you idiot. *I'll* send someone, not you. But you have to make sure the cops in YooHoo, or whatever the hell it's called, will release him to my man."

"Oh, right," said the voice.

"Will my guy need paperwork? Identification? A GBI tattoo?"

"I'll email you a letter of introduction. Hang on while I find out who's on the case. Your man will have to use that name." He puttered about while Benjamin poured himself a Scotch from a bottle beside the tub, then came back on line. "Bad news. It's a woman: Edith Parise. The same agent I had pulled from the electronics store case. I don't suppose you can send a female, can you?"

"Not for this," Benjamin said. "So, don't include the woman's first name on the document, just use her first initial. The 'E' could stand for lots of names, male or female."

"Okay, no problem. But listen, if Parise shows up in person before your man does...."

"See that she doesn't."

"I can't control that," the voice said.

"Use your head! Call her in for an early morning chat. You can cancel it when she gets there. Just keep her the hell away from Hooterville until my man's done."

"It's *Euharlee*. Folks up there may be a little particular about how it's pronounced."

"Do I sound like I give a shit?" Benjamin ended the call and slipped back into the comfort of his tub, not worried in the least. Jermontae would handle it.

~*~

Margaret assembled the luggage the three women would take to Hilton Head Island, South Carolina. Andi had found a condo for rent on-line. It wasn't far from the beach, and they planned to leave as soon as she crammed everything into Margaret's car. It would be crowded, but they could take their time on the drive and stop as often as they liked.

"I'm so glad you're coming with us," Margaret told her. "You've been through a lot lately; you need some, what's it called? R and R?"

Andi agreed.

"Listen, before you help your grandmother to the car, I just wanted to say how happy we are that you and Erik seem to be getting along so well. I really hate to take you away from him right now, but under the circumstances...."

"It's not like we're dating or anything, Aunt Mags. I like Erik, and I think his little girl is the most amazing thing ever, but I don't need to get ahead of myself. He and I had dinner together *one time*. And it was take-out. At his house. With his daughter present. Not exactly a date."

"Well, it's a start, isn't it? After two failed marriages, I know I'm not exactly the best source of information when it comes to romance, but—"

Andi shut the trunk and stuck the car keys in her pocket. "I'll take the first shift behind the wheel, if that's okay with you." She didn't wait for an answer. "And seriously, I'm not looking for romance right now. I'd like nothing better than to stretch out on the beach knowing some raghead isn't sneaking around in the dunes waiting to shoot me. Come to think of it, I'll probably just lay out by the pool. Sand doesn't appeal to me all that much anymore."

"Bad memories, huh sweetie?"

"The worst."

Margaret looked at her niece and realized she had no inkling what the girl had been through while in the service. She wished she knew what to tell her or how to provide counsel. She had been briefed on Andi's PTSD and told what to expect. She had no reason to doubt the diagnosis as she'd heard Andi talking to herself on several occasions. She loved the girl, but she still worried about her.

"Do me one favor, please," Andi said.

"What's that?"

"Please tell Gran I don't need or want a matchmaker. I'm not ready for anything like that. Maybe someday. Maybe soon. But not right now. Not while all this craziness is going on. I need to be able to think straight if I'm going to keep you safe."

"I'll have a chat with her," Margaret promised. "No problem." As if that meant the girl would quickly shake free of whatever demons she brought with her from the fighting in the Middle East.

~*~

Tanner had no illusions about what would happen if he were arrested—for anything. He'd be on his way back to the slammer faster than a fly found shit in sewage. That realization eluded him, however, until he sobered up and took stock of his situation. A holding tank wasn't exactly the same as a prison cell, but there were enough similarities to trigger severe depression.

It didn't help when a black guy the size of the Lincoln Memorial came to collect him. Any thoughts Tanner might have had about overpowering his captor evaporated on the spot. He was totally and irrevocably screwed.

The only words the huge GBI agent uttered toward him were, "Shut up, and come with me."

Tanner managed a weak, "Yessir" in response.

Handcuffed, he walked beside the towering agent and was summarily dumped in the back seat of an unmarked sedan.

"Look straight ahead," the giant said. "Don't do anything, and don't say a damn word."

I won't, ya big asshole. But when we get outta town, I'm gonna choke you to death from right here in the back seat. Tanner relaxed and waited for his opportunity. He prayed it would come soon. Once they hit Interstate 75 and headed south, it would be too late. He didn't fancy his chances of surviving a crash at 70 or 80 miles per hour.

"Just sit tight. I'll unlock the cuffs in a bit," the

giant said as they cruised through downtown Euharlee.

"What'd you say?"

The huge driver shook his head. "You deaf? I said I'd unlock the cuffs. But I won't do it in front of the friggin' cop shop. You got that? Just sit and chill for a while. Mister Benjamin wants to talk to you. God only knows why."

Tanner's world seemed to have suddenly reversed itself, though he had no idea why or what he might have done to cause it. "Who the hell is Mr. Benjamin?"

"He's the guy what saved your dumb ass."

"Uh, okay, and who're you?"

"You can call me Tay; it's short for Jermontae, something most white folk can't seem to pronounce. Don't ask me why. Anyhow, I work for Mr. Benjamin. If you're lucky, you will, too."

"And if I'm not lucky?"

"You'll be dead." Tay's laugh was short and devoid of humor. "There's worse things."

"Worse than death?" It was Tanner's turn to laugh. "Like what?"

"Bein' dead's not bad. Gettin' that way sucks."

They rode in silence until they were several miles away from the little town, then Tay stopped the car, unlocked the handcuffs, and waved Tanner into the front passenger seat.

"What can ya tell me about this Benjamin guy?" he asked.

Tay's eyes closed to slits as he looked from the road ahead to Tanner and back. "Not a damned thing, son. Not a damned thing."

They drove for a short while before Tay's cellphone rang. "It's Mr. B," he said and pulled to a stop on the dirt shoulder of the road. He put the phone to his ear and listened briefly before responding, "Yes, sir. I got him. No problems."

Tanner couldn't make out the words Tay heard, and the big man said very little until the call ended. He looked straight at Tanner and asked, "Where'd you leave your car?"

"Off that way, somewhere," Tanner replied, waving his finger past Tay's head.

"You were so drunk you can't remember where you left your damned car? You're even dumber than I thought."

"I can find it," Tanner said. "It may take a while though. The cops said I had twenty-four hours to get it before they hauled it off."

"They can have it when we're done with it."
Tay started the car and turned back the way they'd
come. "Just tell me which way to go."

"No problem."

"Mr. Benjamin also wants to know where
you've been livin' since you got out of the joint."

"What does he care?"

"He doesn't, unless it could lead back to him."

Tanner shrugged. "Whatever. I grabbed a
little trailer and hid it in the woods. It ain't great,
but—"

"Take me there after we burn your car."

"*Burn my car?* What the hell are you talking
about? I'm gonna need it. I got things to do!"

Tay remained calm. "You stole it, didn't ya?"

"Yeah."

"From some punk druggie in Atlanta?"

"Yeah, but how'd you know—"

"If we don't destroy it, the cops will find it
and figure you killed the owner. You want real cops
lookin' for you? No. We'll burn the trailer in case
there's something in there they could use."

Tanner once again felt trapped by

circumstances he couldn't control. "I've gotta have wheels, man. You don't understand."

"Mister B will loan you a car. He needs you to do some work for him. You can take care of your own shit at the same time."

"Well, I'll be goddamned."

"Most likely," Tay said.

~*~

At some point, I'll get used to being pissed off, Edith thought as she stormed out of GBI headquarters after being told by Director O'Keefe's Executive Assistant that her "urgent" meeting had been cancelled.

He could've called me, for cryin' out loud. My phone number's not a damned secret!

The drive from her home on the north side of the metro area all the way to the Bureau's main office on the far southeast side, in rush hour traffic, meant it would be lunchtime before she worked her way back up north to Bartow County and an interview with Tanner Howell.

If this is karma, God, please tell me what I did to deserve it.

In an effort to save time, she'd skipped breakfast and her usual allotment of high-octane coffee, a special blend she purchased on the internet for way too much money. Though she recognized her addiction, she rationalized that she could be hooked on something much worse. That drove her to buy a big cup of java when she gassed up her car. That and a cream-filled doughnut would have to hold her.

It was her first trip to Euharlee, and she was taken aback when she saw four huge cooling towers just outside of town. She felt sure Georgia's nuclear power plants were all located on the Savannah side of the state, but those towers looked exactly like the ones she'd seen in photos of Three Mile Island in Pennsylvania and Fukushima, Japan where nuclear disasters had occurred.

Edith asked about the menacing towers when she stopped for a coffee refill.

"Oh, ya mean Plant Bowen. That there is a coal-fired power generator," said a smiling senior citizen from his perch behind a counter in the PetrolQwik store. "And there's nuthin' to worry 'bout. Folks comin' through here get confused all the time. And lemme tell ya, while it may be big and ugly, that plant provides a whole buncha jobs 'round here."

Satisfied, and more than a little relieved to know she wasn't about to start glowing in the dark, Edith thanked him and drove on until she found the police station. There she was greeted by a friendly officer upon entering the building. "How can I help you today?" he asked.

Is everybody up here nice and polite, or am I dreaming?

"I'm here to see Tanner Howell," she said, flashing her credentials. "I understand you're holding him. He's a person of interest in a case I'm working."

The officer responded with a puzzled look. "That's really strange," he said, "'cause we already turned him over to the other agent who came in here looking for him."

"What other agent?" Edith asked. "I'm the only one on this case."

"I can't remember the man's name, but— Hold on, lemme check the file."

Edith drummed her fingers while she waited.

"Here it is," said the officer, waving a piece of paper. "E. Parise. Signature's a little hard to read, but it's the same name as on the notice we got early this morning."

"*I'm* Edith Parise," she said.

"Well, ma'am, then I reckon there's two of ya. But you're a darn sight prettier than the fella who showed up earlier. He was big, and dark, and mean lookin'. Kinda impatient, too. We offered to let him do his questioning here, but he insisted on taking Howell back to Atlanta."

Edith shook her head in dismay. *What the hell was going on?*

~*~

They're both asleep y'know.

Andi glanced at her passengers. "They had a rough night," she whispered. She had no desire to wake either Mags or her grandmother.

It's nice of you to take care of these old gals, but don't forget, we've got another mission.

"What the hell are you talkin' about?"

Derrick Benjamin, former secret squirrel. He lives in Atlanta. He's practically sittin' in our laps. We've gotta do something about him.

"Like what? Cheat him at cards? That'd show him all right."

You don't get it. He's got some kinda scam goin' on. Insurance. If the insured dies, he gets a piece of the payout.

"How do you know this?"

Gunny had his suspicions. I'm pretty much just goin' on those.

"That won't get us very far in court. You're better off just forgetting about it."

I can't! And you shouldn't, either. Those were your friends who died because of him. They were more than friends, more like brothers. You're lucky you're not dead, too.

"You don't think I know that?" she snapped. "You don't think I feel like crap because I'm the only one who made it outta there? I should've died right there beside them. I should've—"

Don't start that bullshit with me, kid. Be happy you're alive. Be happy you can drink a beer, or have sex, or—

"I didn't make you a ghost, so don't lay your shit on me, either."

Fair enough. But we can't just let Benjamin get away with murder. Or profiting from it.

"Well then, let's just march into his house and shoot his ass. Would that make you happy?"

Believe me, kid, if I could do that, I'd have already done it. They can't prosecute a ghost.

"They can sure as hell prosecute me," Andi said. "They damn near did just because I tried to defend myself."

There's gotta be a way, damn it.

"As soon as you figure it out, let me know, okay? Meanwhile, I'm going to soak up some sun."

Yeah? You got a swimsuit? I bet you'd look pretty good in a bikini.

"Who knew ghosts could be lechers?" She gave a little snort. "It's not like you haven't seen me with little or nothing on. You know where my stupid birthmark is, for God's sake. The last person to ever see that was changing my diaper."

A bikini might not cover it up, but what's the big deal? I think it looks cute. Kinda like a—

"Like a comma."

—I was gonna say a sperm.

"Ew! You're disgusting."

"Andrea? Are you all right?" Stormy asked.

"I'm fine, Gran. Go back to sleep."

"But who—"

"Phone call." Andi lightly tapped the wireless device clamped on her ear. "Wrong number, apparently. I apologize. Didn't mean to wake you."

Stormy nodded and closed her eyes. Mags remained dead to the world.

Andi tried to focus on her driving, but her thoughts kept drifting back to Marietta. She found it increasingly difficult to clear her mind of Erik and Chloe. But, she admitted to herself, it was mostly thoughts of Erik she couldn't shake.

She hoped the police would make quick work of whoever shot up Gran's house. She seriously wanted to get back to Marietta and spend more time with a guy her own age. And his kid. How weird was that? But then, the three of them might work out really well together. There was only one way to find out.

Mags interrupted her musing when she asked, "Is anyone else hungry? I'm starved."

Tanner hadn't expected quite so much thick, black smoke to come boiling out of Lil' D's shitty old car. Tay had dumped a gallon of gasoline all over the interior, taking care not to let any of it splash on himself. "Don't get too close when you light that thing," he warned.

Tanner stepped away and flipped a lit cigarette through an open window, expecting an explosion of some sort. But nothing happened.

"You need a real flame, bro," Tay said.

"I don't have any matches."

"Use your lighter."

Tanner did as instructed, and they were

rewarded with an elephant-sized ball of flame which quickly simmered down to a blaze just big enough to engulf the whole car.

Tay nodded his approval. "That oughta do it. Now let's get the trailer."

Tanner gave him directions and they pulled up next to the tiny camper in a matter of minutes. They could still see smoke in the distance from the burning car.

"Can't believe they caught your ass so close to home," Tay observed.

"Not much of a home," said Tanner. He grabbed what few possessions he had and threw them in the back of Tay's car, then dumped the remaining gas from the two-gallon can liberally inside the trailer.

It made an even more satisfying whomp sound when Tay applied a flame.

They climbed back into the big man's car for the ride to Benjamin's house.

"They won't find a trace of you in those ashes, my man," Tay said. "It's like you were never there."

Chapter Twelve

*"Look, you have to make mistakes. That's how
you learn, and that's how the world works."*
–Naomi Campbell

The condo in South Carolina proved every bit
as nice as its online write-up. Margaret enjoyed the
walks on the beach they took in the early evenings.
Stormy plodded along gamely, and Andi slowed
down, so they stayed together. The weather was
pleasant, and the beach hadn't yet been swarmed.
That would come in a few days when schools let out
for the summer.

They had been hunkered down for three days
before Margaret found an opportunity to talk to her
niece about the safe room and its bizarre contents.
The two sat in the shade of an umbrella near the
complex's pool. Margaret kept her voice down

though few people occupied the water and none sat or sunned nearby.

"They say every family has its secrets," she began, "and our family is no exception."

"Please don't tell me I was adopted," Andi said with a smile as she licked salt from the rim of her frozen margarita.

"No," chuckled Margaret. "It's nothing like that. Nothing so... normal."

Andi turned toward her with one eyebrow dipped.

"Before I get too far into this, I want to make sure you know about an acquaintance of mine. Her name's Edith Parise, and she works for the Georgia Bureau of Investigation."

"Oh, hell. What'd I do wrong this time?"

"Nothing! Nothing at all. It's just that... well, some of what I have to tell you is going to sound... peculiar. And I wanted you to know that Edith is also aware of it. In fact, she urged me to tell you."

"Okay, then. I'm all ears," Andi said.

"Did you know your grandfather had a safe room built in the lower level of the house?"

"Yes," Andi said. "Gran told me about it after Mr. Swenson got shot. She said if someone ever came after us, she wanted me to know how to get into it. I've gotta admit, I was pretty surprised. I thought only super rich people had stuff like that."

The revelation surprised Margaret, too. "I didn't realize she'd said anything to you. I knew of it, 'cause I grew up in that house, but Dad was adamant about keeping it a secret."

"I can understand that," Andi said. "If I'd known about it when I was little, I might have bragged about it, or said something to the wrong person. Gran said she'd have told me once I grew up, but after I joined the Corps, I didn't spend much time with family."

She hadn't spent *any* time with family, Margaret thought, but chose not to comment. "I know your teens were a rough stage for you, sweetheart. I—"

Andi held a hand up and turned her head away. "I'd really rather not talk about it."

"That's fine. I understand. We were all going through a lot back then. But I'm getting way off track. Forgive me. I need to know if Mom told you anything else about the room. When you were down there, did she open the cabinet or say anything about the mirror?"

"Mirror? No. Is there one in there somewhere? All I remember seeing is her collection of nasty little monster statues."

"They're gargoyles."

"Yeah." Andi pretended to shiver. "They're way too creepy. Where does she get them?" She took another sip of her drink. "And more importantly, why in the world would she want to keep them?"

"I had similar thoughts growing up," Margaret said, "and a few bad dreams about them, too."

Andi grinned. "Can't say that's a surprise."

Margaret took a deep breath before continuing. "I need to ask you something that's going to sound really... uhm... strange. But please, just bear with me."

"Okay."

"Do you believe in ghosts?"

"*What?*" Andi reacted with a great deal more surprise than Margaret expected and even spilled some of her drink. Visibly shaken by the question, she reacted defensively. "Why would you ask me that?"

"I didn't mean to upset you," Margaret said as she handed her a napkin. "But it's something we need to discuss."

"I don't know what those damn doctors at the

VA told you, but—"

"This has nothing to do with the Veteran's Administration," Margaret assured her. "This is family stuff, and it started with your grandmother." She paused a moment to rethink what she'd said. "Okay, no. It goes back way earlier than when Mom got involved, but that particular history won't ever be written."

"I have no idea what you're going on about," Andi said. "Seriously. Gran's a ghost?"

"No, of course not." Margaret shook her head in frustration. "This is going to be a bit of a long story, and I think I'm going to need to have a drink of my own before I dig into it any farther."

"From the sound of your voice, and the look on your face," Andi said, "I think I'm going to need another one myself."

~*~

After a short but unexpected trip to Baltimore, home of the insurance company which had been so helpful in fattening his bank accounts, Derrick Benjamin returned home. His first order of business was a discussion with Tanner Howell. He surveyed the man from his lounge chair; Tanner stood in the exact same spot occupied by the previous thug Benjamin had employed. He hoped this one would be better at his craft.

"Jermontae tells me the two of you were able to take care of your vehicle and the camper you were staying in."

"That's right. Burned 'em both up."

"And Jermontae secured adequate quarters for you?"

"In a real nice motel, but not very close by. It's got a breakfast buffet and a pool, too."

"So, you're comfortable?"

"Oh, yes sir. Life's good. Thank you."

"And the car he gave you to drive?"

"It's fine. Nothing fancy. But it's way better'n what I had. So, thank you for that, too."

Benjamin paused to sip his coffee. A lightly buttered croissant lay untouched on a tray in his lap. "I suppose you intend to finish what you started with your friend, the judge."

"I do," Howell said, smiling at Benjamin's reference. "As soon as he gets outta the hospital. Next time, I won't miss."

"I understand there's someone else you plan on giving the same treatment?"

"One or two," he said. "They're family of the guy who got me locked up in the first place. After that, I'm done. Ready for something different."

"It was their house you shot up the other night? Just before you got drunk and let the cops in Dogpatch arrest you?"

Howell actually blushed. "Truth be told, I'd had a little too much to drink before I drove to their house. And... and I admit it was pretty stupid. I'm lucky you and Tay came along."

"Here's the thing," Benjamin said. "I couldn't care less what you do on your own time. If you have scores to settle, by all means, settle them. If you screw those up, it's on you. Don't look to me for help. But there's another difference, and that's when it comes to an assignment from me. I expect you to carry it out quickly, efficiently, and permanently. There won't be any second chances. Is that clear?"

Howell's head bounced up and down in the affirmative.

"Good. Now, here's what I need done in the next couple days. You should find this assignment especially to your liking since it concerns an additional member of the very family you're already going after."

"The Talmadges?"

"Precisely."

He handed Howell a photo of a young, female

marine in dress uniform. "Your focus needs to be on this woman."

"She's military?"

"Was. She's out now, and I'm told she's living with her grandmother, Stormy Talmadge, widow of the late Peter Talmadge, former head of the GBI. The photo is a few years old, but I doubt she looks much different."

Howell gave the image a subdued wolf whistle before looking back at his employer. "How'd you get ahold of this?"

Benjamin dismissed him with a frown. "I have contacts everywhere, including the military. You might want to remember that in case you screw up an assignment."

~*~

Tanner made multiple reconnaissance trips past the Talmadge home, trying to figure out who, if anyone, was at home. He didn't have a great deal of luck. Making matters worse, Benjamin kept pressing him to take care of his primary objective, the young ex-marine, Andrea Vega.

During the daytime, some sort of work vehicle always parked outside the Talmadge home. Often, there were two or three. He assumed the place was being renovated, but whether or not the owners were still there, he couldn't tell. He'd reported as much to Benjamin, who didn't react well, but they both knew neither of them could do anything about it.

Desperate to obtain a timetable for the work, or some other clue that might reveal when the owners would be in residence, Tanner concocted a plan. All he needed was a costume. Dressed as just another worker bee, no one would say a word if he showed up and poked around, provided he could act like he belonged there.

Painters and woodworkers dominated the labor force, so Tanner had to come up with something plausible from another craft. Roofing was out; he needed to be inside the building. He knew as much about wiring as he did about brain surgery, and it would only take one question to prove him a fraud. He mulled the situation over at length before he arrived at a possible solution: floor covering. Damn near anyone could pretend to sell carpeting, or tile, or whatever. Best of all, it wouldn't require that he dress in any particular fashion. About the only props he'd need were a clipboard, a pencil, and a measuring tape.

He grinned at his own cleverness. Halloween had arrived early.

~*~

"You seem a bit restless," her Aunt Mags had

said. "Why don't you go out for a while and have some fun."

"By myself?"

The older woman waved off the question. "A pretty girl like you won't be by yourself for very long. Find some young people you can spend your time with. I'm sure you must be bored stiff after being cooped up with us."

Go for it, kid!

Andi had to admit the idea held a certain amount of appeal. She'd been thinking about Erik a great deal, but had made no commitments, to him or anyone else. She dressed in cut-off jeans and a halter top, items Mags had insisted she purchase from a boutique near the condominium complex, slipped into a pair of funky beach sandals, and headed out.

Nice choice. You've definitely got your hottie on.

"I suppose it's going to be this way all evening. Is there anything I might say or do to get you to shut up for a while?"

I... I suppose I could try to restrain myself. At least as long as you don't do anything stupid.

"How would you even recognize stupid?"

Trust me. It's a skill perfected over many

years.

"Whatever," she said as she once again attached the annoying cell phone gizmo to her ear.

While the island hadn't nearly reached its capacity for tourists, the bars and restaurants still did a healthy business. Andi aimed her steps toward Loco's, a trendy lounge situated right on the beach. Unlike most of the places she'd been to with her aunt and grandmother, Loco's catered to a young crowd. In fact, Andi's age had her closer to the upper limits as a surprising number of the female patrons appeared to be high schoolers.

Wait. Is this a kiddie bar?

"Go to hell," she muttered and ordered a Lance Corporal's classic: Dr. Pepper and Southern Comfort.

You're really going to drink that shit?

"Yep."

The barkeeper seemed amused by her choice but served it up without comment. Andi remained seated at the bar since it gave her a good view of the wide room and its occupants.

A pair of college-age guys worked their way toward her, laughing and spilling their beer as they bumped into each other in what looked like a wobbly race to see who would reach her first. The curly-haired blond lost to his dark-haired companion.

"You looked lonely," he said before taking a long draught of his brew.

"Looks can be deceiving," she said.

"We're pretty sure we saw you come in all by yourself," said the blond. He sidled next to his pal and stood up straight, as if he hoped to match the brunette's height. "Did you bring anyone with you?"

Andi lightly tapped the device on her ear. "Yeah, sorta."

"Your boyfriend?"

"Hardly." She took a sip of her drink.

"Would you like to join us?" asked the taller of the two.

"I think I'll wait for someone my own age," she said. "But thanks for asking."

"Aw, c'mon. You can't be more than a year or two older than we are. Let's party! We just finished up at Clemson, and we're looking to have a good time."

What a perfect pair of assholes.

"I was thinking the same thing," Andi said.

"Well, then. Let's get started!" said the blond.

"We've got a table near the back."

She took another sip of her drink and gently returned the glass to the bar top. "I wasn't actually talking to you."

The brunette elbowed the blond. "She was talking to me, bro. C'mon, darlin' let's go get comfy."

Andi slowly turned her head toward him and gazed into his eyes. After a short span of silence, she said, "I wasn't talking to you, either."

Nice.

"Why not go chat up one of the girl scouts running around in here? They appear more your speed."

"Listen," said the blond, "if either of us offended you, we're sorry. We didn't mean anything by it. We just wanted to have some fun, and you looked like a girl who… Well, you look like you could be a lot of fun. Let us buy you a drink at least. We can talk for a little while, and if you're still not interested, you can walk away. Fair enough?"

Don't do it. You don't know 'em, and you sure as hell can't trust 'em.

Sick to death of Will's constant interference in her life, Andi picked up her drink and downed it in one, huge swallow. "Y'know what? I think I will go with you. I don't have anyone else to talk to, and I really hate having to pay for my own drinks."

You're being an idiot, y'know.

"Right this way," said the blond, offering her his arm.

"I'll be fine," she said, mostly for Will's benefit.

She followed the pair out the rear of the lounge to a table at the back of a wooden deck overlooking the beach. Several feet below and a dozen steps away, a handful of clearly inebriated people attempted to play volleyball in the soft sand. They were fun to watch, due primarily to the fact that some could barely stand, let alone do anything remotely athletic.

The blond introduced himself as Riley and his copilot as Boz. "It's short for Bosworth," the latter pointed out.

"Andi," she replied as she flagged down a waiter.

"Get whatever you want," said Riley. "It's on us."

Though she'd visited more than her share of bars with her fellow marines, she had scant knowledge of the more expensive alcoholic beverages. However, she recalled hearing one of her fellow grunts say that single malt Scotch could be very pricey. She smiled at the waiter and asked, "Got any single malt?"

"Yes, ma'am. Would Johnny Walker Red be okay? No. Wait." He pretended to slap his forehead. "That's my bad. Johnny Walker Red isn't a single malt."

Andi didn't know Johnny Walker from Johnny Crawler but decided to push the envelope for the benefit of the frat boys. "Right, of course. Actually, I was hoping for—" she paused to glance at her companions "—something a little more... special."

"We've got a Talisker 18, I know, and probably a 25 in the back somewhere. I'll be happy to look for them."

"Those sound yummy, but... a little pricey," Andi said, her voice edging toward husky. She dipped her eyelids slowly down and back up as she looked at Boz. He went for the bait so fast she almost felt sorry for him.

I didn't know you had such a mean streak. These two haven't done anything to deserve bankruptcy.

"Do it," Boz said. "Get the lady whatever she wants."

"And you two?" the waiter asked.

"Refills," said Riley. "Lights."

"Corona," Boz added.

When their drinks arrived, Andi took a sip of hers and tried not to make a face. It was her first taste of Scotch, and it tasted like mouthwash someone had peed in. "Will you guys excuse me for a minute. I've got to go to the little girl's room."

"Need any help?" Riley asked, playfully.

"You're too kind, but I think I can handle it." She walked away without looking back but confident their eyes were on her.

That was just mean.

"What're you talking about?"

Ordering the most expensive booze in the joint and then running out on them.

"I'm not running out. I have to use the restroom."

I guess we'll see.

"Try closing your eyes."

Very funny.

When finished, she washed her hands and checked her make-up, though she'd used only the bare minimum.

You're okay. You still look sexy.

"Thanks."

But there's something you oughta know.

"Damn. Have I got toilet paper on my sandal?" She took a quick look and found nothing.

While you were taking care of business, one of your boy toys out there put something in your drink. God only knows what it was.

"You mean my two, innocent little drinking buddies?"

The very same. So, how do you wanna play this?

"I'm not sure."

Your best bet would be to just walk out and leave them behind. Go somewhere else.

"Yeah," she said. "You're probably right."

She left the restroom and made straight for the front entrance. A quick look behind as she went through the door revealed both Boz and Riley on their feet and headed toward her. "Well, just shit. That didn't go as planned."

Keep moving. Find cover.

"Why do I feel like I'm back in the sandbox?"

You might as well be.

Her rapid exit brought a question from a man she assumed to be the Loco's bouncer and a relative or either King Kong or Godzilla. "You okay, ma'am?"

"I'm fine," she called back. "I just need some air."

"Hope you feel better," he said. "Come back and see us!"

They're coming.

"Screw this," she said, stopping and executing a 180-degree turn. "If I have to, I can defend myself against those two."

That might prove entertaining.

"Speak for yourself."

Oh, I am. I am.

When Riley and Boz cleared the front entrance, they nearly tripped over the brawny bouncer.

Get ready, kid. But try not to get arrested this time, okay?

Andi set her small, clutch purse on the ground and rolled her shoulders in anticipation of combat. A moment later, their waiter flew out the door as well, yelling for his two customers to come back and pay their tab.

The bouncer reacted much faster than the collegians. He burst into a quick run and shoved Boz into Riley's back as they tried to hurry away. Both went down hard. King Kong's cousin hailed the waiter, "Do I need to call the cops?"

"Only if they can't pay their bill," he replied.

"All right, assholes, up you go," the bouncer said as he lifted the two smaller males to their feet. "It's time to cover your tab."

Riley pointed at Andi and shouted, "That bitch cheated us!"

"You can take it up with her after you've settled your bill," the waiter said.

"And make damn sure you add a generous tip," added the bouncer.

Seems like a good time to roll.

"Couldn't agree more," Andi said.

Thanks to Mr. Benjamin, Tanner had some decent clothes. Not fancy, but functional. He clipped the tape measure on his belt, stuck the pencil behind his ear, and slipped the clipboard under his arm. He felt somewhat naked without a gun, but the knife in his pocket offered some reassurance. He could kill quietly with it. If he'd brought the little automatic, he might have been tempted to use it. Thus prepared,

Voices

he walked into the old house as if he belonged there.

The craftsmen toiling on the interior paid little attention to him as he went from room to room taking measurements and making notes on a badly drawn sketch he'd scrawled on the notepad. He finished the first floor and started up the stairs to the upper level. A painter with lacquer and a tiny brush stood in the middle of the stairway touching up scratched surfaces on the woodwork.

"You lookin' for the boss?" he asked as Tanner tried to slip past him.

"Not really," he lied.

"The old broad was up in the master bedroom last time I checked. Be careful with her; she's a real pain in the ass."

"Good to know," Tanner said. "Thanks."

He continued to the top landing and paused to look at a collection of doors lining both sides of the hallway. "Damn big house," he muttered and entered the nearest room.

Furniture had been pushed to the center of the space and covered with a drop cloth. He couldn't tell from the room's fixtures and decor who might have occupied it. On closer inspection, he located a dresser and casually went through the drawers hoping to find something of value, if not a clue to

Josh Langston

who normally slept in the room. Most of the drawers were empty.

After checking the closet, he moved on to the next room via a connecting bath and found little of interest there. He stopped when he heard movement from down the hall.

Moving cautiously, and as quietly as he could, he followed the sounds. When he reached his destination, he gently pushed the door open and peered inside. An older woman, her grey hair fully fluffed as if she hoped to mimic the shape of her body, stood at the entrance to a walk-in closet, oblivious of his presence.

Tanner couldn't believe his good luck. Not only had he found Talmadge's ancient wife, she had no idea he was coming for her. He wondered briefly if he should take the time to taunt her before he slit her throat. The thought appealed to him, and he smiled at the prospect as he removed the knife from his pocket and unfolded the blade. Still new, he recalled the advertising on the package boasting of the weapon's razor-sharp edge, supposedly tough enough to cut through a bolt if driven by a hammer strike.

He'd have no need of a hammer.

He crept closer, hoping the hundred-year-old floorboards wouldn't betray him. They didn't, and he came within two paces of her when she suddenly turned and faced him, startled at first and then angry.

"Who the hell are you, and what are you doing here?"

"Where's your granddaughter?" he demanded, brandishing the blade. "Tell me and save yourself a great deal of pain."

Her eyes grew wide at the sight of the blade. "I'll scream!"

"And I'll cut your throat."

The old woman's mood rapidly changed from surprise to terror. He could see it in her face, though her entire body trembled.

"What do you want?"

"I want Andrea Vega," he said. "Now!"

The woman appeared confused. "Andrea who?"

"Seriously? You're going to try and pull that shit on me? She's your damned granddaughter! Now tell me where she is."

"I honestly don't know anyone by that name. I'm—"

Tanner'd had all he could stand. Just looking at the heavyset matron reminded him of the woman who'd beaten him with a belt when he was a child. He'd have delighted in killing this old sow even if she wasn't married to the man who'd worked so hard to get him convicted.

Reaching out, he closed the distance between them and slashed her throat with a single backhanded swipe.

The woman flailed her arms at him, seemingly unaware of the blood coursing down the front of her dress. By the time she noticed and tried to staunch the bleeding with her hands, she'd already grown faint.

Tanner stepped back as she dropped to her knees, still clutching her neck, her mouth and eyes stretched wide. A barely audible gurgling sound broke the silence.

As gore dripped into a red pool around her knees, the color drained from her face. She fell forward a moment later and lay still as the last of her blood seeped out on the floor.

"Take that, bitch," he whispered. "I'll find your damned grandkid on my own."

Chapter Thirteen

*"Isn't it astonishing that all these secrets have
been preserved for so many years just so we
could discover them!" –Orville Wright*

In a perfect world, Edith Parise would have
been alerted through GBI channels that a woman
named Olivia Ingram had been murdered in the
Talmadge home. Instead, she heard about it on the
news a day later. She didn't need a reason to be in a
bad mood; the Bureau managed that by repeatedly
letting her down.

Edith felt obliged to contact Margaret about
the incident, assuming the Marietta police hadn't
already done so, at least by phone since the three of
them remained out of town. Margaret and her family
would surely have questions, and Edith doubted the
local investigators would have shared much beyond

the obvious. But before she called, Edith wanted a better understanding of just what had happened. If this incident hadn't proved the wisdom of her advice urging Margaret and her family to go into hiding, nothing would.

She arrived at the crime scene long after the local investigators had cordoned off the area, conducted their forensic exams, and removed the body. Paint cans, tarps, ladders, and other redecorating gear littered every room. None of the workers remained on site, nor would they be returning soon.

Ignoring the sole police officer left to ensure the crime scene wasn't disturbed, Edith dialed Margaret's number but got no answer. Doing a slow turn, she viewed the home as if she were a camera, panning in a complete circle. The maneuver accomplished little beyond reminding her she had spent precious little time upstairs during her only other visit. The focus of that trip was the installation of the CCTV camera in the basement which would allow Margaret to spy on her dear old Mom. The memory spurred her to revisit that floor once she'd concluded her look at the murder scene and the other rooms in the house.

Once in the lower level, she tried to recall how Margaret had gotten the bookcase wall to slide open and reveal the windowless safe room behind it. After fiddling with several possibilities based more on old detective movies than anything she actually remembered, she gave up. If she ever needed to get in and face the frightening visage in the mirror, Margaret would have to show her how. The prospect of conducting such a visit would never find a spot on her bucket list.

Adding disappointment to her frustration and foul humor, she got back in her car and headed for the office. She would review copies of the notes the local investigators took, assuming they were sent to her without delay. That could take a few days. More than anything, she wanted to show Tanner Howell's mugshot to the workers who had been on site when the murder occurred. She couldn't understand why the Bureau hadn't made the photo available to the local authorities. *Yet another failed step in protocol by an organization which prided itself on following its own rules.*

Frustrated by her inability to do anything useful with regard to the murder, she put in a call to her pal in the forensics lab, Dan Wolfram. If nothing else, she hoped he might be able to brighten her day.

"Hey, Dan? Edy. You doin' anything important?"

"Nah," he said. "Just contemplating a little surgery."

She couldn't mask her concern. "Surgery!

What's the matter?"

"With me? Nothing, much. But there's a guy in the Bibb County morgue who was a marathoner and a serious Iron Man competitor."

"A weight lifter?"

"Triathlete. Big time competitor. He's one of those people who'll swim a mile, bike fifty more, and then run a marathon, all on the same day. They're frighteningly healthy. Anyway, this poor guy got run over by a pie wagon or something, and I thought, 'Whoa, if I could get a heart, lung, and leg transplant from him, it would change my life.'"

"Sometimes I wonder about you, Dan. I really do."

"That's funny; Kathy says the same thing."

Edith chuckled. "Say hi to her for me."

"No problem. So, what can I do for you today, dissect another devil monkey?"

"It was a gargoyle, and no, I didn't have anything specific in mind. Just thought I'd say hello."

"Did I really just hear you say that?" He exhaled dramatically. "That's a first."

"Well, actually...."

"Here it comes."

"Lately, I'm beginning to think someone at the Bureau doesn't want me to get any work done. I got bumped from a case I'd been working on; paperwork hasn't been forwarded as it should, and in general it feels like someone's been trying to keep me from making any progress."

"So, who'd you piss off? O'Keefe?"

"It's unlikely. I've never met the man."

"You haven't missed much," Dan said. "He's more politician than policeman. Is there something you want me to do? I know a couple tech guys in support; I could talk to them about the improperly forwarded paperwork, but I'd need a little more to go on."

She explained about the problem she had in Euharlee when a bogus agent collected her person of interest before she could reach him.

"That's just wrong," he said. "That kinda thing should never, ever happen. I'll take it to my techie friends. I'm sure they'll be interested."

"Be careful. If there's a mole in the GBI, there's no telling who it might be or what kind of connections they have."

"Let's not get ahead of ourselves, okay? There might be a logical explanation for all this."

Edith doubted it but knew she'd be unable to

investigate it on her own. "Thanks, Dan. Lemme know what they find out, if anything."

~*~

After a pleasant brunch in town, Margaret, Andi, and Stormy returned to their condo. Stormy took a nap while Andi announced she had a date with a recliner at poolside.

Margaret was content to settle down with a paperback she'd found in their rented quarters, but first checked her phone and discovered she'd missed a call from Edith Parise. She dialed her back immediately.

"What's up?" she asked when Edith answered.

"I guess you haven't heard the news," she said, then paused for a short but uncomfortable moment. "Do you know a woman named Olivia Ingram?"

"Sure. She's the head of the Historical Homes Society. She agreed to oversee the renovations of my mother's house. Why do you ask?"

"I wish I could sugarcoat this for you, but there's just no other way to say it. Ms. Ingram was murdered yesterday, in your mother's house."

Margaret's heartbeat had quickened steadily while Edith spoke and reached a crescendo when she heard where the crime had been committed. It took her several seconds to gather her wits enough to respond. "Who did it? How? I mean— What possible reason would someone have to do such a thing?"

"All of that is under investigation, and I'm afraid I can't reveal many details. What I can say is that it occurred during the day while several workers were in the building. None of those interviewed had any idea something like this had even happened. Supposedly, no one heard a thing. The body wasn't found until late in the day when one of the workers went looking for a ladder."

"Oh, that poor woman. I don't know what to say. I'm just—" A thought blitzed through her head and short-circuited her speech. "You don't think... Did the guy you told me about—Tanner something—do you think he did it? Was he the one who shot up the house? Oh, my God. He might have killed Olivia thinking she was—"

"We don't really know much more than I've told you," Edith said. "Speculation isn't terribly helpful. But what I would suggest is that you stay right where you are for the time being. If whoever did this was looking for your family, they obviously don't know where you are. We need to keep it that way."

"I... I guess you're right. But it doesn't make

Josh Langston

me feel any better."

"One last thing," Edith said. "It's about the camera I set up for you."

"I thought we resolved all that."

"I've had second thoughts about it. There are two things, actually. First, since the camera sends a wireless signal, someone else could receive it. I don't know how it could be encrypted to keep it secure, and we can't let just anyone see it, can we? Secondly, what happens when your mother finds out about the camera? She will, you know, sooner or later."

Margaret had no answers. She possessed less technical knowledge than Edith, and she doubted the camera could be better hidden or camouflaged somehow. When Stormy realized her daughter had been spying on her, whatever goodwill they'd developed would dissipate like so much fog. "So, what are you suggesting?"

"It needs to come down. I can do it, easily. Wouldn't take much effort at all."

"And," Margaret added, "you could do it while the renovation is going on."

"Well, then," Edith said, "I think we have a plan."

~*~

"Consider yourself lucky," Benjamin told

274

Tanner who stood before him on the patio of Benjamin's Buckhead estate. "You were hoping to kill the elder Talmadge woman, not the younger one I've been expecting you to deal with."

"I can explain," Tanner began. "I—"

"There's no need. You screwed up. You didn't bother to confirm just whose throat you were cutting. And now there's going to be a police presence at that house for a good long time, at least while it's under an active investigation."

"I'm... It's—"

"You're an idiot."

"I—"

"Just shut up." Though sorely tempted to have Jermontae disconnect Howell's skull from his spine, Benjamin thought better of it. The man was still a weapon, though deeply flawed. When the time came, he could still be depended upon to dispatch a target. The trick would be to ensure he had the proper one. That, Benjamin concluded, had been an oversight of his own. He wouldn't make the same mistake again.

"Do you still have the knife you used on the woman?"

Tanner nodded. "It's in my room."

"Get rid of it. Throw it in the Chattahoochee or the deepest lake you can find. How 'bout your clothing? Did you get any of her blood on it?"

"A little," he said. "It spurted out. Got my shirt sleeve."

"Burn the shirt. In fact, burn everything you wore that day. Understand?"

"Yeah. Sure. No problem."

Benjamin remained less than confident the man would follow through. "Do you want me to send Jermontae along with you?"

"No. No, sir. I can handle it. No problem."

"See that you do."

~*~

Andi awoke early, as usual, and decided to do something nice for her aunt and grandmother. She left a note on the kitchen counter saying she'd gone out to get something "special" for breakfast, then slipped into her running shoes and headed for the door.

This isn't exactly the Land of the Deli.

"I know. But there's a bakery in a grocery store not far from here, and it gives me the opportunity to run off some calories before I gobble down more."

Yeah, that whole calorie thing. I've been meaning to say something to you.

"Like what?" Andi deliberately put a hard edge on her question.

You've probably put on a couple pounds since your time in the Stan.

"You noticed that, did you?"

It's pretty obvious.

"Whether it's true or not has nothing to do with it. Your input isn't needed. Period. Like my Mom used to say, 'If you can't say something nice about someone, shut the fuck up.'"

She sounds like my kinda gal.

"Yeah? Well, just be glad you're a ghost, or I'd kick your brains out, assuming you had any. And just so you know, Mom would have, too."

She jogged on for a few blocks before coming to a stop. A cab had pulled to the curb near the entrance to one of the fancier beachside resorts, and two young men disembarked who looked all too familiar.

Oh shit. I was hoping you wouldn't run into those two again.

"Me, too."

Josh Langston

So, turn around and go the other way.

"It's too late," she said as Boz and Riley stood side by side staring at her. They looked anything but happy. "Think they've been out partying 'til now?"

My guess is they spent the night locked up. Mommy and Daddy couldn't bail 'em out any earlier.

"Serves 'em right."

Boz nodded at her while he engaged in a discussion with Riley that she couldn't hear.

Oh, man, are they ever pissed.

"*You* can hear 'em?"

Sure. They're trying to figure out where they could drag you that's out of the way. They don't want anyone to see them.

"Assholes," muttered Andi as she began walking toward them.

Are you out of your mind?

"I dunno. Maybe."

Wake me when it's over.

The cab pulled away as she approached, and the two college kids began smiling, utterly unconcerned. Boz called out, "It's Andi, isn't it? As in handy Andi?"

"That's right." She smiled back at them and stopped several feet away. "And you two are... Lemme guess. Beavis and Butthead?"

They both tensed, but neither moved until Riley managed a hoarse, "Get her!"

Boz came at her with both arms stretched out in front of him. Andi swiveled on one foot and drove her heel into his midsection. He folded like a lawn chair, but his momentum caused her to shift off balance and gave Riley an opening to grab her hair. She responded with an elbow to his throat that stopped him where he stood.

Having recovered enough to stand upright, Boz tried again to grab her, but she backed away, out of reach.

Bouncing lightly on the balls of her feet, she taunted them both to come for her. "If you haven't had enough, I've got plenty more to share."

Now would be a really good time to retreat. Just sayin'.

"Bitch!" yelled Boz.

"Oh, please." She gave her hair a little shake. "Is that the best you can do, frat boy?"

Must you always poke the damn bear?

Riley was in no condition to comment and

appeared content to massage his Adam's apple. Boz called to him. "We can take her. We've just gotta work together."

"Blondie's busy digesting his vocal cords," Andi said. "Would you like to taste yours, too?"

Boz lunged at her, but she dodged to one side and shoved him into the center of the road. With a look of sheer hatred on his face he spun around for another charge when a car came to a screeching halt a few feet away from him.

The driver, a man considerably smaller than her attackers, emerged from the vehicle with a snub nose revolver in his hand. He looked from Andi to Riley, and then to Boz. "What's going on here?"

"Ask her," Boz growled. "She attacked us."

What a dumb ass!

"That's not exactly what happened," Andi replied calmly. "They came after me, and I defended myself. They're upset because I didn't let them drug me last night."

Boz and Riley exchanged looks of surprise.

"That's why I bailed on you," she said.

The driver of the stopped car waved his pistol at the two young men. "Go on, now," he said, "while you can still do it under your own steam. I'd really hate to have to explain why I shot two more knucklehead tourists in the middle of town. My brother, the police chief, gets so tired of hearing it."

They turned and hurried back toward the resort.

"Your brother is the top cop?" Andi asked.

"Aw, hell no. I buy 'em coffee when I can, but I'm not related to any of them." He chuckled. "'Course, those two yahoos don't know that." He slipped the handgun into a holster on his belt and smiled. "So, is there anything else I can do for you, miss?"

Andi returned the smile with her thanks. "I can manage from here. I was just out to grab some stuff for breakfast."

"Can't help you there," he said, "but if you get hungry for lunch or dinner, drop by my restaurant." He handed her a business card. "Drinks are on me. I'm a big believer in self-defense."

Andi watched him drive away feeling good about herself. She'd remained calm under potentially dangerous circumstances and handled things without killing anyone.

You really are crazy.

"Sometimes crazy isn't a bad thing."

She began running once more and made it to

the grocery store without further delay. The only thing they had that interested her were some bagels since they were still warm from the oven. She bought a half dozen and some cream cheese, then jogged back to the condo.

Over breakfast, Mags discussed the call she'd had with her friend from the GBI. "Olivia Ingram's dead. She was killed while overseeing our renovations."

Stormy's jaw dropped. "Killed? Why? By whom?"

Mags shook her head. "We don't know. Maybe the same jerk who shot up the house. The police are investigating, and my friend Edith promised to keep me up to date."

Andi tossed her napkin on the table. "That's it. I'm goin' back home."

What? Now's not the time to be stupid, kid. Or crazy.

Both Mags and Stormy looked at her in surprise. "Why?"

"Because anyone who's irrational enough to do something like that is crazy enough to come back. And if it's the same guy who went after Erik's granddad, then that whole family is in danger, too."

"And what do you intend to do about it?"

Mags asked.

Great question.

"I'll do whatever needs to be done, but I need you two to stay here. I'll grab a flight home from Savannah."

"Do you think that's smart?" Stormy asked.

"It certainly doesn't sound safe," Mags added.

"I'll be fine," Andi said. "Whoever's doing this is the one who should be worried."

Spoken like a true nitwit.

~*~

Edith's return to the Talmadge home the following day held little of the appeal she normally experienced when engaged in law enforcement. In fact, sneaking into a building and removing a camera felt more like criminal behavior or, at the very least, espionage. Pretending to carry out a lawful function while actually poking around in someone else's personal business made it even harder. But poke she would.

While wandering outside and down the steps to the building's lowest level, workers hailed her twice to advise that all the renovation was being conducted on the two upper floors. She tossed off an excuse she would never have believed if offered by a

Josh Langston

suspect, and kept on moving.

Once she'd picked the lock on the exterior door and made her way to the wall-sized bookcase which concealed the Talmage safe room, Edith had to draw on the memory of her only other visit, with Margaret. Edith had been operating in her "Chad the Electronic Store Pseudo-dude" guise, a memory she found distinctly distasteful. The very thought reignited her displeasure with the powers-that-be who ran the Bureau.

Still, she had a job to do, and she aimed to get it over with as quickly as possible, provided she could recall just how Margaret had gotten the bookcase to slide aside.

"Who the hell are you, and what are you doing in here?" asked a young woman who had moved within striking distance of Edith without making a sound.

The aggrieved voice and suddenness of the query startled the normally unflappable agent, but she managed a weak, "I can explain" as she turned to face the speaker.

"You'd damn well better," said an athletic-looking woman in her twenties. She hefted a discarded spindle from the railing of the stairs leading from the home's foyer to the top floor, and she seemed completely comfortable with the makeshift weapon.

"I hope you aren't planning to whack me with that," Edith said, gesturing at the short length of wood.

"Haven't decided yet," said the girl. "And you haven't answered my questions."

Edith introduced herself as a GBI agent and produced her badge for identification. "Now, may I ask who you are?"

"Andi Vega," she said. "My aunt told me about you." She set the makeshift weapon aside. "There's been some seriously weird shit going on around here lately. Guess I'm a bit on edge."

"That's understandable. Thanks to Margaret, I've got a fairly decent handle on what y'all have been going through." She nodded at the bookcase. "That includes the secrets hidden behind this false wall."

"Have you seen it?" Andi asked. "The magic mirror?"

Edith responded with a grim smile. "Yes, but only... uhm... from a distance. I haven't experienced it first-hand."

"I kinda think we should, don't you?"

"Right now?"

"Yeah. You got anything better to do?"

Edith tried not to squirm. "Actually, no. Not much, anyway. I need to do something for your aunt, but it won't take any time at all."

"In the safe room?"

"Yes."

"Do I need to know about it?" Andi asked.

"Not really."

"Okay, then let's get started."

Andi moved purposefully toward the far edge of the bookcase and reached for a gargoyle sitting on the top shelf. "Aunt Mags told me the switch was under this nasty thing." She flipped a switch hidden in the base, and the huge bookcase rolled aside.

"Can I look at that thing real quick?" Edith asked.

Andi handed it to her.

Unlike the gargoyle Margaret had given her in exchange for hooking up the CCTV system she was about to dismantle, this statuette had a false bottom glued to it in which a wireless switch had been embedded. Clever, she thought, and handed it back.

Together, the two women entered the room.

"I don't see any mirrors," Andi said.

Edith pointed to the locked cabinet. "They're in there. Margaret said she'd leave the key on the shelves with the other gargoyles."

"Fine," said Andi, "you go ahead and root around in the collection. I'm afraid I'll catch something."

"Heebie-jeebies?"

"One can never be too careful," she said with a smile.

"Okay, kiddo. I'll look for it."

"I know this will sound picky," the girl said, "but I'd really rather you didn't call me 'kid.' I— There's someone else who does it, and I find it pretty annoying. *Very* annoying, in fact."

"No problem. You can return the favor by not calling me Chad."

"I— Uh. *What?*"

"I'll explain later," she said as she unlocked the cabinet and swung the doors to the side revealing the elaborately decorated reflective surface.

"Holy crap," Andi said. "That thing's spooky just sittin' there."

"Wait until it comes to life."

Andi appeared to squirm. "I think I need to use the restroom."

"Go," said Edith. "I'll wait here."

While she was gone, Edith stood on a chair and quickly disconnected the little CCTV camera from the ceiling and slipped it into her jacket pocket. She finished just before Andi re-entered the safe room.

"Still all quiet on the front?"

"Not anymore," Edith said as a ghostly image began to form on the mirror's surface.

"Oh, shit," Andi whispered. "Aunt Mags was right. The damn thing's for real."

Within moments a wispy, surreal figure appeared from the smoky depths of the mirror. Edith felt more than a bit unnerved but knew she had to remain strong and confident for Andi's sake. The girl wasn't handling the experience well at all. In fact, she appeared to be talking to herself as much as she spoke to Edith.

"Who's there?" asked a voice from deep within the mirror. "Where is Stormy Talmadge?"

"She's not available," Andi said, surprising Edith with her confident tone. "Who are you?"

"My name no longer matters," said the specter. "What do you want?"

"An update," said Edith. "Is there anything we need to do? Have you any information we need to pass on?" She almost asked if there were any crimes to report but resisted the urge.

"I hear nothing but the usual whining of the unhappy dead. Their constant complaints are of little concern."

"Of little concern to who?" Andi asked.

The face nearly solidified, and the scowl it wore looked ominous. "Who asks?"

"We do," Andi said. "I know who you are."

The girl's response could not have shocked Edith more. "You do?" she whispered.

Andi nodded, then continued to address the mirror. "I know you're a coward and a spineless piece of shit. What I don't understand is why you aren't already burning in hell."

"Send the young woman away," demanded the voice. "I will only converse with those who remain civil. I deserve respect."

"You deserve to burn for fucking ever!" Andi cried.

Edith scowled at her and pointed toward the door. "I'd like you to leave."

"But—"

"Go. Now. I'll finish up here."

"I have nothing more to say," said the Keeper of the Portal. "Begone. Both of you!"

Chapter Fourteen

"On the night of the winter solstice, when the dead get their annual reprieve, they go up to the 24-hour donut shop and wedding chapel to get hitched. Marriage is a good and proper pursuit for dead people. For a while, it relieves the dark, shuddering loneliness of the afterlife." –Rachel Swirsky

"So, what was that all about?" Edith asked. "I thought you were gonna throw a gargoyle at that jerk."

"I was tempted," Andi said.

Keep it to yourself, kid.

"What made you so angry?"

"That... that asshole in the mirror. I know him." She exhaled and rolled her shoulders like a prizefighter. "It's more like I know *of him*. From back in the sandbox. He was a small-time chief, the head guy in a village of a few dozen people. Thought he was hot shit 'cause he could speak English."

"And?"

"He worked with one of the intelligence types in our camp, we called 'em secret squirrels. They were always trying to make deals that would expose the Taliban. Or, at least, that's what they were supposed to be doing."

Easy now. Don't give away the farm. We don't know shit about this woman.

"The guy's name was Al-Maudi, or Al-Mahoody, something like that. One of our supposed intel experts, a guy named Benjamin, gave him a camera for a wedding present. An expensive one, so thank you American taxpayers. I expect he planned to use it on the honeymoon."

"So?"

"His so-called 'bride' was a ten-year-old girl."

"That's gross."

"It gets worse," Andi said. "A short time later he claimed she had dishonored him, supposedly for accepting a candy bar from one of the guys in my unit."

That's enough.

"He *whipped* her. In public. Tore up her back badly. Wouldn't let anyone go near her."

Andi!

"Her wounds went septic, and she died."

"My God, that's awful!" Edith put a hand to her cheek. "What a complete animal. I almost wish you hadn't told me."

Yeah, me, too.

"That's not all."

"Oh, Christ. There's more?"

Andi, stop! You've said enough.

"I heard some scuttlebutt about him and our shithead secret squirrel. Some folks think Benjamin told Al-monkey about one of our missions so he could arrange an ambush."

Great. Now you've gone and linked yourself with Benjamin. If something happens to him, they'll know you had a motive.

"Are you saying this Benjamin character *intentionally* ratted out our troops?"

"That's the theory, but no one can prove it. I heard he'd been discharged, and not honorably."

The GBI agent squinted at her. "Do you know this Benjamin character's first name?"

"Dirk maybe, or Derrick. I'm not sure."

Edith looked as if a 1,000-watt bulb had just lit up inside her head. "I need to get back to the office. There are some things I need to look into."

"Sure," Andi said. "I've got things to do, too. You go on. I'll lock up here."

What the hell do you think you're doing, telling her all that?

When Edith was safely out of earshot, Andi replied. "'Cause if that bastard weren't already dead, I'd kill him."

You've got to learn restraint, kid; quit wearing your heart on your sleeve.

"I can't believe you aren't just as pissed at that monster as I am."

Oh, I'm pissed at him all right. It's just that now's not the time to do anything about him.

Andi responded with a snort. "As if there ever will be."

We'll see about that. In the meantime, we need to keep our eye on Benjamin. I'd bet anything he's still getting people killed.

Neither spoke while Andi walked to her rental car, but she couldn't remain quiet long. "I find it pretty strange that you haven't said a word about the mirror. You weren't even surprised when the asshole inside it started talking. Why's that?"

It's not important.

"The hell it's not. Spill. You owe me that much."

I owe you? Hardly.

"Just this once, how 'bout telling me the whole story?" She felt her jaws tightening. "Do you realize I don't even know your last name?"

Since when does knowing my last name matter? If it did, you would've asked about it a long time ago.

"It just never seemed important."

And now?

"C'mon, Will. Don't be such an ass."

My last name is off limits. I don't want you trying to look into my past. It's none of your business.

"Says the guy who's never *not* in my business."

You're never going to give up on this, are you?

"Not a chance in hell."

Geezus. Okay then, before you drive me

completely nuts, here's what I know, but it ain't much. The mirror is more than a communications device. That said, I don't know where it came from, or how it works. I don't think it's the only one, but I don't know how many others exist or where they might be. On the other hand, the one you saw could be the last of them.

"And it's *more* than a communications device?"

Yeah. It's a portal; you know, like a door. Voices aren't the only things that can go through it.

"I don't get it. Who'd want to go to whatever's on the other side?"

Someone who can't stand it on this side, I suppose.

"This is all too weird. You're telling me creepy shits like Al-moudi could just walk through that damn thing?"

Not exactly. It takes a profound act of will, 'cause on the other side, that's all the souls really have. It's a strange kind of strength, but it's something.

"And you know this… how?"

Because I came through a portal just like that one. Not here, obviously. It was… far away.

"You just willed yourself through? Just like that?"

Actually, no. Someone with a stronger will than mine did it. He tossed me through.

Andi blinked as the information rolled around in her brain. Eventually, things began to come together. "Your name. It's not really Will, is it?"

Nope.

"Well, what the hell is it then, Casper? Holy?"

I told you already; my name's off limits. You don't need to know.

"So, someone tossed you through the portal, and then what? You waited around for some poor slob to wander by so you could climb into his head?"

It doesn't work that way. By my count, about a dozen souls have come through the portal in your grandmother's basement.

"How could you possibly know that?"

I counted the gargoyles on the shelf in the safe room. Oh, and the one on the bookcase outside.

Not for the first time, Andi wished she had someone or something to look at when talking to Will. She squinted just the same and said, "Huh?"

Think of the gargoyles as... I dunno... Kinda

like space capsules, only a helluva lot less reliable. When a soul is propelled through the portal, they come out into the world of the living sort of attached to a gargoyle. If there's a human present when they come through, they're immediately transferred to them.

"And if there's more than one?"

I'm guessing they latch onto the closest one. I dunno. It could easily be driven by something else. It's not like there's a manual somewhere which explains all this.

"And what if there's nobody around?"

Then that soul ceases to exist. It disappears.

"How long can a soul last locked up in a gargoyle?"

I don't know exactly, but it's not very long. When the soul departs, one way or another, the gargoyle becomes even more dense and rigid.

"And can a soul, like you for instance, go back the other way?"

Honestly, I have no idea.

Andi unlocked the car and climbed in, taking some time to settle herself before she started the engine.

Where to now?

"I'm worried about Erik's dad. I need to make sure he's okay, so I'm going to drop by the hospital. And if Erik's there, maybe he'll let me spend the night at their place." She waved a hand at the workers still moving around inside of the house and out. "I sure as hell can't stay here."

You really are hot for that guy.

"And you really are a jerk."

~*~

Weary of continually driving by the Talmadge home, hoping to catch a glimpse of the owner or her granddaughter, Tanner almost missed his chance by leaving for an early dinner. He couldn't help but smile when he caught sight of a slender, dark-haired female coming from the backyard of the building to the carport where she'd left her car. A quick glance at the photo Benjamin had given him confirmed the sighting. There was no doubt he'd found the elusive Andrea Vega.

He watched as she leaned back in the driver's seat and spoke as if someone else was in the car with her, but that wasn't possible. She hadn't been accompanied by anyone else.

Though tempted to pull up next to her and shoot her where she sat, there were simply too many workers hanging around. He had no intention of being seen. Instead, he waited until she backed out of the drive and drove down the street. He followed her at what he considered a non-threatening distance, not that she'd have any reason to believe she'd picked up a tail.

The thought of "tail" made him laugh. Andrea Vega had a very nice tail of her own, one he wouldn't mind spending time with. And why not? Mr. Benjamin hadn't said anything about how she was to be treated before he killed her. Why waste the chance to experience some Grade-A snatch? Especially if he didn't have to pay for it?

Grinning like he'd just won the prize at bimbo bingo, Tanner gleefully followed as she made her way toward the hospital. Along the way, two cars managed to get between him and his target, and no amount of swearing at them made a difference. Fortunately, he caught sight of her turning into the visitor parking area but had to wait before he could make the turn himself. In the process, she zipped up a ramp and out of sight.

Gunning his car, he attempted to catch up but had to stop again when someone backing out of a space had to execute more maneuvering than a barge on the Mississippi. Once again, he took to swearing though it worked no better than before.

He drove all the way to the top of the lot and surveyed a largely vacant area. She'd either parked somewhere along the way, or she'd left altogether.

Lacking other options, Tanner parked his own car and hustled toward the information desk. If he couldn't locate Vega, he'd check in on his earlier target, retired District Attorney Robert Swenson. With any luck, he'd be able to finish the old bastard off.

The woman at the info counter gave him a suspicious look before announcing, "Only family members are allowed in his room."

"No problem," Tanner said. "I'm an... uhm... nephew."

"And your name?" she asked after placing her finger on a list of names.

Totally unprepared to respond, Tanner backed away from the desk and started coughing. He had to force it and feared he might give himself a sore throat before the woman took pity on him and offered to get him some water.

"Thanks," he gasped, clutching his throat as if he'd tried to swallow a gym shoe.

"Go, sit down," the woman said, pointing at a bank of chairs in the lobby. "I'll be right back. The fountain's just around the corner and down the hall."

He waited long enough for her to make the turn, then raced to her desk and reviewed the names on the list. There weren't many, but he found one he thought he could use, then hurried back to the chairs and sat down.

She returned with a paper cup full of cold water. Tanner gulped it down and thanked her as she took her seat, adjusted her glasses, and waited for him to regain control.

"Now then, your name?"

"Erik Swenson," he said.

She stared down at the page. "According to this, Erik is his grandson, not his nephew."

"Must be some mistake," he said, not missing a beat. "His grandson's name is spelled with a 'C.' Mine's spelled with a 'K.' Which one have you got?"

"Erik with a K."

"That's me," he said, smiling, with the tip of his thumb aimed at his heart. "Somebody must've recorded it wrong. Happens more than you'd think."

She squinted at him, shrugged, and gave him the room number.

He entered an elevator intending to go straight to Swenson's floor, but the machine stopped several levels short, and the doors opened to reveal the Intensive Care Unit. Medical personnel wearing surgical masks wandered everywhere. The thought of having to wear such a thing at work, every single day seemed ridiculous. But then he realized that if

Swenson's grandson were in or near the old man's room, he'd recognize Tanner's face in a heartbeat. Suddenly, wearing a surgical mask didn't seem all that terrible, and he helped himself to one from a dispenser in the waiting area before getting back on the elevator.

After donning the mask, he proceeded to Swenson's floor and made his way down the hall toward the designated room where an armed cop stood guard. Tanner pretended to be reading room numbers and walked past the guy, intent on ignoring the officer's keen interest in him. Tanner kept walking, made a complete circuit of the ward, and went back out to the waiting area near the bank of elevators.

He was still silently cursing his luck when Andrea Vega came out of the ward accompanied by a little girl and a man about her age. He recognized all three instantly. Clutching a magazine he'd hastily grabbed from a side table, Tanner hid his face while putting his mask back on. He strained to hear the couple's subdued conversation.

"I'm sure he'll be fine," Vega said, patting the grandson's arm. "If he's survived this long...."

"I don't know. He wasn't terribly healthy before he got shot. And now? I'm just worried, that's all."

The little girl stood between the two adults, struggling to get their attention. "Grampop's gonna be okay," she said. "He told me so."

"See?" Vega said to the man. "There's your proof, right there."

He nodded. "I hope you're right."

"I'm hungry!" said the child.

She smiled at the little girl. "Me, too, sweetheart."

"He's got restricted visiting hours," said the man whose name Tanner had borrowed. "We might as well go home."

The child seemed to be trying to pull him toward the lifts. "Eat now," she said.

"That works for me," said Vega. "My treat."

As they strolled toward the elevator, Tanner casually set his magazine aside and followed them into the enclosure turning his back so they couldn't see what little of his face remained uncovered. He briefly considered killing all three of them there and then, but knew his chances of getting away unseen were zero. Instead, he continued to eavesdrop.

"Where are you staying?" Erik asked. "I heard your grandmother was having the place renovated."

"She is," Vega said. "I just got back in town."

"And your grandmother?"

"She and my aunt Mags are still at the beach. I'll call them when the coast is clear."

He chuckled. "You make it sound so dramatic."

She answered with a tiny groan. "You heard what happened at Gran's house, right? The head of the historical society was—" she lowered her voice to a whisper "—murdered there."

He sounded surprised, then apologetic. "I'd heard that, and you must think I'm the world's biggest dope for not saying something. I apologize. That must've been a terrible shock. I'm afraid I'm not handling stuff these days as well as I should."

"I completely understand."

"If you haven't already made other arrangements," he said, "why don't you come stay with us?"

The little girl jumped up and down sending small shock waves through the elevator. "Please? Please? Will you come spend the night? We'll have so much fun!"

Vega laughed. "I'd love to."

"It's settled then," said Erik.

Tanner smiled to himself. It was settled for

him, too.

~*~

Edith returned to her office and immediately called Dan Wolfram in the Bureau's laboratory. "How're those new legs of yours?"

"Pardon me?"

"Last time we spoke, you mentioned a transplant from some big-deal athlete."

He chuckled. "Yeah. About that. Kathy said if I was gonna have all that done, I needed to have his brain transplanted, too. She didn't think mine was functioning all too well."

"Smart girl. Listen, as much as I'd love to discuss your surgical options, I wanted to see if your tech pals had found out anything about the message to the Euharlee police."

"They did," he said. "And I've been meaning to give you an update."

"I'm all ears."

"Apparently, a blind copy of that correspondence was sent to a civilian. Hang on, I've got the name here somewhere."

She listened to him shuffling papers and could easily picture the mess on his desk, something he attributed to "all great minds." Edith had her doubts.

"Here it is," he said. "The email address isn't very revealing, but they checked, and it's registered to someone named Derrick—"

"Benjamin!" she said, cutting him off.

"Who's he?" Dan asked. "And why did he get a copy of our internal correspondence?"

"Because someone in the Bureau doesn't want me to have anything to do with him." She paused to gather her thoughts. "Much as I hate to do it, I need to ask another favor of you."

"Name it," he said.

"When I did a background search of Derrick Benjamin in relation to the bombing of an electronics store, the information I got was very general. I didn't get anything terribly useful. No known associates or anything like that. Can you dig a little deeper? I want to know all I can about this guy before I do anything."

"Sure, I can check him out for you," Dan said. "But what did you have in mind doing?"

"I'd dearly love to catch him breaking a law— *any* law. He's a seriously sick puppy, and very possibly a traitor. Unfortunately, he's extremely well-connected, and I've got no physical evidence of a crime. It won't be easy to make a case against him.

For anything."

"Are you sure this is a wise career move? I mean—"

"Trust me, Dan. This guy's a prime dirtbag. Just make sure you don't raise any red flags in the penthouse."

"Got it. And you keep your head down, too."

~*~

Andi followed Erik back to his house. Chloe insisted on riding with her, despite Erik's assurances that her new adult friend would, indeed, be coming to their house for a sleepover. This necessitated the removal of a child safety seat from Erik's car and its subsequent installation in Andi's rental. While that took place, she and Will had a quick exchange.

If you were smart, you'd have gotten a kiddie seat from the car rental agency.

"Right on top of things, as usual," she responded. "And how would that have looked when it came time to load her in the car? Just because I hoped to spend a couple nights with them, doesn't mean I wanted to look like I planned it all from the beginning. I'm not that... needy. So, how 'bout staying quiet while Chloe's with me? I'm tired of making excuses for talking to someone who isn't really there."

But I am here.

"And I'm all too aware of it. Now, hush!"

After drinks on the deck of the Swenson home, Erik suggested that they have réchauffé for dinner.

"Ray-shaw-fay?" Andi had no idea what he meant but took a stab at it anyway. "I'm pretty sure I've never had that. I'm not big on seafood."

Chloe giggled.

"What's got you so tickled?" Andi asked.

"Daddy means leftovers."

Andi glanced quickly his way.

"It's old French, I think. My Dad used to say it. He claimed it made anything reheated taste better. Anyway, we've got some lasagna from Constantine's in the 'fridge, and it's always better the second time around."

After dinner they found an animated film on TV which completely distracted Chloe while Andi and Erik made small talk. From time to time Chloe would turn to them and put a finger to her lips in the universal sign for silence. The two adults always complied, but it never lasted long.

Andi learned that Erik owned a company which leased heavy machinery. "Like bulldozers?"

Josh Langston

she asked.

"Yep. And front-end loaders, graders, dump trucks. Cranes, too."

"How in the world did you get involved with that? Aren't all those huge machines expensive?"

He laughed. "I got hooked on construction stuff when I was a kid. I majored in business and engineering, but my heart was always in diggers and scrapers. Mine isn't the biggest operation in town, but I do all right."

"I'm trying to picture you putting a bulldozer through its paces," she said. "It looks difficult. Don't you get hot and sweaty?"

"You don't have to be a genius to dig dirt, even with a huge machine. But it's hard work."

"How hard?" she asked in a whisper as she slid her hand across his chest. She could feel his heart beat beneath a layer of muscle.

He smiled. "Hard enough." Then he leaned in close, lowered his own voice, and added, "Would you like to find out?"

"Are you suggesting a test drive?"

"Something like that." He drew little circles on her leg with his index finger. It felt oddly wonderful.

"Actually," she purred, "I think I could go for a demonstration." She nodded toward Chloe. "How soundly does she sleep?"

"Like the dead."

I'll pretend I didn't hear that.

Andi said nothing and tried not to grit her teeth. She closed the distance between them and kissed Erik on the lips, then casually stood up. "I'll be right back. Where's the loo?"

"Just down the hall. First door on the left," he said.

Andi strolled to the bathroom and quietly closed the door. "Damn it, Will," she whispered fiercely. "I thought you were going to keep quiet. Please don't ruin this for me."

I'm sorry. I didn't mean anything by it.

"I had almost convinced myself that I was alone with Erik, and then you piped up. You're an ass, you know that?"

I said I was sorry. And besides, Chloe was still in the room, wide awake as far as I could tell. Or were you planning to rip Erik's clothes off and have your way with him while she watched?

"You're about as funny as a gas chamber."

Okay. I promise to keep quiet, unless....

"Unless, what?"

Unless there's something you need to know about. Like a prowler or something.

"Erik said the house has a really good security system. If anyone even wanders into the yard or up the driveway, lights go on all over the place, and an alarm in his room goes off. For all I know, he keeps a shotgun in bed with him."

I imagine that's something you'll find out pretty soon.

"We'll see," she said. "Provided you leave me alone."

~*~

"I've got some good news," Tanner said. He stood before Derrick Benjamin on the patio of the man's stately home. Trevontae, his huge associate, had taken up a familiar position nearby, ready to assist Benjamin if needed.

"Good news, eh? That's refreshing." Benjamin took a sip of his drink. Tanner guessed vodka tonic, but he couldn't be sure.

Tanner waved the photo in front of his face as if it were an oriental folding fan. "I found your girl."

"Is she still alive?"

"Yes."

"Why?"

"Well, see, she's not— What I mean is, getting to her requires planning. She's not alone, and there's a security issue. But I know exactly how to draw her out. I'll take care of it tomorrow. Around lunchtime. Guaranteed."

Benjamin did not appear reassured, and Tanner tried not to reveal his disdain. The sooner this job was done, the sooner he could disappear, hopefully with a generous chunk of Benjamin's wealth. In Tanner's world, men like Benjamin didn't trust banks.

Chapter Fifteen

*"They say revenge is a dish best eaten cold,
but for most people, by the time it's ready to
eat, they just don't fancy it anymore."*
–Jo Brand

Andi woke up in a pleasant mood. With Erik's warm, bare arm draped across her stomach, she lay on her back looking up at the ceiling. Her mind wandered back to the night before, to the laughter, the relaxation, and the sex. Especially the sex. Erik had fulfilled her dreams, and she felt confident she had returned the favor.

"Breakfast?" he asked, his voice husky.

"What'd you have in mind?"

"It depends."

"Oh yeah," she purred, "on what?"

"On whether or not Chloe's awake. If she's up, I'll have cornflakes. If not, I wouldn't mind having another helping of you." He rose up enough to kiss her, then nuzzled her breast, his beard just the tiniest bit scratchy.

Oh please, dear God, let Chloe sleep! "I'll be right back," she said, as she rolled out of the bed and tiptoed to the bathroom.

When she returned, Erik was on his side, elbow bent, with his head on his palm. "You've got the cutest little birthmark. It looks like—"

"A comma."

"I was gonna say a polliwog. You know, a tadpole."

Andi grinned, slipped between the sheets, and snuggled close to him. "I guess I can let you live. Consider yourself special. All the other men who've seen it are dead."

"Whoa. I had no idea. I didn't know a peek at your backside could end badly. *Ever!*"

"You're safe," she said, in her best imitation of royalty. "For now, anyway."

From down the hall came the sounds of a flushed toilet.

"That'd be Chloe," Erik said, dejectedly. "We'd

better get dressed. If you hurry, you can slip back into the guest room before she gets here. She's a little pokey in the morning."

"Pokey, hm?" She let it slide without further comment and made her way to the guest bedroom. The idea of sneaking around held zero appeal, but Andi reasoned it was for the best, at least until she and Erik arrived at some sort of permanent arrangement. She prayed there would be many more evenings like the one she'd just experienced.

Not much later, Erik and Chloe were at work in the kitchen when Andi joined them. Chloe raced straight to her, wrapped her arms around Andi's legs and gave her a hug.

"Good morning, Sunshine," Andi responded. She knelt down to return the little girl's embrace. "You look happy this morning."

"I'm making special breakfast. Daddy's the helper."

Erik gave a dramatic nod.

"What're we having?"

"Pana-cakes," declared Chloe. "With choc-lit chips!"

Andi smiled but sent Erik a questioning look.

"I control the chips," he said. "We rarely overdo 'em."

After breakfast, Erik walked Chloe out to the street in front of the house where they waited for her carpool ride to kindergarten. Andi intended to go with them, but Erik suggested it would be better if she waited. The driver for this final week of school was a bit of a gossip, he explained, and he didn't want or need her thoughts on their budding relationship.

With Chloe safely off to school, Erik returned to the kitchen and helped Andi clean up. "I need a shower," she said when they finished.

Erik put his arms around her from behind and pressed his lips to her ear. "Want company?"

"I thought you said you had to go to work."

"I'm the boss, remember. I get to call in late whenever I want. Besides, I'd love to get a closer look at your birthmark."

Andi was about to respond when Erik's cell phone buzzed. He took a hurried look at the caller ID, said "I've gotta take this," and answered it.

Damnation!

Temper, temper, kid.

Andi confined her response to a low growl. Erik didn't seem to notice as his previous good humor soured visibly during the phone call.

"Yeah. All right," he said. "I'll be there in a while. Just tell him to wait."

"What's that all about?" she asked.

"One of my clients is pissed about something." He shook his head, a look of genuine sadness coloring his features. "Much as I'd love to stick around and—"

"No problem," Andi said, feigning a bright attitude. "I'm not going anywhere."

He hugged her. "Chloe gets out of school around noon. When Pop's not here, she stays with a neighbor, but she'll be coming straight back here today as long as you're here. I'll try to be back in time for lunch. I promise."

"Can I reach you at work if I need to?"

"You've got my cell number. Call anytime."

He hurried upstairs, showered, dressed, and went out the door in what Andi assumed was record time.

The big old house felt lonely without anyone else in it, until Will ruined the moment.

Have fun last night?

"Yes."

Wanna talk about it?

"With you? Hell no."

Don't I get a word of thanks?

"For what?"

For not providing a running commentary during the evening's events.

"You'd *do that?* Purposely wreck something that matters so much to me?"

He laughed. *Nah. I'd never do something that rotten. Tease you? Sure. Taunt you? Never.*

"Okay then, thanks."

De nada.

~*~

Tanner knew his best bet for drawing Vega out of the Swenson house was to wait for the little girl he'd grabbed during his attempt on the old man's life. She was far too small to offer any resistance, and it was clear Vega adored the child. Grabbing the kid would be as easy as parking near the house and waiting for her to show up. All he had to do was wait, and he had snacks and coffee enough to last all day if necessary.

He pulled up and parked just out of sight of the gaudy Colonial the Swensons lived in. An image of the patriarch came to mind. *Rich bastard. He'll soon find out what all his money is good for.*

Once he'd taken care of Vega and made Benjamin happy, he could head out on his own and ransom the kid. Thoughts of all the money he'd have once it was over kept him smiling while he waited. Money meant freedom. Money meant he could go anywhere he wanted to go and never have to worry about the law again.

"No one deserves it more than me," he told himself.

The time passed slowly, but he kept his eyes open. Whenever the child showed up, he'd be ready. He had grabbed a package of extra-long zip ties at a building supply. One of those would be enough to immobilize a little kid. He brought a washcloth from the hotel to stuff in her mouth so he wouldn't have to listen to her scream. Traffic was light; the weather was fine, and Tanner was as ready as he'd ever be.

By lunchtime, nothing had happened, although Erik Swenson drove past him and pulled into his driveway. Tanner hadn't known he wasn't in the house the whole time. He assumed Vega was still there, but he began to worry that she wasn't.

As he cursed his luck, a car he didn't recognize soon pulled to a stop in front of Swenson's house. The driver got out, opened a back door, and the little Swenson kid slid out. The driver then got back in the car and drove off. Tanner was already on the move, racing toward the child as she lollygagged across the half acre front yard toward her daddy who sat on the front steps with Vega.

Though deep in conversation with the woman, Erik spotted him running into the yard and grabbing his daughter. Tanner didn't even slow down as Swenson began to give chase.

Tanner decided the zip tie could wait until he'd gotten away. After throwing the girl into his car, he followed her in. She screamed and carried on until he slapped her, then he focused on making his getaway.

The frantic man chasing him got close to his car, but not close enough. Tanner gunned the engine and quickly left him behind. He watched in the rearview mirror as Swenson made a hurried phone call. Vega was nowhere to be seen.

Tanner relaxed for the first time since the race for the girl began. Everything was fine now; he had all but reached the winner's circle.

~*~

Andi wasted no time and headed for her car the minute she saw the man scoop Chloe up and run away. He looked vaguely familiar, but she couldn't place him.

If you hurry, I may be able to track him. But he's moving awfully fast.

"I'm tryin', Andi said as she fumbled the car keys from her pocket, unlocked the door of her rental, and climbed in. "We still good?"

For now, yeah. But you'd better get your ass in gear.

She rolled her window down and yelled to Erik as she passed him in the driveway. "I'll try to catch up with him." She brandished the cellphone hardware she normally wore on her ear. "I'll call you!"

A hard pull on the wheel let her slalom out of the drive and onto the street. Fortunately, no one occupied a lane in either direction. "Okay," she panted, "which way?"

Will directed her to the main road leading to the Swenson's subdivision. *Take a hard right and then goose it. He's pulling away!*

Andi complied, pressing the accelerator to the floor. "Can you see him?"

Yeah, but not well. He's weaving in and out of traffic. What a moron. It's like he's begging for a cop to pull him over.

"Better him than me, but I have to do the same damned thing."

Driving in such a competitive fashion didn't make it easy to clamp the phone to her ear, but she somehow managed and called Erik.

"Can you see him?" he asked.

"Just barely." She could hear the roar of his engine as he joined the chase.

"What's his license plate number? I'll tell the police."

"I can't read it at this distance, but I'll keep trying. Looks like we're headed for Atlanta. I've gotta concentrate. I'll call when I can." She disconnected without waiting for his response.

He's in front of some big ass trucks.

Andi drove like a woman possessed. Other drivers honked and shook their fists, but she ignored them and remained intent on catching up to the kidnapper.

Wish I could tell you to slow down.

"Yeah, me, too."

Don't worry kid, we'll catch him.

"I hope to God you're right."

~*~

Edith Parise camped next to Dan Wolfram's desk, waiting for him to divulge anything new he had discovered about the leaker.

"I'd probably get more done if you weren't breathing down my neck."

"I thought you liked it. Heavy breathing, I mean."

"A subtly different kind, maybe."

Edith backed away a few inches. "Better?"

"Oh, yeah. Huge difference." He gave her the stink eye, then refocused on his computer screen. "The problem is, you can't be sure if the person who notified the civilian is the same person assigned to the computer used to send it. The standing rule is we're all *supposed* to log out when we leave our offices." He gestured at his cramped cubicle. "That even applies to spacious ones like mine."

"Yours is bigger than mine," she said.

"Yeah, but you get to go outside from time to time. You're not trapped here like me."

"Poor baby," she cooed. "So how do we find out who sent it?"

"I'm workin' on it. Be patient."

"I had patience once; I got over it. So, you keep at it, I'm going to get a warrant for Derrick Benjamin. At the very least, I want to bring him in for questioning." She patted his shoulder as she left and returned to her own desk where she filled out the electronic forms required for an arrest warrant and clicked the SEND button.

She knew the process required time, though she wasn't happy about it. The paperwork had to go up the chain of command and pass muster before it could be presented to a judge or magistrate. She had no choice in the matter. That didn't change the fact that the sooner she got her hands on Benjamin, the better.

The lunch hour had crept up on her, and she was contemplating where she might grab a bite when her phone rang.

"Agent Parise," she said.

"This is Gregory Moncrief," said the voice on the line. "Executive assistant to Director O'Keefe."

"Yes sir," she said. "What can I do for you?"

"You can forget this ridiculous warrant request. What's the matter with you? Mr. Benjamin is a well-known and well-respected citizen. Nothing in your request suggests he's done anything outside the law."

"I'm still waiting for a final bit of evidence, sir, but there's been a delay."

"What kind of evidence?"

Edith squirmed in her chair, unwilling to reveal who might be looking for the missing nugget of damning information. "I'm reluctant to say, sir."

"Oh, really? Interesting. How eager are you to remain employed?"

"I'm afraid it's confidential, sir. Much as I'd like to share it with you, I can't."

"Then know this, *Agent* Parise. If you waste even a moment of Mr. Benjamin's time, I'll see you on the street, and you'll be in no position to collect unemployment. Do I make myself clear?"

"Crystal clear, sir."

<click>

Damn!

~*~

Andi followed the kidnapper's car all the way to the trendy north side of Atlanta, better known as Buckhead, where the traffic got heavier and staying within Will's all-too-vague range had her on the very edge of her nerves.

"I can't see him!"

You're doing fine. Don't panic. Turn right, up ahead.

Andi responded robotically. "Now what?"

Just keep going. I'll tell you when to stop or turn.

"He's bound to be headed to an address somewhere around here."

I'm guessing he's going to Derrick Benjamin's place.

Andi hastily dialed Erik. "We're in Buckhead."

"Geez," he said. "I just came from there. I've got equipment on site close by. Any luck on the license plate?"

"I never got close enough to read it. I'll let you know the address when he stops."

"Be safe, okay? Let the cops handle it."

"He's got Chloe! I'm not going to wait for anybody."

"Then, for her sake, please don't do anything stupid. Promise me!"

"Okay," she said, mentally crossing her fingers.

Turn left, here. Now!

"Hang on. It looks like he's stopping. And... Holy crap! You won't believe the size of this place."

"Address?" Erik asked, desperation in voice.

Will gave her the street and number which she relayed to Erik. "Listen," she said, "I've got an idea. How long would it take you to bring one of your big machines over here?"

"Not long at all. I've got a couple units on trailers right now. But why would—"

"I'm going to need a diversion. A big one."

"What the hell have you got in mind?"

"You want Chloe back?" she asked.

"Of course, I do!"

"Then bring a bulldozer or something. We need to tear down King Asshole's castle."

"*We what?*"

"Big machine. Now. Trust me on this. Okay? I won't do anything until you get here." She didn't wait for his answer.

~*~

Benjamin was lounging on his patio, as usual, when Tanner arrived. He set the child on the paving stones directly in front of his employer. She struggled against the zip ties binding her, and the washcloth in her mouth stifled any screams. Binding and gagging the kid had not been much of a challenge.

"You finish your assignment?"

"Not yet, but soon," Tanner said.

Benjamin stared at the little girl. "Who the hell is this, and what's she doing here?"

"She's bait. All I have to do is call and arrange a meet. That Vega broad you're so hot to dispose of will drop everything to get the kid."

"I can't believe you're stupid enough to bring the brat here! The cops are bound to be looking for her."

"No one followed me," Tanner said. "I'm sure of it. I was very careful."

"Tell me why I shouldn't have Trevontae shoot both of you."

"Because then you wouldn't get what you want, which is Andrea Vega. I'm telling you, all I have to do is arrange a meeting. It can't miss. I'll take care of the kid later. Her granddad is a rich bastard. He'll pay anything to get her back."

Benjamin frowned. "No, don't worry about that. I have associates who would be interested in her."

"What d'ya mean?" *Do you think for one skinny minute I'd let you cheat me out of a ransom? Screw that!*

"A couple of my contacts are quite keen on little girls." He squinted at the child squirming at Tanner's feet. "They'll be happy to pay for her. I'll see that you get a cut."

"Sick bastards," mumbled Tanner.

"You're one to talk," Benjamin said. "What do you care as long as you get your revenge and a bonus from me?"

Their conversation continued in that fashion for several minutes before Trevontae galloped through the patio doors, a look of consternation on his face.

"What is it?" snapped Benjamin.

"Somebody just pulled into the driveway with some kinda steam shovel."

Benjamin stared at him. "What the hell are you talking about. A steam shovel?"

Travontae shrugged. "You know, one of them big scooper things."

Rising to his feet, Benjamin yelled, "Go get rid of the damn thing before it ruins my driveway!"

"Where do you want me to put the girl?" Tanner asked.

"Lock her in the basement, then get your ass out front and help Trevontae take care of the nutcase out there."

"Sure, sure," Tanner said. "In a minute. How much do you think you'd get for the kid?"

Benjamin appeared to be restraining himself, but his face reflected outrage. "I said, get out front!"

Tanner had his back up, too. "And I said, how much for the kid?"

"I don't know, you idiot. Now, do as I told you."

"Ya know what," Tanner said, casually pulling the .32 automatic from his pocket. "I'm gettin' kinda tired of you bossing me around."

"I'll have Trevontae tear you to pieces."

"No, you won't," Tanner said as he racked a round into the little automatic's chamber.

"Don't be stupid. I swear, I'll have you killed."

Tanner responded with three rounds, all aimed roughly at Benjamin's midsection. Two found their mark. The man stared down at the wounds, then collapsed into his chair without taking his eyes off the little holes near the center of his paunch.

"Funny thing," Tanner commented. "Your man Tay and I were talking just the other day about how *getting* dead is worse than being dead. I reckon you'll find that out. I'm told gut shots are a real bitch."

"You bastard," Benjamin groaned, but without moving. "Don't think I'll let you get away with this."

"I already have."

He hustled the little girl into the house. Once he found the basement and locked her in, he'd go out and take care of Tay before he knew what hit him.

~*~

With Will's help, Andi managed to sneak onto Benjamin's property without raising any alarms, although they encountered, and avoided, several security cameras. The large, heavily wooded lot shielded the house from the street and provided a reasonable amount of cover. Andi reached a spot of comparative safety and waited for Erik to arrive. With any luck, the police would get there soon, too.

When Erik finally made his entrance, he did so in grand fashion. Seated inside the cab of a gigantic backhoe, Erik had both a bulldozer style scoop and a huge excavator arm at his disposal. While she watched, he drove as close to the house as he could get and swung the great steel arm of the excavator toward it. He revved the massive diesel engine and slammed the scoop into the front of the building, shattering windows and rocking the walls.

Within moments a tall, heavy, black man burst from the house waving a gun and shouting at Erik to stop. By the time he stopped and took up a shooting stance, Erik was well ahead of him. Without a pause, he swung the huge bucket toward the shooter and slapped him ten feet away from where he'd stopped.

Meanwhile, the man who'd grabbed Chloe appeared, surveyed the scene and fired off several rounds from his gun. The bullets clanged harmlessly off the machinery as Erik pivoted to keep a great deal of steel between himself and the shooter.

With the kidnapper distracted, Andi worked her way toward him using the sculpted shrubbery in Benjamin's front yard as cover. Erik backed his machine toward the downed black man writhing on the lawn.

The kidnapper dodged around a parked car and angled toward the cab of the earth mover.

Andi stayed low until the shooter stood facing Erik with his back to her. He advanced with his weapon drawn and held in front with both hands. Erik appeared stricken as he realized the shooter wanted to get closer before he fired again.

Now!

The noise of the heavy diesel engine all but drowned out Will's voice. But it was enough. Andi darted from cover and slammed into the kidnapper's back, sending him sprawling. His gun skittered under the earth mover.

Only momentarily stunned, he ignored Andi crawled under the huge machine to retrieve his weapon.

Erik jammed levers, revved the engine again, and turned the massive piece of machinery.

Thankfully, the sound of the engine obliterated the sound of the kidnapper being crushed between the vehicle's steel treads and the concrete driveway. Very little of the man remained recognizable except his right hand, which still held the little .32 automatic.

~*~

Edith arrived sometime after the police, whose presence had somehow been delayed due to overlapping jurisdictions. Edith wondered if those delays had also been encouraged by an overzealous GBI executive assistant.

She spotted Andi sitting beside a man and a little girl in the shade of some meticulously maintained ornamental trees. Andi had her arm around the child; the man had his arm around Andi. It all looked stunningly domestic.

An ambulance blocked a direct path to the trio, and Edith paused long enough to view two patients. The larger of the two had been sedated and appeared to have been hit by a locomotive. The smaller of them remained awake, though he doubtless would have preferred unconsciousness.

"He'll be lucky to move someday," said the EMT gesturing toward Benjamin. "I think his spine's shattered. As for the other one? I don't even know what to call his condition." He shook his head. "Now, if you'll kindly step aside, we've gotta get these two into the ER right away."

Edith stepped back as the ambulance pulled away, and a faded gold sedan took its place in the driveway. A police officer quickly moved to prevent the newcomer from exiting his vehicle. Edith almost ignored the confrontation until she realized it was Dan. She flashed her badge and assured the LEO that Dan was with her.

"What's up?" she asked him. "I thought you never got to leave your cubby."

"We figured out who copied Benjamin in on the Euharlee paperwork."

"Lemme guess. Gregory Moncrief?"

Dan appeared crestfallen. "How'd you know?"

"They pay me to do detective work. Go figure."

"Killjoy."

She patted his shoulder. "You proved what I could only suspect. C'mon, let's take a look around."

As soon as she turned, Andi and her companions came back into view. "Hold that thought," she told Dan. "I'd like a word with these folks first."

She walked over and greeted Andi who introduced Erik and Chloe Swenson.

"How're you holding up?"

"I'm okay," Andi said. "I've seen my share of... You know." She gave Chloe a squeeze. "My best little buddy here is going to be okay; I think. Erik's still a bit shaky."

"I— I didn't mean to kill that guy. I was just tryin' to move, get out of range, or something. He had a gun—"

"And he got what he deserved," Andi said. "He's not worth the worry." She nodded at the remains still drawing flies beneath the earth mover though covered with a blanket.

Edith added, "She's right. Don't waste any sympathy on him."

She signaled for Dan to join her. "We've got some investigating to do. With all the cameras spread out around this place, I suspect there's some sort of security office or desk inside where we can sort through any video Benjamin captured. We'll need to review all of it."

"What about that mean man?" Chloe asked.

"He won't hurt anyone else, ever, sweetheart," said Erik.

Chloe pointed at the blanketed corpse. "Not him, Daddy. The other bad man."

"You needn't worry about him, either," Edith said.

Chapter Sixteen

"Love is blind; friendship closes its eyes."
–Friedrich Nietzsche

Andi finally had some time to relax. The house would remain hers alone until Margaret and Stormy returned at the end of the week. Andi had told them how nice the place looked now that the renovation had been completed. She had moved back in when Erik's grandfather was released from the hospital.

The shrink at the VA hadn't changed his opinion of her PTSD diagnosis, but he'd failed to convince her. Even Will agreed, something that actually did surprise her. They'd had time to talk about it on the way to and from her appointment and concluded that the head examiner needed someone to take a good, long look at his.

You're okay, kid. I've been around a long time, seen a lot of whack jobs, and you aren't one of 'em.

"I'm glad to hear that, although I have no idea where you got your psychiatric training."

And you're unlikely to find out.

They said little to each other for most of the rest of the day. The silence no doubt prompted by Will's decision to try and use the mirror in Stormy's safe room as a way to clear out of Andi's head.

"I've got mixed feelings about this," she told him after she'd unlocked the secret room and plunked herself down in Stormy's big easy chair. "I can't believe Gran sat in this thing for so many years. It's uncomfortable as hell."

Funny you should mention hell, considering that's where I might soon end up.

"I can't believe that."

I don't have any control over it.

"Okay, but hell is where bad people go. That Howell jerk is down there."

And no doubt many, many more that I could name.

"So why take the risk?"

Mostly, just to give you a little peace and quiet. God knows you've complained often enough about not having any.

"That was mostly just talk. I never thought you'd actually do something about it."

Well, I'd like to give it a try.

"What if it doesn't work?"

And I stay stuck in your head?

"Would that be so awful?"

More so for you than me.

Andi remained quiet for a moment, knowing that what he'd said was true. Still, a part of her didn't want to let him go.

C'mon, kid. It's time to do something. Shake things up, change the status quo.

"You sound like a labor organizer. Or maybe a politician."

And here I thought you had a high opinion of me.

"Yeah, well…."

Open the cabinet. See if you can wake up the dirtbag who runs the portal, and let me do my thing.

"But, what if—"

Hush now. Let's get this over with.

Andi leaned forward, unlocked the cabinet, and pulled the doors open. The mirror appeared dark and lifeless. "Anybody home?" she called.

Cute.

For a long while, nothing happened. Andi stared at the mirror, waiting. Will said nothing. The silence weighed on her, and her patience waned. "This is dumb. Al-numbnuts isn't home, seems like. We should try again later. Next year, maybe."

Be patient.

"Not my best attribute."

True. But you're growing up. You'll get better at it.

"You have such a lovely way of making me feel bad."

The mirror began its lightshow, and a shady face emerged from a swirl of milky fog. Before long a voice droned from within. "What do you want? I'm busy."

"We've come to see you," Andi said.

"Who's we? I see only one person."

Good, he can't detect me.

Andi grimaced. "Give it some time."

"I have little to spare, for you anyway. Where is the old woman? I prefer speaking with her. You may go. Now."

Here goes, kid. See ya in the funny papers. And listen, when you're done here, don't open the cabinet again for at least a week.

"Why?"

One week, kid. That's all. Just promise.

"Okay, fine. I'll leave it locked at least that long."

Great. So, I guess this is goodbye.

"Will, wait."

What is it?

"I don't have a good feeling about this."

I know what you mean.

"Who are you talking to?" demanded the portal keeper.

"Not you, that's for sure."

Gotta go.

"I know, I just... Can you give me one minute more? Please?"

She waited, but Will didn't respond.

"Will?"

"We're done," said the voice in the mirror. "You've wasted my time. Do not summon me again. Next time, send someone wiser. I will no longer respond to you."

Andi gave him the finger, but he had already begun to fade, and she wasn't sure he'd seen it. "Not my best moment," she said, expecting a sarcastic rejoinder from Will.

But instead, she heard nothing at all.

~*~

Edith set her tumbler on a small, glass-topped table that graced the patio in Dan's backyard. "This is delicious," she told his wife, Kathy. "I've never had a Pink Panty Pulldown before."

"It's such a silly name," she said. "I'll leave it up to Dan to tell you where it came from. But they sure taste good."

"I was happy to see they offered him a field agent training opportunity. I think he'd be good at it."

Kathy shrugged. "I heard you got a promotion, too."

"A little one; I'm a supervisor now. Thanks to the evidence we found in Derrick Benjamin's house, we'll be able to put him away forever. But he's got bigger worries. I'm told he's now a paraplegic."

"Yeah, Dan mentioned that. Can't say I'm bothered by it."

"Me, either. Best of all, we busted Greg Moncrief, too. And there's talk of replacing Director O'Keefe, his former boss."

"Good news all around. I know Dan's pleased."

"Where is he, by the way? I thought he was going to join us for a drink."

"You know him, if he's not out playing tennis or golf, he's walking the dog. The man just can't stand still."

~*~

"To be completely honest," Stormy said as she, Mags, and Andi entered the safe room, "I was hoping I'd never have to come back in here. I'm tired of it. Tired of that idiot, Donovan O'Keefe at the GBI, and I have absolutely no use for the current Portal Keeper."

"I know what you mean," Mags said. "He's a bit of an ass."

"Just the bit in the middle," Andi said. "The hole."

They all giggled while Andi unlocked the cabinet. She paused and took a deep breath, remembering Will's admonition that she leave the cabinet shut for at least a week. It had been closer to two since she'd last spoken with him, and she missed his voice more than she ever thought possible. "Here goes," she said.

The doors came open with ease and all three women were startled by the gargoyle which dropped on the floor at their feet with a heavy thud. Mags uttered a startled, "Geez!" Andi put a protective arm in front of Stormy in case the thing bounced or committed some other weirdness.

"It's okay," Stormy said. "It's dead." She pointed to the shelf where roughly a dozen others reposed. "Please, stash it over there for now."

Andi complied, though she wasn't terribly keen on touching it. Mags hadn't moved a muscle.

"I'm afraid you'll need to sit here and talk to the jerk in the mirror," Andi said. "His last words to me were something like, 'Go take a hike and never come back.'"

Stormy smiled and eased herself into the big chair. "Let's see how chatty he is today."

All three watched as the mirror went through its morphing process from darkness to creepy light. Andi hadn't gotten used to it and doubted she ever would.

"I hate this part," Mags said.

Slowly a face emerged from the dense, dark background. It lacked anything close to sharpness, but there was enough to suggest it was definitely a different face.

"Can you hear me?" asked Stormy.

"Yes," came the response.

"And who am I speaking with?"

"Andi," the voice said, "why don't you tell them?"

"*Will?*"

"Hey, kid. It looks like the portal goes both ways. Who knew?"

~End~

About the Author

Josh Langston's fiction has been published in a variety of magazines and anthologies, and two of his short story collections have reached the Amazon top 20 for genre fiction. His many action-adventure novels range  from ancient European history to contemporary American fantasy with frequent humorous forays into modern day life. Here he is with his charming bride, Annie.

Josh also loves to teach. His classes on novel writing, memoir, and independent publishing are filled with students eager to learn and have their work perused by a pro. His textbooks on the craft of fiction, memoir, and novel writing provide a fun and easy-to-understand approach to the subjects while imparting valuable tips and techniques.

If you're a member of a book club, you may want to ask him about making a guest appearance at one of your meetings. He can be reached at: DruidJosh@gmail.com. Be sure to visit his website, too: www.JoshLangston.com

And now, in case you missed the prequel to **Voices**, turn the page for a bonus preview: the first chapter of **Oh, Bits!** where this odd little tale began. The story unfolds smack in the middle of the 1940s....

Oh, Bits!

Chapter One

Perfidy, Peril, and Predilections

"You can't be serious," Angelica said. "The *mayor* did that? *Our* mayor?"

"Seems so," came the muffled reply. Digby Doolan rarely raised his voice, which made his foghorn-in-the-distance growls even harder to understand. The shocking value of Digby's revelations made the inconvenience easy to overlook. How he sounded didn't matter so long as what he offered remained juicy.

Angelica Rohrbach scratched a concluding line on her notepad. It was nearly full, just like the other eight such notebooks she kept locked in a strongbox in the root cellar, the closest thing she had to a bomb shelter in a time of war. Though it was unlikely any German or Japanese bombers would ever reach Georgia, it never hurt to take precautions. She took similar care in recording the dates and times of each notebook entry. Later, when she wrote up her column for the Atlanta *Clarion*, she would enhance the details and obscure their source. No one ever knew where she got her information, and she aimed to keep it that way.

"What do I owe you?" she asked.

Digby shuffled his feet and fiddled with his cap, mannerisms Angelica had learned to accept along with the cemetery caretaker's odor and his dirt-stained attire. Not that she ever let him in the house; just being in his presence provided all the nerve-jangling she could handle.

"Hun'erd?"

Angelica recognized the inflated first offer and shook her head. "Don't be silly."

"It's about the dadgum mayor," Digby grumbled. "That's worth more than usual."

"It would be if we could prove it. That a man like him would spend time with a—" She paused. "A *streetwalker*, doesn't surprise me. How's fifty dollars sound?"

"Pretty danged chintzy. The information's worth a helluva lot more. Now that I think on it, I reckon it's worth more like *two* hun'erd."

Angelica pursed her lips. "There's no doubt my readers will be delighted to learn that His Honor provided a hussy with a furnished apartment. I, for one, would like to know how he paid for it, and whether or not he used tax money. But in any case, I need proof before I can print any of it."

Digby stopped shuffling and pushed his short-brimmed cap to the back of his head. A shock of unkempt gray hair slumped forward and covered his weathered forehead. "You've started with rumor before. You kin do it again."

"I suppose," she said, trying to reconcile accepting his opening bid with her native frugality. "Let me get my purse." She slipped away and took a grateful breath of air not tainted by the gravedigger's aroma. She found her pocketbook and dug out half of what she needed then hurriedly returned to the back door. "I'll have to go to the bank to get the rest," she said, pushing the money into his outstretched hands. "There'll be fifty more tomorrow; I promise."

"There's only fifty here now," he said. "I told ya two hun'erd."

"Now see here, Digger, we've been doing business for—"

"A long time," he said. "And if you'd like to continue doing business, you'll pay what I ask."

"But—"

"A hun'erd an' a half. Tomorrow. Bring it by at lunchtime. I'll be in the shed."

"But—"

"See ya then," he growled over his shoulder as he sauntered away. "Don't be late."

~*~

Still fuming, Digby clambered into his ancient Ford truck and nursed the rusting relic to life. As a cloud of thick exhaust fumes rolled over the Rohrbach residence, he shifted into first and eased his foot off the clutch. Had he been a younger, more impetuous man, he might have tried to spin the tires and spew gravel across Angelica's neatly raked driveway. He knew, however, that such an effort would likely have caused the engine to seize and possibly cough up one of its four dinky pistons. As crappy as the truck was, it was the only vehicle the owners of the cemetery provided for him. If he tore it up, they'd take forever to replace it.

And in the meantime, he'd still have to haul his tools around to care for the old graves when he wasn't digging new ones. They called it landscaping. He wasn't sure what the hell it was. Grass-cutting and flower planting, sure, but the worst of it was hauling off deadfall from the acre upon acre of hardwoods that shaded the place and made digging graves so damned difficult.

Even worse, the owners were too cheap to hire additional labor. If they had more than one burial in a day, they'd give him a little extra cash to hire "independent contractors." These were usually winos and/or other down and outs who'd work for the pittance he had to offer. Granted, at fifty cents an hour, it was twice the minimum wage, but who wanted to earn it digging holes big enough and deep enough for caskets?

Thanks to Hitler, Mussolini, and the Emperor of Japan, able-bodied men were scarce, and those willing to dig graves in the summer heat of Atlanta were rarer still. Rather than pocket some of the cash for his trouble, Digby often had to pay double to avoid killing himself with the extra labor.

Years before, when still a young man, Digby entertained thoughts of getting a desk job of some kind, but he'd seen what that did to people, turned 'em into pasty-faced weaklings who spoke like they were always in church. He knew better. He'd gotten the word. Lots of words, actually. Many of which he'd shared with a local paper's gossip columnist. No, he thought. Make that a local paper's *cheapskate* gossip columnist.

He had a good mind to cut her off entirely. No more scoops, at least for a while. It'd serve her right. If she had nothing interesting to write about for a few months, maybe she'd realize how valuable his information was and actually pay him for what it was worth.

That was somewhat problematical, however, because he needed the extra cash she provided in order to pay for a few of the finer things in life which weren't possible on his caretaker's salary.

Impasse. He'd heard Angelica use the term. It meant you and somebody else were going head to head, and neither party was willing to back off. He'd avoided locking horns with her for ages on account of her being female and him being single. She'd been married once, way back, and got a house out of the deal. He'd always hoped the two of them might get along better, but it never happened. She always seemed glad to see him, but once she heard what he had to say, she grew standoffish and acted as if he had some dread disease. Measles maybe, or the clap. It pissed him off, but he always got over it. *Before*. Their meeting that day, however, hit him the wrong way, and harder than ever.

She wouldn't get away with it this time. Nope. This time he'd keep his tips to himself until she came around to the fact that she couldn't cheat him anymore.

If only he had the option of selling the information somewhere else, but the city of Atlanta, and *The Atlanta Clarion* in particular, could only support one gossip monger.

What the town really needed was a newspaper with an alternative gossip columnist.

~*~

Stormy Green sat in her 1928 Willys Whippet coupe with her forehead pressed against the steering wheel. Though the car could squeeze more miles out of a gallon of gas than most other vehicles, it couldn't do so forever. Her little two-door had wheezed its last and shuddered to a stop *almost* off the road. Close enough, she hoped, that people would think she'd just done a lousy parking job. She had one gas ration coupon left and no idea how to get the fuel or where to go once she had it.

She straightened, and with a puff of determined

Josh Langston

breath, fluffed the bangs covering her forehead. The time had come. No sense putting it off any longer. But then she glanced at her legs, bare from mid-thigh down, she still couldn't make herself comfortable in the outfit her former roommate, Lorraine, had sewn for her.

"It's called a romper, and it's all the rage," Lorraine said. "As slim as you are, you'll look spectacular, and not just at the beach." She handed Stormy a page ripped from a Hollywood fan magazine. It featured three starlets in matching rompers, all styled to look like sailor suits.

"They're cute," Stormy admitted. "And would be great for a long trip in a hot car. But go out in public dressed like that? I dunno."

"When did you turn into Mrs. Grundy?" Lorraine handed her a cream-colored romper with green trim. "Try this on. I made one for each of us, only yours is about five sizes smaller."

Stormy smiled at her plump friend. "You're too good to me."

The exchange had occurred three short weeks earlier, and now the cream-colored jumper was the only clean piece of clothing she owned. It couldn't be helped, she'd have to wear it for her interview.

The editorial offices of *The Atlanta Clarion* stood half way down the block. While not exactly a prestigious publication, it had a respectable circulation for a small city's second daily. Stormy hoped her credentials as the assistant editor of her college paper would be enough to wrangle a job. Though less than optimistic, based on failed attempts with five other newspapers in as many towns, Stormy tried to ignore her ridiculous outfit and focus her thoughts in a positive fashion. Failure meant going hungry, sleeping in her car, or worse—going home, hat in hand, to an avalanche of I-told-you-sos from her family. She wasn't above working any reasonable job to survive, but she'd always dreamed of becoming a journalist, and she wasn't about to give up on the idea. At least, not yet.

After a last check of her hair and make-up in the Whippet's minuscule rearview mirror, Stormy slipped out from behind the wheel, grabbed her portfolio from the passenger seat, and aimed her steps toward the future. Or what she hoped might be her future.

~*~

Angelica Rohrbach realized she'd made a mistake in bargaining with Digby for his information, but she'd become accustomed to the practice. And he never seemed to mind. It was a game, that's all. If he couldn't see it, that wasn't her problem.

At least, it hadn't been before that day. Now the old reprobate seemed determined to not only set his prices high, but to stick with them, too. It wasn't fair. How was she supposed to keep up with the vagaries of an old man's mind?

Maybe it was time for her to teach him a lesson.

She had already heard everything he had to share about the mayor. Now it was up to her to find some way to confirm it. Maybe it would be best if she held off paying him another nickel until she had some solid proof about the mayor's shenanigans. On the other hand, Digby had never been wrong before. He might have gotten a detail or two confused, and sometimes the reality didn't measure up to its potential, but he never gave her bad information.

The phone rang as she ruminated on her plan to put Digby Doolan back in his place.

"This is Angelica," she said.

"Your column was due an hour ago, Angie. What am I supposed to do, make something up for ya?"

She found her editor's voice nearly as grating as Digby's, though for different reasons. Though Nathan Sparks ran The *Clarion* like the ringmaster of a circus, his vocal range was much higher than Digby's. It was also significantly more nasal and came accompanied by a good deal of wheezing and coughing, no doubt the product of his three-pack-a-day habit. Angelica maintained the same odor-isolating distance from both men.

"Well?" Nathan said, his voice rising an octave over the course of a single syllable.

"I'm workin' on it, but I've got some things to nail down, first."

"So, I should just leave a blank space where your words are supposed to go? Readers will love that."

"Of course not, Nate. I just need you to be a little patient."

"There's no such thing as patience in the news business. You've been around long enough to know that."

"Obviously."

"Then why do you drive me to utter distraction every week? You know what your deadline is. Why must I call you every time to remind you of it?"

"But you *don't* have to do that!"

Nathan's response was part cough and part wheeze. Angelica wondered if he was having another heart attack. "You okay?" she asked.

"Hell no, I'm not okay!" he roared back. "I've got a paper to put out, and all I have to go on your page is a furniture ad and fifteen column inches of empty space."

"Calm down, Nate. I'll come up with something. I always do."

He exhaled heavily.

"Seriously," she added. "All I need is a couple hours more."

"Oh, no problem. I'll tell the gang in the press room to sit back and relax 'cause Angie needs a couple extra hours. They'll love hearing that. It means they'll get overtime. It means my whole damned budget goes up in flames. It means everyone else on staff will wonder why they have to get their shit in on time when you don't. It means—"

"Okay, okay. I get it," she said. "Just use my back-up column. I'll keep working on the juicy new stuff I've got, and next week you'll be all smiles. I promise." She couldn't actually remember seeing him smile.

"I used your back-up column the last time you missed your deadline, remember?"

"Oh." She actually *didn't* remember, but she didn't dare tell him that. "You know I don't just make this stuff up. It takes time and effort to get to the truth."

"You're a regular Horace Greeley."

"Now you're just bein' mean."

"Angie, I swear, the only reason I put up with your crap is because it usually pans out, and sometimes I can get an actual news story from it. I don't suppose that'll happen this time."

She chuckled. "When I said 'all smiles' before, I meant it. This new story could be huge. Gigantic!"

"I'm getting too old for this," he muttered.

"I'm serious!"

"And I don't really give a shit," he said. "Get me something in an hour. That's all the time I can spare. Your usual five hundred words of inspired innuendo will do."

He was *definitely* being mean. She'd have to make it a rumor and be careful not to identify the subject of Digby's revelation. Digby, of course, would remain anonymous as usual. No way she'd ever give up her source.

"So, you'll do it? You won't let me down?"

"I swear, Nate. You won't regret it."

He grunted. "I already regret it."

Angelica raced to hang up before he could.

~*~

Digby Doolan liked the tool shed. He thought of it as his office, even though it more closely resembled a metal-roofed barn. He had walled off a section for his personal use and installed a folding cot with a thin but useable mattress, a cupboard for his beer and snacks, and a radio so he could keep tabs on his favorite teams. College sports ruled the south, and he could usually find a game if he tried hard enough. One could be a fan without ever having been a student, and that description fit Digby perfectly.

Sports and coffins, he mused. He never seemed to run out of either.

The most valuable thing in the shed, however, was neither a tool nor a domestic convenience. That designation belonged to an ornate mirror which had been left behind by his predecessor. Digby had no idea where it had come from originally though he suspected it had been imported from Europe or some obscure part of the Orient. Way before the war. He didn't know exactly when, and if the man who trained him was aware of its history, he never bothered to share it.

Certainly, the old timer hadn't said anything positive about the mirror. Quite the contrary; he feared it and even swore it was cursed. He kept it covered with an old blanket and made Digby promise to leave it that way. That had changed over the years, but truth be told, using it scared the crap out of him, too, if not as badly now as it had the first few times.

He glanced toward it, hanging on the wall above a workbench. He kept a towel draped over it to keep the dust off. Whether that mattered to the inhabitant of the mirror he didn't know. He'd never asked. There were many questions he'd never asked.

Sometimes it was better not to know all the answers.

In a carefully hidden set of German command bunkers nestled in the wooded splendor of Bavaria, Axel Schmidt looked at the orders he'd been given for his new mission, one which had but two possible outcomes: disaster and suicide, probably both.

His thoughts were shaped in large part by the debacle known as "Operation Pastorius." In that ill-fated effort, a team of eight highly trained and well-funded saboteurs secretly entered the United States with the goal of blowing up factories, power plants, military installations and Jewish-owned businesses. Their success was intended to terrify the American population and force them to withdraw manpower and equipment from the war effort and put it to work guarding their homeland.

The plan could not have failed more miserably. Instead of spreading terror across the land, the mission whimpered to an end when the leader of the team turned himself in to the FBI. The other seven operatives were arrested, and all were put on trial and convicted. Two went to prison for life; the other six were executed. In Germany, they would have been shot. The Americans used their "electric chair." Axel's sphincter tightened to a pinprick at the thought.

While similar in nature to the failed Operation Pastorius, Axel's mission had a much narrower focus. The Americans were building a factory which would soon be churning out long-range bombers at an alarming rate. The massive aircraft would be flown by female pilots to bases near the war zone where they would be loaded with bombs and crewed by veteran airmen intent on laying waste to the fatherland. Axel's family had perished in Berlin, burned to ash along with countless thousands of other innocent civilians when the British and American bombers dropped their devastating loads on the unprotected populace below.

Der Führer himself had been rumored to say a few more such raids would force Germany to stop fighting. For Axel, that was unthinkable. The Americans had to pay for the misery and death they inflicted on his family, and that sentiment had propelled him to volunteer for the mission. He would have preferred to personally dole out retaliatory death and destruction, but he was enough of a realist to know that a covert operation had the capacity to do far greater damage than could one man, no matter how well armed.

The Americans had developed a high-altitude, high-speed airplane which carried a vastly bigger bomb payload than any other. The B29 could turn Germany into rubble; Axel and his crew were expected to slow down if not stop their delivery. The team would be dispatched onto American soil via U-boat as had their unfortunate predecessors. This time, however, the mission wasn't being planned by the craven leaders of the now-defunct *Abwher*. Every step of the complicated plan had been worked out by the *Schutzstaffel*, or SS, to which Axel had dedicated himself.

America *would* pay.

~*~

Stormy tried to brush some of the wrinkles from her skimpy outfit as she waited to see the *Clarion's* managing editor. A bony woman with gray hair and severe clothing had told her to wait, though she couldn't say for how long. The look she had given Stormy—or more accurately, Stormy's outfit—had screamed disapproval, though she settled for an obviously unneeded sniff. She claimed the staff had production deadlines to meet, and she couldn't be sure the managing editor, or anyone else, would have time to interview a potential trainee.

Stormy didn't even get the chance to correct the trainee reference. She was there for a real job. She'd had all the training she needed; she was ready to write.

Sitting in the empty room, she whiled away the time by filling out an employment application. She felt as if she'd gone through a hundred of the damned things since she received her college diploma, a handshake from the dean, and his mumbled good luck wish. He almost got her name right.

It was okay though; she was done with what her father called "higher education." She was on her own at last, free to pursue her dream. She never realized getting a paying job in the industry would be so hard.

"Miz Green?"

Stormy almost jumped to her feet but caught herself in time. No need to appear over-eager, though she knew the effort was hopeless. Her face always gave her away. Everyone said so.

"Mr. Sparks will see you now." The gray-haired stick figure smirked at her as she gestured for Stormy to follow, then turned and marched away. Stormy scrambled to catch up, chasing the real-life version of Popeye's girlfriend, Olive Oyl, down a hallway.

"He's in there," the woman said, aiming a skeletal digit toward a room that bore an atmospheric haze.

Is it safe?

"Hope you don't mind the smoke," said her gray guide. "Someday they'll pass a law about smoking in the workplace, and he'll be out of a job. Assuming he lives that long."

Stormy didn't believe Congress would go along with anything like that; aside from the fact they were focused on a world war, there was simply too much money being made in the tobacco industry. Everyone in Hollywood smoked, or so it seemed. If opinions were based solely on what the movie stars did, everyone would think smoking was glamorous. Many of her friends in college smoked, but she'd only tried it once. That was enough. She'd heard of some who'd tried marijuana, too, but she figured if she couldn't handle tobacco, she'd never handle anything stronger.

"Well, c'mon in," said a voice from within the smoky room. "I'm not gettin' any younger."

Stormy eased into the cramped, messy room, most of which was occupied by a wide wooden desk. The speaker remained hidden from view behind a handful of yellow copy paper. She recognized the stuff from her time on the staff of her college rag.

"Siddown," he said. "Be with ya in a minute."

There were two chairs in the room. Mr. Sparks filled one of them, and a stack of files filled the other.

"Uh—"

"Hang on. I'm almost done." He dropped the

paper on his desk and attacked it with a blue pencil, drawing a huge "X" on one paragraph and several lines through another. He circled a word here and there, drew some arrows and added a couple symbols she'd never seen before, then tossed it in a metal tray marked "Out." In the same motion, he pressed a button on the corner of his desk which summoned a runner. The boy, a couple years younger than Stormy, dashed in, emptied the "Out" box and departed without a word.

While Stormy observed the runner, Sparks observed her.

"Just set that stuff on the floor," he said, watching intently as she followed his instructions.

When finished, she handed him her resume and the partially completed job application. "I didn't have time to answer everything."

While he perused her paperwork in silence, Stormy glanced around his workspace. A dozen black and white photos and a handful of wooden plaques adorned the walls. She didn't recognize any of the awards, though some of the people in the photos looked familiar. Among them were the governor, a state court judge, who she was reasonably sure now occupied a cell in a federal prison, and some other supposed notables.

A poster featuring the face of Franklin Roosevelt bore a quote from his 1940 re-election campaign: "I'll say it again and again and again: Your boys are not going to be sent into any foreign wars." A feathered dart protruded from the left side of the president's forehead. Numerous tiny holes in the poster testified to previous assaults.

"Stormy, huh?"

"Yes sir," she said, steeling herself for the inevitable snide comment about the notorious burlesque queen who performed under the name "Stormy Weather." She didn't have to wait long.

"I'm pretty sure there's a fan dancer by that name."

"I think the term 'stripper' is more accurate, but I assure you, that's where the similarity between us ends."

Sparks cleared his throat and lit up a Lucky Strike. His ashtray overflowed with snuffed out butts and burnt wooden matches. After taking his first deep drag, he smiled at her in a way that suggested a measure of respect. "So, you wanna be a reporter."

"Yes sir," she said, relieved that he hadn't said anything about a trainee position.

"We already have a trainee. You saw him a minute ago when he came in."

The room suddenly felt a great deal warmer than it had before, and the volume of cigarette smoke made her lightheaded. "Actually, I've already done some practice jobs. I'm ready for a real one."

He regarded her closely, paying significantly more time on her face and figure than on her resume. She suddenly wished she'd worn pants. And a parka.

After an uncomfortably long silence he once again focused on her paperwork. "Says here you maintained a regular column on your school paper. Got any samples?"

"You bet," she said, digging into her portfolio. She had divided it by story types: news, features and opinion. She grabbed everything in the opinion section and handed it to him.

"Nice photo," he said, holding up the clipping to compare the headshot in it with her actual, in-the-flesh, flesh. "Very nice."

"Thanks."

"We don't use headshots in our opinion pages."

"Oh." *Crap.*

"But if the folks writing for us looked as good as you I'd be tempted to change that." It appeared he wanted to say more, but once he started coughing it took him a good long while to regain his voice.

"Can I get you some water?" she asked.

"No," he said, red-faced. "I'll be okay."

He reached down beside his chair and retrieved a thermos jug from which he poured two fingers of something dark into a coffee mug. Stormy wasn't close enough to identify the fluid by smell, especially since the room reeked of cigarettes and other odors she chose not to think about.

"Which of these is your best?" he asked, holding up her columns.

"I think they're all pretty good," she said, "but the one I like the best is about problems with the nursing program. Those were—"

"This one?"

"Yes."

He handed it back to her.

"Which one do you like the least?"

She was trying to get a handle on his game, but had little confidence. "The one on women's sports, I guess."

He thumbed through them and finally held one up. "This it?"

"Yes."

He handed the rest back to her and started reading.

"I—"

"Shhh. Gimme a sec."

Trying not to do a slow burn or squirm too much in the straight-backed chair, Stormy waited until he finished.

"Not bad," he said at last. "A little overly dramatic, maybe, but not bad."

"Thanks." She managed to avoid adding, "I think."

"So, why do you want to work for the *Clarion*? Why not a big-time paper like the *Constitution*?"

"I'd love to work for a big paper," she said, "but from what I've seen, they only want writers with years and years of experience."

"And the *Clarion* doesn't?"

"I didn't say that!"

He smiled at her. At least, she thought it *might* have been a smile.

"Tell ya what," he said, "I'll take a chance on you. Your writing isn't bad. It isn't great, either, but we can fix that. What you need is seasoning—a little time in the saddle and exposure to some real editing. Before you know it, you'll *be* one of those experienced writers, and then I'll probably have to bribe you to stay here."

"You won't regret it," Stormy said, flushed with relief. "I promise."

"I'd rather you promised something else."

She blinked at him, her suspicions as taut as a harp string. "Like what?"

"Promise you'll continue to wear short skirts. Seems like everybody who works here is a couple hundred years old. Seeing a pretty girl in nice clothes will definitely improve the atmosphere around here."

Stormy paused, her mind racing. "Uh, okay. But I confess, this is the only short outfit I own, and I probably won't get paid for—"

Sparks smiled and dashed off a note. "Give this to Audrey, she prefers 'Miz Banks' by the way, she's the woman who showed you in. It's an advance on your first paycheck."

I won't have to sleep in the car!

"Be back here at eight o'clock, sharp. I'll have an assignment for you. Screw it up, and you can return the advance before you leave in the afternoon."

"I won't screw it up," she said, forcing every bit of determination she could into her voice.

"Let's hope not," he said. "Now, skedaddle."

~End of Excerpt~

www.ingramcontent.com/pod-product-compliance
Lightning Source LLC
Chambersburg PA
CBHW051444260626
47162CB00001B/239